I0524989

NO SHELTER

THE HOLLY LIN SERIES

NO SHELTER

A HOLLY LIN NOVEL

ROBERT SWARTWOOD

RMS PRESS

Copyright © 2011 Robert Swartwood

Cover design copyright © 2016 Damonza

This is a work of fiction. Names, characters, places and incidents are either products of the author's imagination or used fictitiously. Any resemblance to actual events, locales, or persons, living or dead, is entirely coincidental. All rights reserved. No part of this publication can be reproduced or transmitted in any form or by any means, electronic or mechanical, without permission in writing from Robert Swartwood.

ISBN-13: 978-1945819001
ISBN-10: 1945819006

www.robertswartwood.com

For my wife

PART ONE

LESS THAN HUMAN

ONE

My flight gets in at McCarran a few minutes before midnight. Nova picks me up in a black Escalade reeking of stale cigarette smoke.

The first thing he says to me: "I know what you're thinking and no, this isn't stolen."

The second thing he says to me: "You ready to kill some bad guys?"

He drives us to our temporary base of operations, a cinderblock storage garage on the outskirts of the city. Inside the garage are a table set up with computers, a card table covered with weapons, and what looks like a brand new Lincoln Town Car.

"Like it?" Nova asks me as we get out of the Escalade. "It'll be your ride tonight."

"Can't wait." I walk over to the card table, look at the mini-arsenal of rifles and pistols. Then I glance over at Scooter on the computer. "What's up, handsome?"

He smiles at me, chomping away at his Bazooka Joe. "Hey, Holly, how was th-th-the flight?"

"Too short. They didn't even serve me one of those tiny bags of peanuts I like so much."

Nova walks up to me, holding a manila folder. "So you want to know who the target is?"

"I thought you'd never ask."

He clears a space at the table and pulls up two stools. I take one and he hands me the manila folder. Inside are surveillance photos of a middle-aged man in a suit, balding with bushy eyebrows and glasses.

"Where'd you take these?"

"Those were taken just outside the MGM Grand."

"That's where he's staying?"

Nova shakes his head. "He's staying at the Bellagio, but he's been making stops at all the major casinos the past week."

I look up from the pictures, glance at Nova, then at Scooter. "Just how long have you guys been here?"

"Week and a half."

"Walter never mentioned anything to me."

Still typing at the computer, his back to us, Scooter says, "Th-Th-That's because we weren't sure yet whether we'd need you."

"You really know how to make a girl feel special, Scooter." I look back at the pictures. "So who's the woman—his girlfriend?"

In almost every photograph there is a tall, thin, blond woman beside the target, carrying a briefcase.

"That little hottie right there," Nova says, "is Delano's personal assistant. Her name's Alayna Gramont. Believe it or not, she used to be a model."

"Do I need to worry about her?"

"No. She won't be there tonight."

I nod once, give Nova a serious look. "So what's the deal?"

He clears his throat. "The deal is he and his associates are having a party."

"And?"

"And they've requested girls."

"Of course they did," I say. "And I just bet this guy right here—what's his name again?"

"Roland Delano."

"I just bet Roland Delano has a thing for Asian chicks."

"Actually," Scooter says, his back still to us, "the guy with the Asian fetish isn't the target. It's the target's buddy."

Nova hands me another manila folder. Inside are more surveillance photos, this one of a large black man, his head bald, wearing wraparound shades.

"The bodyguard?"

Nova nods.

"And he's the one that likes Asian chicks."

He nods again.

I glance once more from Nova to Scooter, Scooter to Nova. "I'm going to be completely alone on this thing, aren't I?"

Nova says, "At least on the inside, yeah."

"Great." I cross my arms, take a breath. "So what's the plan?"

TWO

Nova thumbs through the photographs of Roland Delano until he finds the one he wants. He sets it on the table, taps his finger on a specific place.

"See this?"

"The guy wears bling."

"It's not bling," Nova says, keeping his finger on the spot just beneath Delano's neck, where a golden coin hangs off a chain. "It's a flash drive."

"A flash drive," I say.

"This is a two-part job, Holly. Taking Delano out is part one. The second part is ensuring you walk away with this flash drive."

I look up from the photograph, glance at the two incongruous men, Scooter small and thin and wearing glasses, Nova big and strong and gorgeous. "What does this Roland Delano do again?"

"Your run of the mill terrorist."

"And what does he specialize in?"

"Arms."

"Big arms or small arms?"

"Massive."

Nodding, I say, "So security is going to be tight."

"Very," Scooter says. He waves me over to the computers. "Delano's st-st-staying in the Chairman Suite of the Bellagio. Apparently he'd wanted one of the villas but th-th-they were all booked and he got pissed. As you can imagine, th-this is a guy who always gets what he wants."

Scooter opens up a window on the screen, types rapidly and brings up the Bellagio's website.

"Wow," I say. "It's impressive all the legwork you've accomplished in the past week and a half."

"Keep laughing, keep laughing." He clicks and clicks until he brings up the page for the Chairman Suite. "You have to keep in mind this isn't a George Clooney movie. Infiltrating a casino is pretty much impossible, especially with my limited equipment. The best I could do was determine his floor, his suite number, and tap into his room phone. Th-Th-That's how we know about the party tonight and the girls he requested."

"And how did I get my invite?"

"He requested an Asian from one of the agencies," Nova says. "We called a few hours later, giving them all the same information, told them to cancel the order but that we'd still pay in full."

"An Asian," I murmur, shooting a glare at Nova. "You guys are so racially sensitive."

"Anyway"—Scooter moves the mouse and clicks something else—"th-this is the basic floor plan. You have the foyer leading into the living and dining area, the wet bar and conference room on the right. Two bedrooms, one on the left, the other on the right, both with His and Her Baths."

"You sound like you're pitching me an advertisement." I stare at the screen a moment, then ask Nova, "How much more security does he have?"

"At least a half dozen."

"And I'm walking in there with no weapon."

"Yeah, that sounds about right."

"So if I break a nail and need backup, how long before the cavalry arrives?"

Nova looks away, scratches the back of his neck. "That's kind of another issue we need to discuss."

"Kind of," I say.

"The suite elevators are exclusive. You need a key to use them, and unfortunately, we don't have a key."

"It's not something I can easily override either," Scooter says. "Not with th-th-the Bellagio's level of security."

I cross my arms, scowl at them both. "Okay, so let me get this straight. I'm going in there with no weapon, no protection, no backup. Does that sound about right?"

Nova looks away again, gives a short nod.

"So where *are* you two going to be?"

"After I drop you off," Nova says, "I'm going to park the Town Car in a garage, change, and start working the casino."

"Great. So while I work you play."

"I'll be in radio communication the entire time. So will Scooter."

Scooter nods. "I'll be in the parking garage, in the Escalade, monitoring their security."

I glance back at the screen, thinking about the "at least a half dozen," the fact that I won't be seeing Roland but his bodyguard.

"How many other girls are going to be there?"

"At least a half dozen," Nova says. "Maybe more."

"Oh, I see. A boss who likes to share his wealth."

Nova gives his head a little shake, keeping his gaze on me level. "No, they're all for him."

"Oh. So he's a selfish bastard."

"From what we hear," Scooter says, "he's more th-than just selfish."

Nova pulls a pack of Camels from his pocket, offers me one.

"You know I'm trying to quit," I tell him, but take one anyway. Once he's lit both mine and his, he looks down, looks back up, but before he can even open his mouth, I beat him to the punch.

"He likes to play rough, doesn't he?"

Nova nods. He doesn't break his stare with mine.

Scooter pulls a fresh Bazooka Joe from his pocket, unwraps it, places the piece of bubblegum in his mouth. He'll keep adding to the same piece he's already chewing until he gets eight pieces, sometimes ten, before spitting the large ball of gum out and starting over with a fresh piece. The comic inside he'll save and add to his collection. Now he leans back and glances up at me, and I see the same thing in his eyes that I see in Nova's.

I let the moment pass a beat, then say, "Don't worry about it."

"Holly—" Scooter starts.

"I mean it. I'll be cool."

"Walter knows this isn't going to be a clean hit," Nova says. "But he doesn't want it to get out of hand."

Right. If I were a United States general in charge of a non-sanctioned mission—especially one on U.S. soil—I wouldn't want things to get out of hand either.

"What's his definition of out of hand?"

"You know it changes with every job. But I believe his exact words this time were something like if it's going to be news, he'd rather it be local than national."

"I can't promise anything."

"No, but you can promise you'll at least try."

"How does he want me to take out Roland, anyway?"

"The way we figure it," Scooter says, "th-th-the bodyguard

might try to play rough with you too. He tries to slap you around, you fight back. Simple self-defense."

"I don't know," I say, glancing back at the photographs spread out on the table. "He's a pretty big guy."

His cigarette finished, Nova drops it on the ground, grinds the cherry with the heel of his boot. Doesn't say anything, just keeps watching me.

I realize Scooter is watching me too, leaning back in his chair, and then it hits me.

"Roland's not here strictly for pleasure, is he? He's here on business."

"Some people are flying in from Argentina tomorrow afternoon," Scooter says. "They're going to make the deal then."

"Do we know what for?"

Nova says, "Most likely what's on that flash drive around his neck."

"Okay," I say, nodding again, "and I'm guessing this is the kind of deal that can't be made."

"Of course not." Nova reaches out to pat me on the shoulder but pauses, his eyes lighting up. "Oh shit, I almost forgot."

"Forgot what?"

Grinning now, he glances at Scooter. "Want to give it to her or should I?"

Scooter is already jumping out of his chair, starting over toward the other end of the garage.

Nova says, "The guy that requested you, he requested something else."

Scooter comes back, a cardboard box in his hands. He sets it down on the table, pushes it toward me. "Happy birthday."

Frowning at the boys, I reach out and open the box. Glance at what's inside. Start to shake my head. "No fucking way."

"Yes," Nova says.

"No. I'm not wearing that."

"You don't have a choice."

Scooter pulls out his phone, points it at me. "Can I get a picture then?"

I just stare back at Scooter, then glance at Nova when he finally pats me on the shoulder.

"So," he says, "you ready to party or what?"

THREE

Nova drives me in the Town Car to the Bellagio. He doesn't speak once. He just drives and I sit in the back, watching the bright lights and the people still awake at two o'clock in the morning, finding it hard to imagine how just five hours ago I was at my mother's place for family dinner. It's her monthly excuse to get me and my sister and my sister's husband and their two boys together, so she can learn what's new and interesting in their lives and subtly hint at her disappointment in my life, what with me being almost thirty with no boyfriend or solid job or even secure future.

God how I hate those family dinners.

As Nova turns up the long drive to the casino, I close my eyes and take a deep breath. Then we make it to the front and he stops and one of the attendants hurries over to open the back door.

I step out into the cool dry air of the Las Vegas desert. I smile and nod at the attendant, and in broken English say, "Tank you."

I'm wearing a thin cashmere overcoat that comes down to my knees, and as I walk toward the entrance, as I enter the hotel and make my way toward the elevators, I transform myself into tonight's character: a Japanese working girl, limited high school education, speaks very little English. Just the type of girl who knows what guys like to hear and feel and is willing to give it to them for the right price.

At the elevators a man in a suit approaches me. I can tell at once he's not hotel security. The suit is Armani, much too nice, and the look he gives me is intense.

"You here for the party?" he asks, and I nod, my lips pouted, like I only understand half of what he's saying. "Okay then, follow me."

He leads me to one of the farther elevators. He swipes a key card, and the shiny, spotless doors open.

"Go on up, honey," he says, "have a good time," and as I walk into the elevator he gives me a quick pat on the ass.

My first impulse is to spin around and pop him one in the face, break his nose, send him to the ground with his eyes watering and blood dripping into his mouth. But I let this impulse slide, remembering that I'm a professional, and I only turn, smile at him, give him a half wave until the elevator doors close completely and then the smile fades and I turn my hand around and drop all my fingers except the middle.

As the elevator ascends I step back and look at myself in the shiny doors. I open the cashmere overcoat to reveal tonight's requested outfit. Black four-inch heels, white knee-high stockings, a green and blue plaid miniskirt, a white button-up top that's opened at the chest to reveal my cleavage. Not at all what I was planning on wearing tonight, but if a Japanese schoolgirl is what this bastard wants, a Japanese schoolgirl is what he's going to get.

Scooter says, "Are you alone?"

I'm wearing a wireless transmitter in my ear, a tiny thing smaller than a pebble.

"In the elevator, yeah. What's up?"

"Listen to th-th-this Bazooka Joe comic I just opened."

"Scooter, I don't have time for this."

"But I th-think it's a good omen. It's my favorite one, comic number twenty. Joe's grilling and he says to his buddy, 'Hey, what happened to th-the hot dogs? Who took the hot dogs?' And in the next panel Joe's dog is leaning against a tree, a toothpick in his mouth, and says, 'It just proves it's a dog-eat-dog world. Get used to it, kid.'" He pauses. "What do you th-th-think?"

Nova's voice comes over the line, saying, "I think you need to quit bothering Holly so she can concentrate."

"Yeah, I know, but don't you two see the life lesson in the comic? It's brilliant. And the fortune says it all: We know what goes around, comes around—if you send it, you better duck." He laughs. "Isn't th-th-that just perfect?"

The elevator begins to slow before I have a chance to respond. I look up at the numbers, see I've made it to the thirtieth floor. The elevator stops. I close the cashmere overcoat, take a deep breath. Then the doors open and I start to step forward but pause when I see the gun pointed at my face.

FOUR

"Easy, baby, everything's okay. Just need you to come out slow-like, press yourself flat against this wall."

"Against wall?" I say, using my broken English. At the sight of the gun—a black nine-millimeter Glock—I've raised my hands and do my best to look frightened and confused.

"That's right, baby, against the wall. I need to pat you down, make sure you ain't carrying something."

"Carry something?"

My hands still raised, I move slowly toward the wall. I press myself against it. The man isn't alone; he has two other buddies watching, and they grin as he steps forward, starts to frisk me. I'm surprised at first that he actually does a good job of it, like a professional, but then he has to go and disappoint me by making sure he squeezes my breasts and pinches my ass.

He steps back, says, "Okay, good, you're clean. Sorry about that, baby, but we just need to make sure."

"Okay," I say, stressing it into two syllables.

He laughs through his nose, shakes his head, motions to one of the men behind him. "Phil, take her in."

Phil steps forward, grabs my arm, pulls me not so gently

down the hallway toward Delano's suite. He has on really
strong aftershave that makes my eyes want to water. He asks,
"What you got under that coat there, little lady?"

I smile but don't say anything, knowing that he's not worth
the time. Then we're standing in front of a door and he knocks
twice and the door opens and another man is there with a
Glock pointed at us. He motions me in and the man holding
my arm pushes me into the room.

The smell of marijuana hits me first. It's heavy and pungent
and as I step into the main area of the suite I see a thick cloud
of the stuff floating up by the ceiling.

A man stands up from the couches and raises his arms. He's
wearing a plush maroon robe and smiles at me. "Welcome,
welcome," he says, and I know at once this is Roland Delano,
my target. Around his neck the gold coin of his flash drive
shines in the light.

There are six other girls lounging on the couches or
standing by the windows. Two are white, one is black, the rest
are Hispanic. They wear tight dark dresses, so short they barely
cover their crotches, and all of them have on stilettos.

Delano's bodyguard, the large black man with the fetish for
Asian women, sits on one of the other couches. Unlike his boss,
he's wearing a suit. His eyes meet mine and he gives a slow,
steady nod, like he approves.

Roland Delano approaches me, his arms still raised. It's
clear that he's drunk by the way he stumbles, and when he
takes me into an embrace, tells me how very happy he is I
could join him, I can see the residue of cocaine around his
hairy nostrils.

"Please, please," he says, "let me take your coat," and before
I know it the coat is being ripped off my body, revealing me in
my schoolgirl outfit. I lock eyes again with the bodyguard and
see another nod of approval, this time even a slow grin, the
man showing off a gold-capped tooth.

I look around the room again and notice the other girls noticing me. Their glares are full of menace. I doubt any of them are over twenty-five, but the years of work have worn them down, trampled their spirit, their dreams. And while many of them could be called attractive—I have no doubt both Nova and Scooter would think so—they also have a rough edge that I've managed to keep off.

Roland takes my arm and leads me to the wet bar, saying, "A drink, please, won't you have a drink? And please indulge yourself in some of our other party favors. I insist. I have everything—weed, coke, even some X. Please, please, I want you to enjoy yourself."

One of his men stands behind the wet bar, looking bored. I smile at him, say, "Beer?" and he produces a bottle of Bud.

When I turn around, Roland has disappeared, gone back to the couch where two of the girls are waiting. He sits down and places his arms around their shoulders, smiles at them as he continues telling a story my entrance must have interrupted.

I take a sip of the beer and look around. Music is coming from the sound system, a rap beat, and on the widescreen TV a porno shows some lesbian action. The fireplace is on, the flames dancing inside.

The bodyguard catches my eye. He motions me to come over to him. When I get there he tells one of the girls beside him to scram and then I'm sitting on his right, his large arm around my shoulders, the man telling me his name is Jerold, what's mine?

"Cho," I say. When he smiles—the gold-capped tooth gleaming in the light—and says that's a beautiful name, what does it mean, I tell him, "Means butterfly."

"Butterfly, huh? That mean you like to fly, or are you tasty like butter?"

I do my damnedest not to roll my eyes and just smile, take

a sip of my beer. In my ear, Scooter says, "I think I'm g-g-g-gonna puke."

The Hispanic girl on Jerold's left glares at me, angry that the attention has been taken off her. What I wonder is why she cares, she's being paid either way, but I'll never understand hookers.

Jerold takes his arm away from my shoulders, places his warm hand on my thigh. "I really dig the outfit. Nice touch. Didn't know I could have requested that shit or else I definitely would have. I'll have to remember that next time."

I smile at Jerold but say nothing, while in my ear both Scooter and Nova chuckle softly. Fucking assholes, I swear I'm going to break their pinkie fingers when I see them next.

Jerold raises his bottle of Perrier, taps it against my bottle. "Cheers," he says and leans forward, plants his lips against mine. It's a quick kiss, a peck, but it's enough for me to taste absolutely nothing. No alcohol, no liquor, not even weed, which just adds another hurdle.

Five minutes pass, ten minutes, and I do my best to nurse my drink, to only take limited hits of the weed when it's passed my way. I smile and smile and listen and listen but keep my eyes open for all possible exits, weapons, interferences. It looks like all of Delano's men are packing, maybe even Jerold.

Finally the rest of the girls arrive, two of them. Roland Delano does his greeting act again, taking their coats, leading them to the wet bar. Jerold's hand hasn't left my thigh. It stays there, squeezing, rubbing, working its way toward my crotch but quickly moving back, like it's a game.

I've sized him up and figure breaking his neck is out of the question. A big guy like this, he's protected by layers of fat and muscle.

Roland silences the rap music with a remote, letting the porno run for a few seconds, two girls on screen playing with a dildo. He watches it for a moment, a wry grin on his face, and then shuts that off too. He clears his throat, pats his chest, then speaks.

"Welcome again, ladies. It's my pleasure to have you join us tonight. The party has begun, yes, and now it is time for the main attraction. Some of you will be coming with me, some of you will be going with my associate. Some of you will have to wait your turn. But don't you worry, ladies"—smiling even wider, winking—"you'll all get to play."

Then the smile slides off his face and he points at three girls, motions for them to get up and follow him toward the one bedroom.

Jerold's hand leaves my thigh for the first time tonight. He stands up, turns, extends his hand to me and helps me up. I'm already visualizing the bedroom, the possible weapons, the different ways I can take Jerold out, and I turn and start that way.

I only stop when I hear Jerold's deep voice behind me— "And you too, sugar"—and turn back to see him helping the Hispanic girl up him from the couch, smiling as he takes her arm and leads her toward me.

FIVE

This Jerold is one sick bastard.

The first thing he has us do is bend down at the end of the bed, leaning so our asses stick out. He shuts the door, dims the light, turns the music up on the stereo. I expect rap but what comes out of the speakers is some kind of jazz, a contemporary number with saxophones and drums and bass.

"You know what you girls are?" He takes off his suit jacket, lays it across the back of one of the chairs. "You're my slave girls. And like all bad slave girls, you need to be punished."

He unbuckles his belt, slips it out from around his waist. He folds the two ends together, then steps forward and raises it back behind his head.

He does the Hispanic girl first. One solid slap with the belt across her ass. From the corner of my eye I see her jump, clench her jaw, squeeze her eyes tight. She tries to hold back a yelp but still it escapes her mouth.

"Yeah, baby, you like that shit?"

He steps behind me, raises the belt behind his head. I brace myself for the impact, staring ahead, and then —*WHACK!*—it's over with and I grit my teeth against the pain, I manage not to yelp or make any noise at all even though I know it's stupid.

It's stupid because it makes Jerold want to hit me again.

Which he does a second time—*WHACK!*—and then a third.

Still I don't make a sound.

"So you think you're tough?" Jerold chuckles. "Okay, baby, we'll see just how tough you are."

He steps close, grabs a fistful of my hair, yanks me back. He puts his tongue against my cheek, gives it a good lick, and whispers, "I'll save you for last."

He pushes me away. I stumble backward at a bad angle, lose my footing with my heels and fall to the floor. He looks at me and laughs, then leans forward and whispers something to the Hispanic girl. She whimpers. He laughs even louder. Then he's leaning back, dropping the belt, loosening the knot of his tie.

He grabs the girl's hair, yanks her back, says, "Ready to have some fun?" then pushes her down on the bed.

I'm frozen on the floor. My heart is pounding.

Jerold gives me a glance. He grins, showing me that gold-capped tooth of his, then winks.

He gets onto the bed, slowly, like an animal approaching its prey.

He grabs the front of the girl's dress, pulls it down.

I look around the room once more, try to spot something to use as a weapon, but the lighting isn't good, it's too dim.

The girl whimpers again and Jerold whispers, "Shh, baby, shh," and my eyes fall on the belt he's dropped on the floor, the thick leather thing he used to punish us, his slave girls, and with the jazz playing from the stereo and the girl whimpering as Jerold places his big hands on her breasts, I jump to my feet, grab the belt, and launch myself onto the bed.

I come down hard on his back, wrap the belt around his

throat. I cross it behind his neck and squeeze, the best I can, I squeeze even as he tries to stand back up, tries to buck me off. His hands move away from the girl. They reach beneath the belt, try to give his Adam's apple some breathing room, try to give his fingers some kind of leverage. He keeps one of those hands there and with the other grabs at me, finds my hair, pulls, yanks, rips.

But I don't let go. I can't let go.

Jerold is big, and strong, and determined, and with me holding onto his back he steps off the bed, twists back and forth like he's a bull and I'm riding him for eight seconds, and then when he realizes that won't work, he rushes backward into the wall.

It knocks the wind out of me. The back of my head strikes the wall, making me see stars. The world tilts. I start to lose my grip. Just a little slack but it's enough for Jerold. He rips the belt away, turns, lets me drop to the carpet. He kicks me in the gut with the tip of his designer shoe.

"Stupid fucking cunt," he says, and kicks me again, and again, and again.

The world tilts even more. My wind still hasn't returned and I keep wheezing. The pain is intense. And still he keeps swearing, spitting, kicking, kicking, kicking.

The girl attacks him without a sound. She comes from the left, the house phone in her hand, and smashes it into the back of his head. It doesn't drop him, it hardly even fazes him, but it's enough to make him pause in his kicking, to allow me to get my wind back, to make the world slow its spinning.

He turns away. Glares at the girl. Balls his hand into a fist. Raises that fist—

I reach out and grab his ankle, sit up and shove the heel of my palm into the center of his shin. It's a bad angle but I'm a pro and the bone snaps, just a little, enough to cause the body-guard to cry out, stumble, fall to the ground.

I'm on my feet a second later, the world still spinning, the floor tilting back and forth, but I step forward and raise my right foot, bring the sharp end of my heel down on his head. He tries getting back up but I do it again, and again, and again.

The girl drops the telephone. She places her hands to her face. I glance at her briefly and see tears in her eyes.

I have a crazy thought that I don't want to ruin my heels more than I already have. So I step away, bend down and grab the phone, turn back and smash it once into Jerold's face.

The girl is murmuring something. I can hear it just beneath the jazz that keeps going and going, someone now doing a saxophone solo. Her hands are still to her face and it takes me a moment to realize she's murmuring the Ave Maria.

I start to stand but the room tilts again and I have to throw a hand out to the wall to stay balanced. I look down at what's become of Jerold, all his blood soaking into the plush expensive carpet. I place a hand on my stomach, know I'm going to be sore for a couple days.

Watching the girl, I say, "Scooter, can you hear me?"

"Yeah." His voice soft and tinny. "You all right?"

"I've been better." I clear my throat, take a breath. "The bodyguard's out of the picture. I'm going for the target next."

"Good luck."

I turn to the girl. Her wide eyes are like spotlights shining down on the darkness that was Jerold. She looks at me and even in the dimness I can see the fear and terror there.

"Hey," I tell her, as quietly and calmly as I can. "It's okay."

She keeps murmuring the Ave Maria.

It hits me then she doesn't speak English, and that if she does it's not very good. I speak seven languages and Spanish is my third best. I take a step toward her, slowly, and in Spanish tell her that everything is okay.

Her eyes go wider, and she takes a step back.

I say, "I'm not going to hurt you."

She stops murmuring the prayer. She shakes her head quickly, says, "Never like this."

"I know"—taking another slow step, then another, the world still spinning—"but he was a bad man. I had no choice."

"They will"—she places her thumb in her mouth, starts to bite at the nail—"they will kill me."

"Don't worry about these men." My voice has gone calm. The pain is still there but I'm to the point now where I don't feel it. "I'll take care of them."

"Not these men." More tears come to her eyes. "The men who run the ranch."

"The ranch?" I pause. "What ranch?"

That's when there's a knock at the door, and a voice says, "Yo Jerold, you okay in there?"

SIX

For a moment the world stops spinning. Even the carpet pauses in soaking up Jerold's blood. The jazz has gone silent too, and it's not until another second passes and a new song starts up that I realize it's not just my imagination.

There's another knock. "Don't play too rough, man. You don't want Mr. Delano to have to pay for any damages." The man sounds like he's laughing with his friends.

I glance up at the girl and find that her hands have gone back to her face. Her eyes have grown even wider.

"Jerold?" The man sounding puzzled now. "Jerold, you hear me?"

I quickly dart my gaze around the room, looking for something—anything—to use as a weapon. Jerold wasn't packing, but it doesn't mean there isn't a piece in one of those drawers. Or in the bathroom.

Thinking of this, I whisper to the girl to go in the bathroom and lock the door. She doesn't move. I step forward, point, repeat my order. Still nothing. I take another step, give her a soft slap on the face, and she blinks and nods and hurries into the bathroom.

She closes the door when I hear the man out in the main room clear his throat, then say, "Jerold, man, I'm coming in."

I turn back and jump for a place just beside the door. I flick the switch for the lights just as the knob turns and the door is pushed open. I realize my heels are going to be a burden and slip them off, place the one on the floor, keep the other in my hand. I hold it with the toe pointed toward my wrist, the four-inch heel pointed out.

The door opens wider, yellow light suffusing the plush expensive carpet. The man's silhouette holds a gun at his side.

"Jerold?" he says, caution now in his voice as he takes a step forward.

I wait for him to take another step before I lean out and swing the heel. I aim for his face but luck out and strike him in the throat. His mouth opens and his eyes go wide and his free hand goes to his neck like it will do any good, which it won't, because I've driven the heel right into his larynx.

He tries raising the gun with his other hand but I grab it, turn it around so it's aimed at his chest. I place one bullet there and push past him into the main room, see that with the four girls two men in suits have been lounging on the couches. The men are already scrambling to their feet, already reaching for their guns. I put two bullets in the one guy's head, two bullets in the other guy's, and then I'm running forward, the gun aimed at the guy behind the wet bar.

He ducks behind the glass, comes back up with a SIG MPX K, and lets it rip.

I dive behind one of the couches for cover. I'm barely aware of the girls screaming and the rap music blaring and the deafening blasts of the gunfire. I eject the magazine, see how many rounds I have left, pop the magazine back in, rack the slide and wait a moment, a half second, before I make my move.

The guy behind the wet bar's an idiot—he exhausts the entire 30-round mag, which gives me the chance to pop back up from behind the couch, aim and fire toward the wet bar. He sees me and ducks, but I plan for that and aim low, striking him in the chest.

Two of the girls have been caught in the crossfire, their dead bodies spread out like rag dolls on the floor. The other two girls keep low with their hands to their ears, crying and screaming.

The foyer door opens and the gunfire starts up again, the guy who'd frisked me charging in with his finger pressing the trigger of his Glock. I put it down to a rookie mistake—you never charge into a gunfight, not if you don't know what's what first—and I shoot him in the left leg twice, the guy crying out, falling, dropping his weapon.

I reach him a second later as he tries to stand back up, tries to reach for the gun. I bend down and pick up his gun, knowing he has more rounds in his piece than in mine.

His face is red. It looks like he's hyperventilating. I should tell him to take it easy, just breathe, but instead I point his own gun at his face.

"Easy, baby, everything's okay." I've dropped my dumb schoolgirl act and speak in my normal tone of voice. "You're going to be a good boy and help me out here, okay? Otherwise I'm going to kill you."

He's still hyperventilating. His eyes are huge. He manages to say, "Fuck ... you," and tries to spit at me.

I shoot him a third time in the leg.

He screams, begs for me to stop.

I say, "Then stand up, you sissy."

He raises himself on his elbow but that's as far as he gets. I have to help him with the rest. Keeping the Glock aimed at him, I pull him up then push him forward, toward the main room, the gun digging into his back.

"Believe it or not," I tell him, "I don't plan on killing you.

So listen carefully to me, do as I say, and I won't shoot your spine in half."

He tries to act tough but it's difficult when you have three bullets in your leg. He limps forward into the main room and I direct him toward the master bedroom, the one where Roland took his trio of girls.

The air has become thick and bitter with cordite. I realize the rap music is still blaring. I don't have a remote so I take a moment to shoot the stereo system. That takes care of the music, but leaves the porno going. The thing makes me sick, so I put a bullet in the widescreen.

The guy takes this as his cue to be a hero. He turns and tries to make a play. I block his first punch, push his fist away, step forward and knee him in the balls. He goes down groaning.

"Get the fuck back up," I tell him and use the back of his jacket to yank him to his feet.

The two girls still alive keep crying. One of them realizes the gunfire has stopped and hurries toward the foyer. The other follows. She's in such a hurry she stumbles and falls, for some reason can't remember how to get back up, and sobs into the carpet.

I push the guy farther ahead. The bedroom is ten feet away. The door is still closed.

When we reach it I put the barrel of the Glock to the back of his neck.

"Open it."

"But—"

"Now," I say, and he does, and the moment the door is opened gunfire comes from inside, and I hunch down and use the guy's body as a shield as I push him into the room where all three girls are naked and hiding behind the bed, Roland also naked and standing there with a .45 in his hands, yelling as he fires.

But then the realization hits him that he's shooting one of his own men. He pauses, frowns, and I push my human shield away, take aim, and place one bullet right between Roland's eyes.

The naked girls start screaming. Two of them get up and rush past me. I let them. The last one stays where she is behind the bed, crying.

I walk over to where Roland has fallen. I get a load of how small his junk is and have to suppress a smile. I bend down, grab the golden flash drive, and jerk it away so that the chain snaps.

"Scooter, you hear me?"

"Yeah."

"Target's out and I have the prize."

"Good. Now get th-th-the hell out of there. More are c-c-coming!"

I glance over at the girl sobbing beside the bed, the girl looking back at me with tears in her eyes and her lips trembling.

"How many?"

"At least four."

"Roland's men?"

"Definitely not Bellagio security."

"When?"

"Any second now."

SEVEN

Back in the main room, I stop by the wet bar and grab the dead guy's MPX K. I search his pockets, thankfully find he has another mag. I stuff the Glock in the waistband of my skirt and then eject the MPX K's spent magazine, load the fresh, and hurry around the bar.

The hooker who'd stumbled and forgotten how to get back up is still sobbing into the carpet. I keep the pistol aimed at the foyer door as I reach down and take a fistful of dress fabric. I try to pull her to her feet but her body is dead weight and she just starts sobbing how she doesn't want to die.

"Then stand up and maybe you won't."

She stops sobbing for a moment, looks up at me. She wipes at her eyes, scrambles to her feet. Then she just stands there, her legs shaking, biting her lip.

I motion toward the foyer door, say, "Go," and she takes off, running awkwardly because one of her heels has fallen off and she's too scared to notice or even care.

Then she's gone and I start to head in that direction but pause when I realize I'm forgetting something.

Back in the other bedroom then, stepping over Jerold's

body, hurrying toward the bathroom, I knock once on the door and speak in Spanish, telling the girl that it's okay, it's me. I push the door open. The bathroom is empty. I take another step, confused now, and notice that the shower curtain has been drawn. I step over and pull it aside, find the Hispanic girl lying in a fetal position in the base of the tub.

"Hey," I shout, and when she looks up at me, I say, "Let's go."

She murmurs in Spanish, "Leave me here. They're going to kill me anyway."

Scooter says, "Ah, Holly, what do you th-th-think you're doing? Th-Those men are coming up the elevator right now."

I ignore Scooter and tell the girl nobody is going to kill her, that I'm going to make sure of it.

"You saved my life," I tell her. "Now I'm going to save yours."

She still doesn't look convinced. I extend my hand, keep it there, listening to my heart palpitate in my ears, listening to Scooter telling me to hurry the fuck up. Finally the girl takes my hand and I pull her out of the tub. Seconds later we're in the main room, heading toward the foyer, and the entire time the girl hasn't let go of my hand. Then we're at the foyer door and I open it and step out at the same time there is a ding farther down the hallway and the elevator opens.

I push the girl back into the room, crouch and aim at the elevator. But the people that step out are civilians, a man and woman dressed up for the club, and they're laughing about something until they turn and see me and the gun and their laughter dies.

Before I have a chance to lower my gun, before I even have a chance to tell them to get to their room, another elevator dings and the doors open and men appear, very bad men in suits, and they have weapons in their hands and see me and raise those weapons and begin firing.

The couple dies first. The woman screams and the man yells and they try to duck away but bullets tear into their bodies and then I find myself yelling too, raising the MPX K and returning fire.

I manage to hit one of the men. The other three step back to take cover in the elevator. I glance behind me, see the emergency exit, yell for the girl. Her face appears in the doorway but she looks scared and I know I should just leave her, that she'll slow me down. Maybe these men won't bother with her, will leave her alone, but it's a very thin maybe. And besides, this girl saved my life when she didn't have to and I owe it to her, so I yell at her again to move. She takes a step forward, another hesitant one, and I grab her hand and pull her forward and push her toward the emergency exit just as the three men step back out of the elevator.

I walk backward, firing at the men sparingly since I don't have an extra magazine. They take cover in the elevator again and I turn back around, sprint toward the door the girl has just gone through and slam it shut right as bullets rip into the door and shatter the glass.

The girl is already hurrying down the stairs. Following, I tell Scooter we're in the stairwell heading down.

"I know," he says.

"How?"

"A sensor goes off. Look, the police have been tipped about what's going on. A bunch of th-th-them are already in the lobby."

The girl is one flight ahead of me. I hurry to keep up.

"Nova, you there?"

"What's up?"

"I'll have a package for you to grab."

"The prize?"

"That and another."

Nova asks me what this means but I ignore him and

continue down the steps. I've long since ditched my heels and the thin fabric of my stockings threatens to make me slip. Past the twenty-fifth floor, past the twenty-fourth, I hear the heavy footsteps closing in behind us. I can keep going—running five miles is a regular part of my daily workout—but it's clear the girl is slowing down. She's holding her side, wheezing, and I know she won't be able to go another twenty floors at the same speed.

I push myself even harder, finally reaching up to her. I take her by the arm, and at the first floor we come to—the twenty-first—I open the door and push her into the hallway.

We hurry toward the elevators. Thankfully the hallway is deserted. I know cameras are watching us—have been watching us the entire time—and that the police are probably sealing off every exit.

I press the button for the elevators and start counting—one, two, three, four, five—and then there's the ding and the doors open just as the emergency exit opens and the men appear. I see one of them raise his gun but it's just as we're stepping into the elevator and he doesn't bother firing.

I press the button for the lobby, and the doors close.

"Nova, we're in the elevator headed down to the lobby right now."

"Who the hell is we?"

The girl is having a hard time catching her breath. She asks who I'm talking to.

We pass the fifteenth floor.

"Nova, are you there?"

"Almost."

The girl asks again, "Who are you talking to?"

We pass the tenth floor.

"Nova?"

"You got a weapon on you, Holly, you better ditch it. Expect the police once those doors open."

"How many police?"

"A shitload."

"What's going to happen to me?" the girl asks. "No police. I can't go back. Please."

Three more floors, two more floors, one more floor, and as the elevator slows, I flick the safety on the MPX K and drop it to the floor and kick it to the corner. I feel the press of the Glock against the small of my back, and I flap the back of my shirt to make sure it's concealed. The doors open and I take hold of the girl's arm, begin crying, screaming, telling the dozen men in uniforms that they had guns, they were gonna kill us.

The police have their weapons drawn. Suspicion is in their eyes. But then they see the two of us—helpless young women —and the suspicion starts to fade. Empathy replaces it, and two officers step forward, take our arms, try to hurry us out of the elevators. I don't let go of the girl; she doesn't let go of me. I bring the tears on without any trouble and the girl takes my cue and doesn't stop either. We play a pair of blubbering idiots. People are everywhere watching us. I spot Nova in the crowd. The cops are leading us away from him but then another set of elevator doors opens and then there is shouting and gunfire and the place explodes with activity.

The two cops leading us away let go and turn back toward the action. I hold on to the girl and lead her toward Nova. He opens his mouth but I shake my head and push the girl toward him, say, "Take her back to the garage." He knows better than to argue; he takes her arm and then they're slipping through the crowd of people that is quickly dispersing, everyone running and screaming now that there's gunfire.

I turn back around, inspect the damage. I hold the chain up at my side, the gold coin swaying back and forth. If any of Roland's men are watching, they'll recognize it. If they recognize it, they'll understand what's happened and come for me.

That's fine. My goal here is ensuring nobody follows Nova and the girl.

The gunfire continues by the elevators. It's only been going on now for thirty seconds. Some police are hit, some of Roland's people are hit. The three that were in the elevators don't look like they'll be a problem for me.

But then I see more of Roland's men. It looks like just two of them. Not wearing suits but dressed casually, like a pair of insomniac gamblers.

They're watching me, fury in their eyes.

I look back at them. I wave. I smile. I give them the finger.

They start toward me.

I run.

EIGHT

Believe it or not, sprinting through the lobby of the Bellagio in a schoolgirl outfit at three o'clock in the morning isn't as conspicuous as you'd think. Not while gunfire continues by the elevators. Not while someone has apparently pulled the fire alarm and strobes are blinking and a siren is blaring. Not while almost everyone else is hurrying away, running for their lives. So yeah, me running through the lobby, the gold flash drive swinging from my hand, isn't that strange at all.

I come outside and see cop cars everywhere, their lights flashing red and white. The people closest to the entrance when the gunfire started have already made it out, many crowded around like the violence inside has no chance of escaping. A few police officers stand around, their weapons drawn, looking back and forth frantically.

The Strip is still heavy with traffic, people at Bally's and Paris across the street having no idea the amount of chaos ensuing inside the Bellagio. They're drinking, gambling, not having a care in the world, while right behind me people are screaming and crying and dying.

Coming up the drive is a group riding motorcycles. The

cycles are crotch rockets, what look like Hondas, and I start in the group's direction.

The guy in front has stopped his bike, straddling it as he takes off his helmet. I glance behind me, the entrance now fifty yards away, the pair of Roland's men having just made it outside. I turn my attention back to the guy on the lead bike, say with a seductive smile, "Hey, that's a sweet ride."

He's overly tan and has long dark hair with highlights and probably drinks Red Bull. He smiles and says, "Thanks. Maybe you'd want to go for a ride sometime?"

I'm standing less than five feet away, really putting on the charm, giving him a sexy look as I grab his helmet and say, "Actually, I'd love to go for a ride right now."

Looking surprised, he says, "Really?"

I glance behind me. Roland's men are running now, their guns out and held at their sides.

"Only thing is," I tell the guy, stepping close, "I don't ride bitch."

The smile fades abruptly. He gives me a confused look but by then I've put on the helmet—it's sweaty and smells of cigarettes—and I've grabbed the one handle of the Honda and with my other hand I shove the guy off the bike. He shouts and falls back, loses his balance, hits the ground. I'm already on the bike, applying the throttle, letting go of the clutch, before the guy even has a chance to sit back up.

The Honda's rear tire burns rubber as I incorporate a one-eighty, and then I'm speeding away, hearing a distant pop behind me as one of Roland's men fires.

At the end of the drive I brake and stop and glance back. Roland's men have taken a much less subtler approach in acquiring their transportation. A number of the other riders are either on the ground or starting to get back to their feet, having been thrown off. Both of Roland's men are now on the bikes, turning them around, heading toward me.

Of course they'd know how to ride a motorcycle. How naïve of me to think otherwise.

I give them an extra second to make sure they see me, and then I shoot out onto the Strip.

I'm headed south, swerving in and out of traffic. Some people brake, some honk and shout obscenities. I keep riding. I pass the Monte Carlo, the MGM Grand, and at the main intersection right by New York New York the traffic light flicks to yellow and then red. Cars are stopped in front of me and I swerve up onto the sidewalk, downshift so I don't run into the late-night stragglers.

At the corner I glance back, see Roland's men are right on my tail. They're following my lead, up on the sidewalk now, and I give it an extra second before I pop the clutch and then I'm speeding over the sidewalk onto Tropicana Avenue.

I've been to Las Vegas before at least a half-dozen times, I know my way around the city pretty well, and my plan now is to lose them on the interstate.

So that's just what I do—I merge onto 15 and head north. The traffic is lighter here. A couple taxis, a couple tractor-trailers, a number of cars. As I pass one car I look over just as the car's driver looks over. He sees me on the bike, sees me in my outfit with my skirt and shirt flapping in the wind, and makes a face. Because he can't see my smile, I give him a thumbs-up. Then I glance behind me and see the two of them back there, headed my way. I let up off the throttle, letting them catch up. As they do, I reach behind me for the Glock.

Seconds later the two men are riding right on my tail. We're doing seventy-five miles per hour, almost eighty. They're spread out, one behind me on the left, the other behind me on the right. Both of them have their weapons drawn. I hit the brake just a little and they zoom past, both looking back at me as the same time. I do a quick eeny, meeny, miny, moe, and then I raise the gun, fire at the man to my right. The bullets hit him in the back. He goes down hard, the bike scraping against the highway, spitting up sparks.

The other man points his gun back at me. He starts firing. I duck and swerve off to the left and—shit—lose the Glock in the process.

The man veers wide to the right. He glances my way, starts to drop back. I accelerate. I push it hard, watching the glowing needle go up to eighty, eighty-five, ninety, and I concentrate on the highway, on the cars and taxis and tractor-trailers, swerving from one lane to the next, knowing the man is right on my tail. No way is he going to try to take another shot, not at this speed, but then again I have run into dumber dipshits, so maybe this one will surprise me.

I try calling Nova or Scooter, but my voice is too muffled because of the helmet. Besides, the transmitter only goes up to two miles, and if everything went accordingly, they should already be headed to the garage.

The interchange is coming up fast. I make a split-second decision and veer right, merging onto 515. I continue on for maybe a tenth of a mile and then slow for the exit. Next thing I know I'm back on Las Vegas Boulevard. Driving up three blocks and then pulling over onto the side of the street, I jump off the bike, take off my helmet, and glance back the way I came.

Roland's man has kept up and is coming my way.

Making sure he sees me, I wait another moment and then turn and start down Fremont Street.

Despite the late hour, the place is packed. At this time of night, the freaks have come out. I figure with my outfit I should blend right in, but still I get a few stares, even a whistle. I glance back, expecting to see Roland's man having ditched his bike, following me now on foot. But I'll be damned if the crazy son of a bitch hasn't driven up onto the sidewalk. He's revving his engine as he maneuvers around people trying to scurry out of his way, and he has the gun in hand, as if he isn't making himself conspicuous enough.

If there is a God, he'd have police swarm on this stupid schmuck right now, but maybe God's busy playing craps at the Golden Nugget. I am by myself, surrounded by people, and without looking back—with just sensing it—I know Roland's man has seen me.

I approach the Four Queens, quickly dart into the casino. If I draw some stares, I'm not aware of it, because I keep my focus on the entrance. I position myself to the side, the helmet in my hands. I wait. Listening to the sounds of the casino, listening to the hushed murmur of disembodied voices, I can just hear the motorcycle approaching. I hear it shut off.

Roland's man appears moments later. He still has his gun out in one hand. I figure, what the hell, for anyone watching now it'd be self-defense, and as he takes a step forward I wind up my arm holding the helmet and smash it right into his face.

He goes down hard. The gun clatters to the ground. I kick it out of his reach and keep wailing on him with the helmet. It's just like déjà vu, like I'm back in the bedroom with Jerold. Only now I have a captive audience, people having gone silent watching. The only sounds are the bells and whistles of the slot machines. I smell sweat and cigarette smoke and the distant aroma of the buffet. The man's face has become a bloody mess.

I stand up straight, drop the helmet, and turn back to everyone staring at me.

"This bastard just tried raping me!" I shout.

Then I walk away, dipping low to pick up the gun, concealing it in my shirt as I disappear into the moving crowd of freaks.

NINE

The boys aren't happy with me.

Scooter hasn't spoken to me since I've returned to the garage. He keeps himself busy packing up his computers on the table. Every couple seconds he glances back at me with a scowl as he chomps on his gum.

I guess it doesn't matter though. Nova does enough talking for both of them. Standing in front of me, his arms crossed, he says, "Just what the fuck were you thinking?"

"You mean back at the hotel? I was thinking about staying alive. Besides, what the hell do you care? Not like you had to do any hard work."

"Actually, for your information, your little friend over there and I ran into some trouble. One of Roland's men was hanging out by the garage entrance."

I roll my eyes, shake my head. "God, just how many henchmen did this bastard have?"

"He came at us with his gun drawn. He even aimed the fucking thing at my head."

"Well," I say, crossing my arms now to match Nova,

"judging by the fact you're standing here telling me this captivating story, I'm guessing you made it out alive."

"Just barely. The fucker actually took a shot at us. I had to bat the gun away, hit him in the throat, break his neck."

"Aw, poor baby. You actually had to get your hands dirty for once?"

Nova, his face already red, opens his mouth to respond. But before he can, Scooter slams his hands down on the table. He turns around to glare at us.

"Enough of this shit," he says. "What's in the past is in the past. Each of us is st-st-still alive, which is all we can ask for after a job. Now the only thing left to ask are two questions both Nova and I have been asking ourselves for the past half hour. Just who the f-f-fuck is that woman and why the f-f-f-fuck did you have her brought here?"

I'll admit it—Scooter's intensity catches me off guard. Very rarely does he raise his voice like this. Normally he's the easygoing one, the guy who's always cracking jokes, looking on the brighter side of things, sometimes even making fun of his own stutter. Not the guy who has venom in his eyes.

The girl is standing off in the corner. Apparently she hasn't said a word to either Nova or Scooter this entire time. She hasn't even let them near her. But when I first arrived she ran over to me, wrapped her arms around my neck, murmuring in Spanish how happy she was to see me. Then when Nova came over and started up with me she slipped away to the spot she's standing in right now.

"Well?" Scooter says, and when I glance at him I see his jaw is still and I think it's the first time I've ever seen him not chewing his bubblegum.

"She saved my life. I needed to repay the debt."

"That doesn't answer the questions, Holly." Nova still has his arms crossed, glaring at me. "Who is she and why is she here?"

"She's a prostitute," I say.

"No shit."

"But I don't think she's any ordinary prostitute."

"What makes you th-th-think that?" Scooter asks. "The fact that she's an illegal?"

I ignore him and walk past Nova to the girl. I hold my hand out to her and smile and tell her my name. I ask her what her name is. She says it's Rosalina.

"It's very nice to meet you, Rosalina. Thank you again for your help back at the hotel."

She shrugs and looks away, embarrassed.

I push on. "Rosalina, you mentioned something about men and a ranch. What did you mean by that?"

Still looking at something near the ceiling, Rosalina shakes her head.

"Please," I insist, "I want to help you. But you need to tell me about them."

Her eyes shift to meet my own, and I can see tears are threatening. In a very small voice, she says, "They will kill me if I tell you."

"No, they won't. I promise they won't. Now please. Please tell me."

And so she tells me. Not a lot at first. She's vague and I have to keep asking questions, and when she speaks her words are slow and thoughtful. Then, the more questions I ask and the more she answers, her words begin to increase. Soon she's frantic, telling me everything, every terrible detail, her arms waving around, tears streaming down her cheeks. Then she falls silent. She holds her hands to her face, begins sobbing.

I place a hand on her shoulder, squeeze it, tell her that it will be okay, before turning away and walking back to where Nova and Scooter now stand together.

"So what's the deal?" Nova asks.

"The deal is that she is one of at least twenty women kept prisoner in a place out in the desert."

Scooter is already shaking his head, knowing exactly where this is going. "Don't even th-th-think about it. Our job here is done. Now it's time to go home."

"You know I can't do that."

"Holly—" Nova begins.

"The girls at this ranch only get five percent of what they make. Until they earn five thousand dollars each, not one of them is free to go. They're slaves. Their whole purpose is to be a whore. They fuck and suck and most times they get beat by the men that request them. Apparently that's what the place specializes in—very rough sex."

Both men are silent, staring back at me. I glance over my shoulder and see Rosalina standing right where I left her, still sobbing. Now in brighter light and away from danger, it's clear just how emaciated she is. That was another thing she said, something I don't bother mentioning to the boys because I'm sure they already know the truth: the men who run the place starve the girls, get them addicted to drugs, sometimes beat and rape them if they're bored.

When it's clear neither of the boys is going to say anything, I shake my head in disgust. "You both are cowards."

Nova keeps his arms crossed, his face impassive. "Holly, this isn't our problem. If you want to call the police, be my guest. But we can't get involved."

"You've said that before."

"Yeah, but this time I mean it. Remember what happened in Berlin? I do. We almost got killed working on one of your fucking crusades."

"One of my fucking crusades," I say, nodding. "That's nice, Nova. Thanks for that."

"Holly"—Scooter now, his voice back to normal—"just th-th-think for a moment. Just one moment. I've said this to you before and I'll say it again: You can't save the world. It's just not possible. Yeah, I feel bad for this girl—for all the girls there—and yeah, those men no doubt deserve to pay. But let the police handle it. Our time here is up."

I stare back at them for another long moment. I'm thinking about Rosalina, of course, and the rest of the girls back at what she calls "the ranch." But I'm also thinking about another woman I once knew, someone I'd called a friend, someone who had something terrible happen to her and then killed herself.

It's her face I see now as I stare back at Scooter and Nova, her ragged, sorrow-filled face, and before I know it I'm turning away from the boys.

"Don't," Nova says, and I pause. "Holly, if you go through with this, you're on your own. I'm sorry, but neither of us can involve ourselves. It isn't our fight."

I wait there a moment, just one moment, and then I turn away completely, start walking, staring intently at Rosalina until I come to stand directly in front of her.

"Rosalina, this place you told me about, the ranch—do you know where it's located in the desert?"

Her eyes shift again, this time toward the floor. They stay there for a moment, then shift back up to stare into mine. Wiping at her face, she slowly nods.

I reach out a hand, place it on her arm. "Show me."

TEN

After I let the Town Car roll to a stop, I place it in park and shut off the engine. We just sit there then in darkness, neither one of us speaking. Eventually I look over at Rosalina. She looks at me. After a moment she nods and points out through the windshield, at the rocky hills in front of us.

"There," she says. "It's over there."

Rosalina had taken me down the road that leads to the private drive that leads back to the ranch. I'd backtracked then to the highway, taken that for a half mile north. At some point I turned off the highway, cut the headlights and did a good job of not hitting the brakes, rolling over the dirt and rocks and through the sagebrush for a quarter mile, so that anybody driving by on the highway wouldn't see us. Now we're wrapped in darkness, the moon almost full, the stars bright, and Rosalina has just confirmed what I already know.

"Wait here," I say.

I've already flicked the dome light off, so when I open the door the darkness remains. I open the back door, reach in and grab the sports bag the boys had given me before I left the garage. They may be cowards but they're not complete assholes, and they didn't let me walk away empty-handed.

I've changed out of the schoolgirl outfit, now wear jeans and a T-shirt. The only weapon I have on me is a Kimber Micro 9 Nightfall, strapped to my ankle.

The other two weapons I pull out of the sports bag: a nine-millimeter SIG Sauer P226 Nitron and an FN 15 Patrol Carbine.

Rosalina opens her door and slowly steps out. Despite everything she still wears her heels and they crunch the dirt in the dead silence.

"You are really going by yourself?"

I set the P226 on the roof to check the rifle, ejecting the magazine, slamming it back in.

"These are very bad men," Rosalina says. "They will kill you."

I strap the FN 15 over my shoulder, grab the gun, check its magazine then rack the slide. Reach back into the sports bag for its holster, clip the holster to my belt.

Rosalina persists. "Why are you doing this?"

It makes me pause. Sure, Nova and Scooter asking the same question, that's one thing, but a complete stranger, an illegal who has been forced into prostitution asking why I'm trying to help save her?

Before I can respond, she says, "You are a killer, yes? A ... assassin?"

Actually, when people ask what it is I do for work, I tell them I'm a nanny. I tell them I watch two children, a boy and a girl, who I sometimes wish were my own children and who I sometimes wish would shut the hell up and quit being brats.

The killing people thing, the non-sanctioned government missions, that's just work on the side that I keep to myself.

"Do you not want me to kill these men, Rosalina?"

She takes a moment to think about this, raising her thumb to her mouth, biting the nail. Finally she shakes her head.

"These men," she says, "they are very, very bad. But …"

"But?"

"But us women, we are all here in this country illegally. What … what will then become of us?"

It's like a giant corkscrew jammed into my stomach, being twisted and twisted, this question of hers catching me so off guard. Here is a girl younger than me but yet looks ten years older, who has been forced into a life of prostitution where half the time she is beaten to an inch of her life—here is this girl finding herself preferring this rather than being sent back home.

"Who says you'll be sent back?"

Rosalina gives a soft, sardonic laugh. "Everyone in this country hates people like me. We are … less than human. We are trash. They will send me back to my country without a second's thought or care."

"But wouldn't you rather be back in your country? Don't you have anyone there?"

"I have my husband and children, yes."

Rosalina sees my expression and quickly shakes her head.

"No, no, believe me when I say I love and miss my family more than anything in the world. We came over here four years ago, us and a dozen others. But then the police came and took my husband and children and many of the others away. There were only a few of us left, women, and we had nothing—no money, no shelter, absolutely nothing."

"I still don't understand. Why then wouldn't you want to go back?"

"Because this … this is America." She says this in such an obvious way, a soft light starting to burn in her eyes. "This is the land of wealth and freedom. You have to work to get it, and once I get it, I will send for my husband and children."

I see where she's going with this and ask, "Rosalina, how much money have you earned since you've been at the ranch?"

She looks away, tallying the amount up in her head. "Almost six hundred dollars."

"So that means you need another four thousand four hundred dollars before you are free."

She nods, slowly, that soft light dimming bit by bit in her eyes.

I don't tell her the obvious, something she must already know but something she has blinded herself to. She just stares back at me, her eyes filling again, and slowly shakes her head.

"I cannot return empty-handed."

I reach back into the sports bag, pull out the last toy Scooter has provided me. It's a night-vision scope which I stuff into the front of my pants pocket. Then I softly shut the back door and walk around to the other side, keeping my gaze level with Rosalina. When I reach her I place my hand on her shoulder and ask her to again tell me everything she can about the ranch.

She wipes at her eyes, slowly shakes her head. "Please tell me—why are you doing this?"

I think about that woman from years ago, the one I used to know, the one who called me a friend, and I say to Rosalina, "Because nobody else will."

ELEVEN

The darkness has taken on a greenish-yellow tint. I can distinctly see the ranch house at the base of the desert, a squat brick building with bars over the windows. Adjacent to this is another building, just one room, a shack where Rosalina says the guards spend most of their time.

There is no electricity, no indoor plumbing to either building. A generator growls softly in the night, keeping the lights on inside the guards' house.

I lie on my stomach on top of the rocky hill, the night-vision scope to my eye. I sit up and turn, focus back down to the other side of the hill where I parked the Town Car. Rosalina is inside, the keys in the ignition. I told her if I don't return within an hour, or if she senses trouble, to take the car and never return.

In the heavy and cold silence, a sound comes from down the hill. Rusty hinges screech as a door opens. A man steps outside. I focus the scope on him. He's tall, Hispanic, wearing a holstered gun on his belt. He stands there a moment, looking out over the dark. He pulls out a pack of cigarettes, lights one, then starts toward the sagebrush, unzipping his pants.

I watch the man smoke and piss, then watch as he zips back up, turns away, takes one last drag before dropping the spent butt to the ground, smashing it with the heel of his boot. The man walks back to the building, turns to glance once more at the dark, his eyes roaming like he's searching for something, and then he turns and walks back inside.

Putting away the scope, taking the FN 15 from where it hangs off my shoulder, I grip the rifle in both hands and then slowly start down the hill. I take my time. The light here isn't great, and I put one foot in front of the other, make sure it's solid ground before I place all my weight onto it and continue on. It takes a while, but then I'm less than fifty yards away from the ranch house. Close now, I can hear voices and music inside the guards' building. Someone laughs, someone else coughs. I listen another minute, determine there are at least four men inside.

I start toward the ranch house. I keep the FN 15 aimed at the guards' building as I move. Rosalina said that most times the men lock the ranch house. Sometimes they don't lock it on purpose, to give the girls a false sense of freedom, and any girl stupid enough to try to escape gets raped and beaten.

Tonight the guards haven't played one of their mind games. The door is locked. Maybe it has to do with the trouble earlier tonight. Surely the men know what has happened, since at least one of their girls was involved.

The rusty hinges of the door scream out into the night. Another man exits the guards' house, a different man than before but a man who still wears a holstered gun. I expect him to pull a pack of smokes out of his pocket, but instead he starts walking off toward the same patch of sagebrush, what seems to be the favored pissing ground.

I think about my options. I don't have many.

The guy stops at the edge of the sagebrush, unzips his pants. He stands there a moment, murmuring something in

Spanish, and then I hear the steady stream of his piss splash the dry ground.

I don't have time to think. He's fifty feet away, maybe forty. His back is exposed. He has a gun but I have three, and before another moment of hesitation I start toward him, quickly, doing my best to keep my sneakers from making any sound on the hard dirt. Past the guards' house where I hear voices and laughter and music—someone inside asking, "Anyone else want a beer?"—closer and closer to the man who keeps pissing, now whistling something, a tune I don't recognize.

Twenty feet away ... fifteen feet ... ten feet ...

He hears me when I'm five feet away. He starts to turn, starts to reach for his holstered gun. I come up right behind him, the FN 15 now strapped back over my shoulder. I jab him in the kidneys once, then take his head in my hands, twist it to break his neck. This isn't as easy as it looks in the movies. The guy's at a bad angle and my twist does nothing more than help him turn around. He's still reaching for his gun, his hand on the handle, trying to pull it out. He wasn't done pissing and his dick is exposed, dripping.

I punch him in the gut, step around him, elbow him in the back of the neck. He goes down. I come up behind him, ready to give this one last try.

I put one arm around the front of his face, another arm around the back of his head. He tries to bite me, cry out, but then I twist and this time hear the satisfying snap of his neck. He's not dead, though; just paralyzed. On the ground, his eyes dart around, his mouth is open and he tries to shout but can only just wheeze. I search his pockets. I don't find the keys I'm looking for but I find a switchblade. I flick the knife open, bend down, and ram the tip right into his throat.

He doesn't die quickly. His body convulses first. He makes a sound like he's choking. Then, after a minute, he goes still.

I stand back up, pull the rifle off my shoulder. I flick off the

safety and start toward the guards' house. I can still hear them
inside. They haven't heard a thing. None are wondering where
their friend has gone.

The main door is open, only a screen door protecting them
from me. Light spills out onto the dirt. I place my hand on the
door, wait a moment to breathe, then open it.

Inside three men sit around a card table. Bottles of beer
litter the table, along with bags of chips and pretzels. First
someone says, "Rico, what took you so long?" and then that
man looks up, sees me, throws his cards down and pushes back
his chair. The other men follow suit.

I shoot each man three times. Two of them get hit in the
chest and go down without any trouble. The last man moves
too fast and my bullets hit him in the shoulder. He goes down,
but he's alive, and he reaches for his weapon, tries to come back
up with it aimed.

I move closer, aiming for his head just as the brings his gun
up. He's fast but I'm faster, and I shoot him right between the
eyes.

For a moment I don't do anything but just stand there. My
heart is racing. I can smell their sweat and cheap beer as well as
the bile that has been released by my killing them. I start with
the man whom I killed last. He doesn't have any keys on him.
The next man does. He has a ring of jangling keys and I take
them back outside and hurry over to the ranch house.

I try a number of keys, come up with the right one, open
the door and step inside. I reach out, fumble for the light
switch, flick it on.

The place is lined with cots. There are at least twenty of
them. More than half are filled. In those that are filled,
battered-looking women peek out from beneath their sheets.
They're expecting one of the guards, not a woman with a rifle
strapped over her shoulder. Rosalina said that most of the girls
there were Mexican, so first I speak Spanish.

"It's time for all of you to leave. Hurry and get your things."

None of the girls move. They must think this is some kind of dream.

"Now!" I shout, and like that they blink and realize this is no dream. They scramble out of their cots. They start running around. Many are smiling. I just stand there, watching them, while one girl with a black eye walks up to me.

"Who are you?" she asks.

"It doesn't matter. I'm here to save you."

"What about the others?"

"Rosalina is fine."

I expect her to smile in relief, but she still gives me that look of worry. She says again, "What about the others?"

"What others?"

The girl's eyes go wide, quickly filling with fear. The other girls stop what they are doing. In the sudden silence I can hear what the girls can, what they are no doubt used to hearing every night: vehicles, what sounds like two of them, approaching quickly.

TWELVE

On the drive up here, Rosalina mentioned something about how the girls are transported. Every night they are taken by one or more of the men in SUVs to specific areas around the city. Usually a guard is posted somewhere to ensure the girls don't try to escape. Rosalina admitted she tried this once and they broke her pinkie fingers for the trouble of tracking her down.

So that's what these vehicles are now, the two SUVs filled with armed men and the girls who had been requested tonight. They've returned, and very soon the armed men will enter the guards' house and see what has become of their friends. They will be angry. They will be fucking pissed. And here I am, trapped in a building with over a dozen women who have no weapons.

I flick the lights back out, shut the door. I tell the girls to get back in their beds. Some are murmuring, some are crying. I raise my voice, speak in Spanish and English forcefully, telling them to move it. Act like nothing's wrong.

Outside, the vehicles stop, their engines shut off. There is the sound of doors opening, the voices of men.

My eyes haven't adjusted to the dark yet but I hurry

forward, trying to find a vacant bed. I pick the first one and lie down on it, pull the covers up to hide the FN 15. At once the reek of body odor hits me, and I wonder just how many nights pass before these girls sleep on clean sheets instead of lying in their own filth.

In the dark, one of the girls speaks in Spanish. "What are you doing?"

"Quiet," I say.

Outside, the crunch of feet on the ground.

"They will kill you," another girl says.

"Shut up," I whisper.

A key slides into the lock. There is a pause, and then the key slides back out. A voice murmurs something, another voice answers.

I close my eyes, take a breath.

The doorknob turns.

I take another breath, tighten my grip on the rifle.

The door pushes open.

One of the girls is still sobbing. My grip tightens even more.

Someone flicks on the lights. I have to squint, turn my head slightly like all the rest of the girls. Here they come, stumbling on their stilettos, all in skimpy dresses. One of the girls is chewing gum, making me think of Scooter for an instant, and it's in that instant the girl's gaze and my gaze lock and she stops walking altogether.

Two men have entered with the girls. Though neither of them carry a gun, it's clear they're packing. One of the men grumbles, "Gloria, get in your fucking bed."

Gloria stares at me for another moment, then starts walking, chewing the gum again. But it's already too late. The half-dozen or so other girls have noticed me too, and they pause, uncertain who this new face is, why I'm here, what's wrong.

But nothing comes of it.

Because it's right then the other men from the SUVs find what's waiting for them in the guards' house. Shouting starts, two or three men outside yelling that there's been an attack, and then the two men in the ranch house reach for their weapons.

Fuck it. Time to work.

I throw the sheet off, jump to my feet as I raise the FN 15. I aim for the guy on the left, who is already drawing his gun, but my bullet just misses him. He ducks, moves to the side. He raises his gun but thinks better of it and bolts back out through the door, leaving his friend who in his panic can't seem to unholster his gun.

Moving forward, snaking through the girls who have started running around screaming, I keep the rifle raised as I near him. My hope is to use him as a shield, but when I'm ten feet away he manages to free his gun and starts to raise it and I have no choice but to fire three rounds into his chest, making his body do one of those crazy dances before he falls to the ground dead.

I jump over him and continue on, slide against the door to peek outside.

At once the men fire, bullets chipping away at the brick. A shard hits me in the face, cuts me on the cheek. I have to turn away for a moment before looking back out, and in the dark I can see the men spread out around the door.

In Spanish one of the men yells, like he's a fucking cop, "Drop your weapons and come out with your hands up!"

I've flattened myself against the wall beside the door. I glance over at the girls, many of whom have gotten on the floor to hide behind their beds.

Silence outside. Then I hear the men begin murmuring. I can't tell exactly what they're saying, but the meaning is clear— they know I'm not going to come out willingly. So the same guy who spoke before, the guy who sounds like a cop and maybe that's because he is a cop, this guy decides to up the ante.

"You girls in there," he shouts, "whoever brings this bitch out is free to leave immediately!"

I glance back at the girls. I see the same thing enter into their eyes at the same time. That promise of freedom none of them ever thought they'd receive.

It enters their heads, sure, but I know none of them are actually stupid enough to believe it let alone consider it.

But one of the girls—she was working tonight, still in her dress and heels—stands up.

"Julio," she shouts, "do you promise?"

I start shaking my head.

Julio says, "Yes, you have my word. Get the fucking cunt out here and you're free to leave. *Anybody* who helps is free to leave."

The girl is moving before Julio's done speaking. Two other girls decide to follow.

"Stop," I say and aim the FN 15 at them.

The two followers stop. The first girl keeps coming. She's lived as a slave for years and now sees a chance at freedom, and no matter how fucked up it is, she's going to take it.

Her face is red and her eyes are dark, like she's hopped up on something, and she's ten feet away from me, then five feet, and of course I'm not going to shoot her, she must know this, but I'm still not going to let her throw me to the wolves.

When she's less than two feet away I lower the rifle, pivot it and smash the butt into her stomach. The wind is knocked out of her. She falls to the floor, wheezing, and the two followers rush me, screaming bloody murder.

I don't have a chance.

Before I know it they're on me, pulling at the rifle, at my gun. The men have sensed what's happening and have hurried inside. They push the girls away, bend down and grab me, and even though I try to kick and punch and bite, they drag me outside.

They throw me down on the dirt.

Someone kicks me in the ribs, another kicks me in the butt.

Then the men stand back and form a circle, their pistols aimed at me, each with his finger on a trigger.

THIRTEEN

"Who the fuck are you?"

I presume this guy is Julio. He wears chinos and a brown shirt with the sleeves rolled up to the elbows. A gold chain hangs around his neck. He grips a Browning 1911, aimed straight at me.

I don't answer him.

He looks at his friends, shakes his head and grins. "Shame, we really could use a tough girl like you. I wouldn't mind testing you out myself."

I slowly start to push myself up from the ground. I put my weight on one knee, my hands raised in defeat.

"The problem is," Julio says, "you seem to be a fucking cunt. And we hate fucking cunts."

There are five men but the guy I'm concerned about right now is Julio. He seems to be the leader of the group. He has a chip in one of his front teeth and this is what I concentrate on as he speaks, no longer hearing his words, just slowly trying to stand back up, acting like I'm hurt. I balance myself on my knee and reach down, as if I'm going to push off the ground with both hands. But while my right hand is down there I reach for the Kimber strapped to my ankle, bring it up, and use one bullet to make Julio's chipped tooth disappear.

His head snaps back, but most importantly, he shuts the fuck up. I shift the Kimber to the man next to him, but before I can pull the trigger, one of the men behind me steps up close and presses the barrel of his gun against the top of my head.

Suddenly there's a crack, then another crack, then another, and at first I don't understand because it's not coming from any of these men's guns. No, it's coming from somewhere else, somewhere in the dark. One of the men jerks, goes down, followed by another man—the barrel pressing against the top of my head disappears—and the two remaining men disperse, returning fire into the darkness of the desert.

An engine growls in the night. Headlights are flicked on, showing a vehicle already coming up the drive to the ranch house. Even from here I can see it's the Escalade, having crawled this far without lights, now speeding forward.

At once I understand who's in the dark shooting, and I figure Nova must be set up on one of the hills with a sniper rifle. The two men continue to return fire, forgetting me momentarily, and I shoot the first man, then the second.

The gun in hand, I do a quick three-sixty, making sure there are no more surprises. The only movement that catches my eye are the girls now huddled in the doorway of the ranch house, the girl I'd popped in the gut glaring at me.

Ignoring her, I hurry over to the guards' house. It's empty, the same men still lying dead in the same positions I left them in. I come back out just as Scooter pulls up the Escalade. Nova hurries down from the hill, his rifle in hand. I sprint forward, more glad than ever to see them.

Nova reaches the Escalade first. He opens the back door, tosses in his rifle, shakes his head at me as he closes the door.

"I thought Berlin was the last time," I say to him, grinning.

Scooter shuts off the engine, opens the door and steps out.

He too is shaking his head, but he's smiling as he chews his gum. "You, Holly, are one crazy bitch."

"Yeah, but I'm one hot crazy bitch."

He laughs, shakes his head again, steps forward to take me into an embrace. It's a rare thing but I allow it, my heart still pounding, knowing how close to biting it I had come. I've been there before, right near the threshold of death's doorway, but always managed to jump back. This time I wasn't sure I was going to make it.

Nova must see it first. My back is to the ranch house, the girls momentarily forgotten. Scooter is hugging me, holding me tight, and Nova is standing behind him, still smiling. Then the smile fades. He starts to open his mouth but it's Scooter I hear shouting. Next thing I know I'm being squeezed even tighter, Scooter grabbing me and turning to the side, letting go as he turns back and faces whatever's coming at him.

It's the girl I'd popped, the one who had first moved at Julio's demand. She's come out of the ranch house, picked up one of the guns, and God help me, I realize it's my gun she has, the P226 now raised as she hurries forward, screaming and firing.

Scooter takes the bullets. He stays in front of me and he takes each bullet, and for an instant I just stand there, paralyzed, not sure what to do.

Then I move. Even before Nova can, I step past Scooter and run at the girl who's running at me. She's still shooting but I don't care. I intercept her, knock the gun out of her hand, punch her in the face, kick her in the knee, send her to the ground. Then I reach down, grab the gun—my own goddamned gun—and stand back up, aim at her face and fire until she no longer has a face, until there are no more bullets, and I'm left pulling the trigger and hearing the dry clicks.

Nova shouts my name.

The woman is dead but still I want to kill her again.

"Holly, help me!"

I turn away. The gun still in hand, I sprint back to the Escalade. Nova is on his knees, holding Scooter. Somehow, Scooter is still alive. His entire chest has been ravaged by bullets but he's still alive.

I fall to my knees. I say to Nova, "Start the truck."

"Holly—"

"Start the truck!"

He gets to his feet, runs to the Escalade. The engine roars to life.

I hold Scooter, whispering to him that everything's going to be okay. He wheezes, coughs up blood.

Nova is back out of the Escalade, hurrying over to pick up Scooter. I run to the back, open the door and get inside to help Nova load Scooter in. Scooter is wheezing even more, and I don't know why I kid myself, but I actually think that it will be okay. That we'll get Scooter the help he needs. That they'll extract the bullets, close the wounds, nurse him back to health.

I even murmur this to him as Nova gets into the front of the Escalade, puts it in gear, spins the tires in the dirt as he does a wild one-eighty and sends us back down the drive toward the road. I hold Scooter close, Scooter who keeps wheezing and coughing up blood, and I tell him that everything will be okay, it will be okay, it will be okay, until at some point he stops wheezing and stops coughing up blood and the piece of bubblegum he was chewing falls from his mouth to the floor.

PART TWO

WORK IS WORK

FOURTEEN

At 5:45 AM my alarm goes off. I'm already awake. I've been awake, just lying here in bed, staring up at the ceiling or at the corners of my room or sometimes, when I felt courageous enough, at Josh sleeping beside me.

He snores, a heavy, steady breathing. Like a hiccup, I wait for him to stop, but somehow find relief after each throaty breath. Despite the sixty-eight degrees I have the thermostat set at, he's been sweating throughout the night. I can smell him— an oddly pleasant scent. His still presence gives me a disturbing comfort.

I could have turned off the alarm but I let it buzz anyway, for Josh's sake. He stirs, mumbles something in his sleep, and turns over on his side.

I turn the alarm off.

I watch Josh for a little while more, this man who is a boy and a friend but who isn't my boyfriend. I've never asked him to stay the night—at least not the entire night—and it's strange to have him in my bed this morning, snoring lightly, his body odor absorbing into my sheets.

The only man I've ever let sleep in my bed is Zane.

But no, I can't think of Zane in the present tense. When I think of Zane it always has to be in the past tense, because Zane is gone, has been gone for two years now, never to return, having not been able to jump back from Death's Door like I had managed all those times before. Zane my friend, my lover, someone who I actually found myself caring about, someone who I envisioned spending the rest of my life with.

I get out of bed, walk through my apartment to the kitchen. I turn on the coffee machine, open the fridge to look at what's inside. Not much besides V8 and leftovers and milk that expired yesterday.

I shut the door, turn back around and look at my cluttered kitchen as if for the first time—dirty dishes in the sink, newspapers stacked on the table, empty cereal and cracker boxes littering the counters—and my gaze falls on the corkboard hanging on the wall. Right in the corner amid pictures and Post-its of scribbled notes, held in place by a sky blue tack, is a Bazooka Joe comic.

Without even looking I know it's number twenty out of fifty, Scooter's all-time favorite comic.

But no, I can't think of Scooter in the present tense anymore either, and it's this realization—what I've been trying to deal with for the past twenty-four hours—that finally brings it all home.

My vision starts to blur as one tear after another fills my eyes. Then all of a sudden comes a deluge, and my shoulders hitch, my legs go weak, and before I know it I'm on the floor, holding my side as I sob.

I sob for Scooter and I sob for Zane and I sob for Karen and I sob for Rosalina, wherever she is now. It's been almost two years since I've cried and it feels strange at first, like I'm not doing it right, always having forced the tears back, no matter what, always telling myself I was strong enough to keep them away, that a woman like me shouldn't cry, cannot cry, because crying shows weakness, vulnerability, helplessness.

It's Scooter I have in my mind, the guy forever chomping his Bazooka Joe, but quite suddenly Scooter's face fades and becomes Zane's face. Zane who taught me how to love and care and understand the world, who made me feel like I had an actual purpose.

No, stop it. I can't think of Zane. I can't think of Scooter. I can't think of any of the people I've lost because they are dead now and I am not and I have to worry about today, about tomorrow, about next week, I have to worry about the next mission and how I can't make any mistakes, I have to—

A floorboard creaks, and Josh says, "Holly, are you okay?"

It's such a stupid, pointless question that I want to ignore him, just stay where I am sobbing on the kitchen floor, ignore him until he goes away and never comes back.

But he takes a step forward, leaving the doorway and coming toward me, dressed only in his silk boxers. I wipe my eyes, start to sit up, find myself leaning against the refrigerator. I lean my head back against its cool surface, my left ear grazing the Universal Studios magnet my mother brought back from Florida last year.

Still Josh continues forward, the sleep completely wiped from his eyes, concern now on his scruffy face. He comes and bends down and places his hand on my arm, places his other hand on my face. Slowly, gently, lovingly, he wipes away my tears with his thumb.

And right then—right at that instant—I want to sleep with him again. Right here on the kitchen floor if need be, I don't care. I just need the closeness, the warmth of another human soul, something to remind me that I am not completely alone in this world.

It's why I called Josh last night and invited him over, Josh who by now knows the score and arrived within the hour. Josh who I went to high school with and who I have stayed in contact with the past ten years, always just casual friends, a nod and hello if we see each other in public. Josh who has been in love with me since eleventh grade, who had more than once asked me out, and who I always turned down because even at sixteen I never liked the idea of dating, of relationships, always seeing the entire process as a huge waste of time and energy.

So after Zane died—was killed, I remind myself—I needed something to bring me back down after every mission, my body so pumped up, my nerves on edge, and so I called Josh and asked him over and seduced him. Afterward, Josh wanted to spend the night but I told him that probably wasn't the best idea, he should go.

For the past two years he has known the score, not understood completely the reasons why I sometimes call him out of the blue to come over, but still he always arrives within the hour, knowing what to expect, having just showered and brushed his teeth, his underarms fresh with deodorant.

And right now, his hands on my arm, my face, wiping away my tears, I want to seduce him again, if not for the closeness then at least to get whatever else is bottled up inside me out. Because in an hour I will be going over to Walter's to see the kids, I will see Walter himself, and I need to be focused and clearheaded and in control of my emotions.

But instead I take Josh's hands, gently push them away. "It's okay. Really, I'm fine."

He stands back up, looks down at me with a frown.

"It's just been a really stressful past couple days." I hold out a hand and he helps me up, and then I look around the kitchen again. "Want some coffee?"

A little while later, after having showered and gotten

dressed, I come back into the kitchen to find Josh washing my dishes. He's put back on his jeans and T-shirt, his white socks with the gold toes, and he's listening to *Good Morning America* turned up on the TV in the next room.

"How does my face look?"

He turns, gives me a squint, tilts his head back and forth a couple times. "Pretty good."

"Liar."

The story I told him last night was that one of the kids shattered a glass Friday afternoon, and one of the shards hit my cheek and cut it open.

I look around the kitchen, see that Josh has done an amazing job of cleaning it up. For a bartender/musician, he should consider doing housecleaning part time.

I have to leave in ten minutes to beat the traffic into Arlington. During my shower I've been thinking about an excuse for my strange behavior, why I'd broken my only rule in allowing him to stay the night, but before I can even open my mouth, he clears his throat.

"Holly?"

"Yeah."

He wipes his hands on a towel, sets its aside, walks over and pulls out a chair and sits down. When I just stand there, staring at him, he motions for me to sit.

I sit.

He clears his throat again. "About last night ..."

"Josh—"

"We can't do that anymore."

I close my mouth. Just sit there, silent.

He reaches across the table, takes my hand in his, gives it a quick squeeze. "You know I like you a lot. And, well, as much as I've enjoyed our booty calls"—he smiles at the term—"I've met someone."

"You have?"

"Yeah." Nodding now, staring at me to gauge my reaction. "Her name is Dawn and she plays the bass in this band that we opened for last month and … I think I'm in love."

I try to smile, I really do, but for some reason my face won't work, all the muscles have gone on strike, and I just stare back at Josh whose own smile starts to fade.

"I figured you'd understand, right? Because, like, this was never anything serious. You'd told me that before and that's what I accepted it as. Just two friends, you know, having a good time."

He's right, of course. That's all it ever was. But the nasty truth is our "booty calls" were designed to help free up my tension, get me grounded, and while I hate to admit it, I always assumed Josh would be there whenever I called, always arriving within the hour. Josh having a girlfriend, well, I guess that was something I knew was a possibility, something that would eventually happen, but for some reason I just never worried about it.

Josh squeezes my hand again. "You're happy for me, right, Holly? It means a lot to me that you get where I'm coming from."

Still I try to smile and still I fail, just sitting there in my slacks and shirt, my hair pulled back in a ponytail.

"I mean, I wanted to tell you last night, before … well, you know, but I just … I could see you really wanted to do it and I figured I'd tell you later, and I guess it means I cheated on Dawn, but if she knew our arrangement and everything, I think she'd understand, even though I'm not going to tell her, I mean, of course I'm never going to tell her about last night, but if she—"

"Josh," I say, and I hardly recognize my own voice.

He looks at me, his eyebrow raised.

"It's fine."

"Really?"

"Yeah." I pull my hand away, start to stand back up. "Now if you don't mind, can you lock up when you leave? I have to go to work."

FIFTEEN

The Hadden residence is a three-story colonial just outside of Arlington. It sits in a neighborhood with several other three-story homes, many that could be considered mansions, and on a clear autumn day, when the leaves have all fallen, you can stand in the Haddens' backyard and see the tip of the Washington Monument.

I turn off Arbor Drive into their driveway a few minutes before seven. I park the car and hurry toward the back door. The back door lets into a foyer, the foyer into the kitchen. The moment I open the door, Sylvia, standing at the dishwasher, turns to me and smiles.

"Good morning, Miss Holly."

"Morning, Sylvia. How are you doing?"

Before Sylvia can answer, David and Casey shout my name in that singsong way of theirs. They're at the kitchen table with their mother, Marilyn, dressed in one of her smart business suits, skimming the *Post* while she takes deliberate bite after bite of her Special K.

I smile at Sylvia and touch her arm as I walk past her, the

housekeeper going back to her duties, and then I'm at the table and Baron raises his old head off the floor, panting with his tongue lolling from the side of his mouth and slapping his tail on the floor.

I lean down and give Baron a good scratch behind the ears, the hound closing his eyes and groaning with pleasure. Then I pull out the only remaining chair and sit down, smile at Casey beside me as she busily eats her bowl of Cheerios with her Big Bird spoon.

David says, "Holly, what happened to your face?"

Marilyn had nodded to me briefly before, but now she pulls down her newspaper, squints to give me a closer look. Forty-four years old, she looks ten years younger, this woman with high cheekbones and blond hair, who does yoga and Pilates in what little spare time she has. She works as a grant writer and deals with mostly nonprofit organizations. If I were a normal person leading a normal life, I'd want to be just like her.

"Oh my," Marilyn says, real concern in her voice. "That's a nasty boo-boo. Are you okay?"

I touch my cheek. "Yes, I'm fine. Just had a little accident over the weekend."

"Can I touch it?" David asks. He's six years old and apparently acts just like every other boy his age, and while he can be a brat most times, I love the kid.

"David," Marilyn says, turning back to her paper, "don't be crass."

Casey says, "What does crass mean?"

"It's the green stuff outside, stupid," David says.

"David," Marilyn warns.

"Don't call me stupid!" Casey says, tears already threatening in her blue eyes.

I turn to Casey just as Marilyn stands and turns to David.

Marilyn does her stern mother thing while I do my gentle nanny thing. I smile at Casey and tell her she's not stupid, of course she's not. Then I widen my eyes, jerk my head back toward David, and whisper that if anyone's stupid, it's her brother.

Casey giggles, the tears forgotten.

Sylvia comes over to the table with a cup of coffee. "Here you are, Miss Holly, with cream just as you like. Would you care for anything else?"

"I'm good. Thanks, Sylvia."

Sylvia smiles, nods and turns away, becomes part of the background like she's paid to be.

Whatever Marilyn said to David, it seems to have had the proper effect. The boy has his head lowered, nods once, then twice. When Marilyn steps back, she says, "Now, David, what do you have to say to your sister?"

He mumbles, "I'm sorry, Casey."

Casey looks at me, the ghost of a smile on her soft face. I nod at her and she looks back at her brother across the table. "That's okay."

Marilyn is already sitting down, giving me that look of hers that says *Just wait until you get a pair of your own*. It must be a mother thing, something I've seen many times from other women, but the truth is I don't plan on ever becoming a mother.

"Oh yes, before I forget," she says suddenly, looking back up at me. "Walter told me he'd like to see you when you arrived. Something about this month's pay."

As far as Marilyn knows, all her husband ever talks to me about is my monthly rate. At the start she had wanted to hire someone with experience, who had a degree in child psychology and whatever else, but Walter had done his best to convince her that I would work out, and while she'd had trepidation at first, she now seems happy with me.

God only knows what she'd think if she knew I almost always carry a gun with me while I watch her children.

"Where is he?" I ask.

"He should be in his study. Don't bother knocking. He's expecting you."

SIXTEEN

But I do knock. I knock and I wait and then I knock again. Finally I hear Walter's deep voice—"Come in"—and I open the door and step inside.

Walter sits behind his large oak desk, typing at his laptop. The window is behind him, letting in the morning light, making it impossible at first to see his face.

"Shut the door, Holly."

I shut the door.

"Take a seat."

"I'd rather stand."

He looks up from his computer screen for the first time, giving me a hard look.

I return the hard look and say, "Let's just get this over with."

He stares at me for another moment, this man in his fifties with intense eyes and somber face and graying hair shaved in a crew cut. He's wearing his uniform with the three stars, and for an instant I'm reminded of the first time I met him and he only had two stars, the both of us on the other side of the world, when he walked into the room the MPs had locked me in after they arrested me.

Walter keeps watching me, not saying anything, so I decide to break the silence.

"Going to the Pentagon today?"

"I have to make an appearance once in a while. And apparently a known terrorist was hit in Las Vegas over the weekend. I need to be briefed on that."

Walter typically wears suits; he only wears his uniform for special functions, meetings, or when he has debriefings at the Pentagon.

"Well?" I ask.

"Well what?"

"Goddamn it, Walter."

"Hmm." He glances down at his screen, moves the cordless mouse around, then shuts the laptop. "'Goddamn it, Walter.' I guess that's appropriate enough for the situation."

"What do you want me to say? I fucked up. I'm sorry."

He stands up, turns away from me, stares out the window with his hands behind his back.

"No, Holly, you didn't fuck up. The mission was a success. The target was eliminated and the prize was recovered and brought home safely."

"If I could go back and change things, I would."

"Don't be childish."

"But—"

He turns away from the window. "Scooter is dead. There's no changing that."

"I never should have gone out there."

"You mean Vegas or to that compound in the middle of the desert?"

I say nothing.

"We've been here before, Holly. At this same exact spot,

this same exact conversation. And to be quite frank, I'm tired of telling you the same thing again and again."

He moves around the desk, walks up to me and places his hands on my shoulders. This close I can smell his aftershave and the Listerine he'd gargled after brushing his teeth.

"You never used to be like this. You always followed the rules. You always knew not to involve yourself in anything but the mission. But ever since what happened two years ago, you've been on this … this gradual decline. I've tried to ignore it, hoping you'd wake up to reality, change back to what you used to be."

I shift my eyes away from his. "And what did I used to be?"

"A great soldier."

"Walter—"

"What was your ultimate goal in going out to that compound? Please, Holly, enlighten me."

I'm quiet for a moment, remembering the cold darkness, the dirt crunching beneath my feet, the guards' house and the ranch house and the rows and rows of cots, the sheets smelling of body odor and sweat and desperation.

In a very quiet voice, I say, "I don't know."

"Okay," Walter nods slowly, taking his hands away from my shoulders. He moves back to his desk and leans against it, crossing his arms. "So what you're telling me now is that Scooter's death was in vain. There was no ultimate purpose for what you were doing, so in his coming to give you backup, he essentially died for nothing. Now tell me—is my logic wrong?"

"Those girls were slaves."

"I know they were, Holly. But so are a million other girls all over the world. And guess what—you can't save all of them."

"But—"

"Besides, you couldn't even save the ones you tried to save Saturday night."

I look at him again. "What?"

"Almost every single girl there was an illegal. When the police arrived, so did ICE. Those girls were sent back to Mexico."

I don't say anything, letting this sink in. I'd figured as much but actually hearing the truth is still like a knife being inserted slowly into my heart. After Scooter had been shot, the thought of those girls had left my mind. Even Rosalina, left by herself in the Town Car on the other side of that rocky hill, had vanished, and all I could think or care about was Scooter, dying in my arms.

"What about his parents?"

"What about them?"

"Do they know?"

"Of course they know. They know that early Saturday morning their son was driving home from a very late night at work. He must have dozed off behind the wheel and swerved off the road and struck a tree. Completely demolished the car, as well as the body inside."

"That's not fair."

"What then would you consider fair? Should we tell them the truth? Should we tell them how their son was secretly working for a top secret government unit? That for the past seven years he has helped keep our country safe from terrorists? That he was in fact a hero?"

Walter takes a breath, slowly shakes his head.

"Those are all truths, Holly, something his parents would be very proud to hear, but something they will never know. As far as they're concerned, their son was just an ordinary citizen who did freelance web design. Nothing more, nothing less."

"When's his funeral?"

"Forget it."

"Tell me."

"It doesn't matter. You were never part of his life. You have no reason to go to his funeral. You have no reason to mourn with his family." He raises a finger at me. "And don't get any stupid ideas, either. I will have surveillance there and if any of them even catches a whiff of your perfume you will be taken away in a matter of seconds."

I cross my arms, glare back at him.

"You can't blame yourself for this," Walter says, his voice slow and deliberate. "Scooter made the decision to go out there just like Nova did."

I glance down at the floor, glance back up at Walter. "So what happens now?"

"Regarding?"

"Regarding me and Nova."

"Nova is on indefinite hiatus. At least until a new team is formed."

"What about me?"

"What about you?"

"Is the new team going to include me?"

"Give me one good reason why it should."

I say nothing, look away from him.

"Just as I thought." He stands up straight and walks back around his desk, lowers himself down in his seat. He seems to think a moment, his mouth half-open, and then sighs. "Holly, what I'm going to say to you now comes from a friend and not from your superior."

"And that is?"

"What happened two years ago was terrible. It shocked us all. And unfortunately you were the most impacted and apparently still are. And ever since then you've had this stubbornness that makes you believe you can save the world. But the problem is you will never be able to do so. Why? Because when it comes right down to it, you can't even save yourself."

SEVENTEEN

Blondie got engaged over the weekend.

She has been with her boyfriend now for three years, they've been living together for two, and over the weekend he finally popped the question—she has already told us about the dinner, the flowers and the wine—and for the fiftieth time in the past hour she extends her hand to us, letting the diamond sparkle in the sunlight.

"Oh my God," Brunette says. "I just *love* it."

"Really," Redhead says, "it's *beautiful*."

Blondie smiles, says thank you, then looks at me.

I've been smiling for the past hour and am getting pretty sick and tired of it. But still I keep smiling when I say, "Absolutely gorgeous."

We're out at a public pool, these three girls and myself, all who put down on their W-2s the profession of nanny (only theirs is true and mine is just a cover). Blondie, Brunette, and Redhead are not their names, of course, but that's how I think of them. I've known them now for two years and we're friends to an extent, always seeing each other during the week while we drag our charges around D.C., and there have even been a few times when one or the other invited me to go out with them partying. I'd gone, just to show face, but had mostly stood in the corner, nursing a drink, declining invitations to dance.

I decided to come up with a cover story from the start that I was already involved with someone, a longtime boyfriend who lives out of state. This way none of the girls would try to fix me up with one of their friends. The only problem was I needed a picture. And, well, I had a picture of Scooter on my phone one day, a pretty cute one, actually, and this was what I had shown the girls.

Scooter, my fake boyfriend, not even dead forty-eight hours.

"So," Redhead says, "have you guys decided on a date yet?"

While the girls talk—Brunette and Redhead already confirmed as bridesmaids—I glance out toward the shallow pool the toddlers now splash around in. In this kind of community, even a pool this size has a professional lifeguard on duty, so we tireless nannies can take an hour break and lounge in the shade of oak trees while one of those nannies works out her wedding plans with her nanny friends.

These girls, they're serious about the work. They've taken classes, have attended seminars, and Redhead has ambitions of one day opening her own agency. I mean, they're nice and everything, they have a lot going for them, but I can't imagine what happened when they were growing up that made them one day decide they wanted to watch other people's children for a living. Then again, I can't imagine what makes other people want to sit behind a desk for eight hours a day, or stand behind a fast-food counter, or wash dishes, or whatever else.

The girls talk and talk and I keep watching the toddler pool. Less than fifty feet away, I can see Casey standing in her bright pink bathing suit, the water wings on her arms. She's in the shallowest part, just a foot. David is with his friends on the other end, what is maybe three feet deep. They're laughing as they throw a beach ball back and forth.

Farther past the shallow pool is the real pool. Nearly one hundred people are either in it or walking around it, kids and adults sharing a leisurely afternoon. The male lifeguards are tan and well built, and even though they're not as hot as the ones you'd find at the beach, the girls still like to ogle them. Normally that's how we pass the time in the shade of this oak tree, picking out which lifeguard is the cutest and daring each other to go talk to him, while the kids we watch tire themselves out in the water.

Earlier today I took the kids to the Smithsonian. For some reason they absolutely love the place. David especially loves the dinosaur display, while Casey likes walking through the butterfly exhibit. So that was our morning, amid hundreds of other children, me trying to keep an eye on both of them while also keeping my eye out for any danger.

"What do you think, Holly?" Brunette asks.

I look back at them. "About what?"

Redhead sighs. "What's with you today?" She asks this in a genuine way, yet I sense a hint of exasperation behind it.

"What do you mean?"

"You just seem"—Redhead shrugs—"distracted."

"My boyfriend and I had a fight over the weekend."

"Is that how you got … you know?" Brunette asks in a low voice, touching her cheek.

I shake my head. "Like I told you, that was just an accident."

"Still"—Blondie reaches out, pats me on the knee—"why didn't you say something before?"

"I didn't want to spoil the mood."

The girls delicately back away from my suffering and return to Blondie's wedding plans. I hear a shout amid the rest of the shouts and recognize it as Casey's. I glance over to see her holding her hands up in front of her face while two kids maybe a year older than her splash her with water. There's no splashing allowed in the toddler pool, but the lifeguard's distracted by a large-breasted woman flirting with him.

I stand up, excuse myself from the girls, and hurry over to the pool.

By the time I get there David has already intervened. Despite the fact he can be a brat sometimes, he always stands up for his little sister when kids are picking on her.

"Knock it off," he says, stepping between the two kids and Casey.

The kids just laugh, start splashing him.

"Knock it off!" he shouts, and this catches the attention of the lifeguard, who has to take his eyes off those massive (and fake, I'm sure) breasts.

"No splashing!" he calls, his voice automatic like a robot's, and the two brats look at him, look back at each other, before stomping away through the water.

David waits a moment to makes sure the threat is gone before turning back to his sister. "Are you okay?"

Casey pouts her bottom lip. She nods.

I'm wearing sandals for the occasion and I slip them off so I can dip my feet into the cool water. I bend down, place a hand on David's shoulder, and say, "Good job."

He looks at me, sort of blushes, then turns and hurries back to his friends.

"I hate the water," Casey says. Her bottom lip is still pouted and it looks like she might cry.

"Do you want to come hang out with me?"

She nods and so I pick her up out of the water and carry her back to the shade of the oak tree where I left my bag and the towels. I give Casey her Hanna Montana towel and dry her off while kids shout around us, music plays from those massive speakers, and the girls keep going on and on about how

Blondie's life is going to change now because she's getting married.

Redhead says, "I mean, once you get married, you guys are going to stop having sex regularly. You know that's a fact, don't you?"

I clear my throat, just loud enough so the girls glance in my direction and see we have virgin ears in our midst.

They lower their voices.

"Holly?" Casey says. We're sitting on the grass now, Casey leaning back on my stomach.

"Yeah, babe?"

"Why do they have to be so mean all the time?"

"I don't know."

The girls start laughing at something and then Brunette says, "Might as well keep your vibrator," and I clear my throat again, really loud this time, but the damage has already been done.

Casey tilts her head back to look up at me.

"Holly, what's a vibrator?"

EIGHTEEN

After my sister takes a sip of her coffee, she says, "So tell me again what happened to your cheek."

One thing about Tina is she always tries to get information out of someone by acting like they've already talked about it. We've only been here at Java the Hut for five minutes now, Matthew and Max at the table next to us, playing their video games, and not once did I tell her about the cut.

"I had an accident over the weekend, that's all."

"What kind of accident?"

"Look, I didn't ask you to meet me here because I wanted to talk about a little cut on my cheek."

"Then what did you want to talk to me about?"

I open my mouth but shut it, not sure yet how I want to continue. I've been thinking about it all morning, ever since leaving Walter's study, but then again maybe that's not true. Maybe I've been thinking about it for a while now. The only problem is I've never had a real job a day in my life and there is a part of me that thinks a nine-to-five will forever be beyond my grasp.

"You said before that Ryan could get me a job at his firm, right?"

Java the Hut is a small coffee shop located in Georgetown. Very bohemian, it has artwork by local artists dotting the walls. My sister has a piece hanging here she made over a year ago, an abstract with a crow standing in the middle of a deserted Times Square. I have to admit it's not bad, but it's not great either, and the price tag on the thing has forced it to keep its place on the wall. I know Ryan tried buying it one time, just to cheer Tina up, but Tina had found out about it and forced him to take it back. Now here it hangs, looking right over our table, where Tina has lifted her large cup of coffee to her mouth to take a sip but now pauses, staring back at me over the brim.

She sets the cup down, slowly, and says, "Are you being serious?"

I nod.

She keeps staring at me, her eyes narrowed. "This isn't one of your lame jokes?"

"I don't know how much longer I can keep working for the Haddens. I mean, the only reason they hired me in the first place was because Walter and Dad worked together. I'm getting, I don't know, just tired of the whole thing."

My sister smiles a small smile. "Not ready for kids yet, huh?"

"Look, you said before he could get me something. An entry-level position or whatever. At this point I don't care what it is."

"McDonald's is always hiring."

Truth is, I'd probably prefer working at a fast-food chain making fries and burgers more than sitting behind a desk for eight hours a day.

I say, smiling, "Quit being a bitch, Tina."

The boys pause in their video games to give their Aunt Holly a wide-eyed look.

"Don't swear in front of the boys," Tina says, her teeth gritted but smiling nonetheless.

"Okay, but first don't be a bitch."

Tina turns to Matthew and Max, tells them to go back to their video games. Then she turns back to me, leans forward, and says, "What's gotten into you?"

"You know what? Never mind." I push my coffee away, start to stand. "Sorry I asked you to meet me here in the first place."

Tina reaches out, grabs my arm.

"If you're being one hundred percent serious," she says, "then yes, of course I'll talk to Ryan and of course he'll set something up. If this is, you know, what you really want."

It's not what I really want, but then again I don't know what it is I really want.

"It is."

"Then I'll talk to him tonight."

She lets go of my arm and I reach into my purse, find a couple dollars, toss them down on the table.

"You're leaving already?" Tina asks.

"Yeah, I have to run." I walk over and kiss both boys on the forehead, tell them goodbye, and then I turn to say goodbye to my sister but pause when I think of something else. "Also … I'm sorry for not being the greatest sister in the world. I'm sorry for, you know, being difficult all the time."

Tina frowns at me. "Okay, who are you and what have you done with my sister?"

"Anyway, I just wanted to say that. I'll talk to you later."

I start walking again, past my sister. I reach the door when Tina catches up with me.

"Holly, what's gotten into you?"

What's gotten into me is my life is falling apart. I got one of my team members killed and now it looks like I won't be doing the only thing in the world I know and am good at. And the one person in the world who I could somewhat trust, the only person I've slept with for the past two years, is dating someone he's in love with and I have nobody right now, absolutely nobody except my family, and even they don't know the real me.

"I've just been thinking a lot lately."

"About what?"

"I have to go, Tina."

My sister stares at me, biting her lower lip like she's thinking of saying something. Then she nods and says, "It was good seeing you. We should do this more often."

"Yeah, we should."

We stand there then, neither one of us saying anything. Finally my sister forces a smile and heads back to the table. I turn away and push open the door. I step out onto the sidewalk and just stand there for a moment and watch the cars and the people going by, and even though I know they're there, I feel like that crow in my sister's painting, trapped in colors on a canvas that nobody wants to buy.

NINETEEN

My apartment complex is located in Fairland, a good fifteen miles southwest of D.C. It's a little one-bedroom on the third floor. The elevator is almost always being "serviced," which forces me to take the stairs.

It's no exception today.

I trudge up the steps to the third floor. I already have my keys in my hand. I'm thinking about my meeting with Tina, whether I should have gone through with it, and for an instant my mind isn't concentrating on what it needs to be concentrating on.

If it were concentrating on the right thing, it would notice right away that my door is slightly ajar.

By touch I find my apartment key, start to extend it to the lock, but freeze.

Just stand there a moment. Not breathing, not moving at all.

The world suddenly takes on a fourth dimension, warbling in and out of focus, and I'm backtracking through my mind the past ten minutes—driving down Interstate 395, glancing every thirty seconds in the rearview mirror in case of a tail—

and then I'm thinking about parking in the apartment complex lot, walking toward the stairs, and I can't believe that my mind wasn't focused like it usually is, that instead of worrying about covering my back I was worrying about what I should wear to my eventual job interview.

I reach into my purse, grab for my gun—a SIG P320 Nitron Subcompact—but the gun isn't there.

Of course it's not there. Because today we went to the Smithsonian and they make you walk through metal detectors and so I took out my gun, placed it in the glove box, and normally I would have retrieved it right away, but I've been so preoccupied that I forgot it and that's where it is now, in the glove box along with the owner's manual and tissues and my emergency ration of tampons.

I consider backing away, retracing my steps, retrieving the gun, coming back up here properly armed.

The only problem then is I lose a good sixty seconds. Not only that, if whoever is inside is a pro, they've heard me coming —maybe even watched me pull into the parking lot—and of course it doesn't help that my keys jangled when I extended them, so now whoever's inside knows I'm standing right outside.

Maybe I'm overreacting—maybe Josh just forgot to close it when he left this morning—but I know that's bullshit because Josh is smarter than that, especially with other people's stuff, and then I think maybe it's Josh inside, having come back because he decided to dump that stupid bitch and keep what we have going, but I know that's not the case either and I know that the closest weapon I have to me right now is in the kitchen, a butcher block full of sharp carving knives.

Five seconds have passed. The world warbles back into place, losing that fourth dimension.

I raise my right foot and kick the door and immediately pivot away, place my back against the wall, waiting for a gunshot. When a second passes and nothing happens, I peek inside. Nothing; all the lights off. I hurry in, staying close to the wall, keeping my breathing shallow, listening for any sound. Four seconds pass and then I reach the kitchen but stop before I enter, crouch down to peek around the corner, because anyone watching will expect me to still be standing and will be aiming for a headshot. Again nothing, nobody at all. I slip into the kitchen, losing my shoes so my socks are silent on the tiles. I go directly to the counter, grab the longest carving knife, and turn back around.

Still nothing.

Now sufficiently armed, I start toward the doorway leading into the living room. The light here isn't great either, not with the shades drawn, but it's not total darkness and I have no problem spotting the person sitting on the sofa.

"Stop right there," I say loudly, the knife held up with the tip pointed straight out.

I take a step forward, squint so my eyes adjust to the dark. Then I lower the knife. "Goddamn you, Nova," I say.

"No lock is too small to keep me out." He gives me a drunken smile and holds up a bottle of Cuervo, shaking it slightly so the tequila inside sloshes around. "Now why don't you help me finish this bad boy off?"

TWENTY

"Walter's a fucking asshole."

"He's just doing his job."

"He's trying to cover his ass, Holly, that's what he's doing. You know what I say? I say fuck him."

We're up on the roof of my apartment complex, sitting on cheap lawn chairs staring out over the buildings at the setting sun. Neither of us speaks for a time, and in that moment or so the only sounds in the world are the traffic drifting up from the street and the rusty wind chimes someone placed up here long ago tinkling as they sway in the breeze.

"Walter's not the bad guy here," I say finally.

Nova takes a swig of the tequila, shakes his head. "No, I guess he's not."

I take the bottle from him. "He saved my ass a long time ago. Did I ever tell you about that?"

"I've heard some but never the entire story."

"It happened in Iraq."

"I know that part, yeah."

I open my mouth to continue but decide now's not the time. Also I'm not sure I want Nova to hear the story. Not because he wouldn't understand—I know he would—but because it's such a personal thing, the one time when I truly failed as a friend and as a human being.

"Walter says I've been on a gradual decline. Have been for the past two years."

Nova says nothing, just keeps staring out at the horizon.

"What—you agree with him?"

Nova stands up suddenly. Stepping forward, he hawks a loogie and lets it fly up over the edge of the building. He watches it a moment, just watches it, and for some reason I picture it in my mind, that wad of phlegm flying down toward the parking lot, coming apart the farther and faster it goes. Maybe it hits a car, maybe it hits the pavement, maybe it hits the grass. Whatever the case, it hits something because that's its nature, its purpose.

When Nova turns back to me, he says, "What do you want me to say?"

"I want you to tell me the truth."

"The thing with your father was fucked up. It would have traumatized anybody."

"Oh, I see. So now I'm traumatized?"

"I didn't mean it like that."

"Then how did you mean it?"

The breeze picks up, sending the wind chimes into a sudden frenzy, clanging and clattering.

"Look, your old man?" Nova says. "He just … flipped."

"I sometimes think I should have seen it coming."

"How?" He takes a step forward, his eyes intense. "Just how could you have seen that coming? There were no warning signs. There was absolutely nothing you could have done about it."

"Still …"

"Still what?"

"Still it never made sense. How he could do something like that. *Why* he would have in the first place."

"Everyone has his price, Holly. Sometimes I think even God would bow out for the right amount."

The breeze dies down and the wind chimes go quiet, still swaying but not making any noise.

"You can't bring God into the equation," I say.

"Why not? It's a good cop-out answer."

"That's exactly the reason."

Nova holds his hands out, the open palms lifted toward the sky. "Then what the fuck do you want me to say?"

I shake my head, wipe at my eyes. "I'm thinking about getting out."

Nova doesn't say anything.

I glare up at him. "This is the point in the conversation you're supposed to tell me that's a crazy idea."

Nova looks down at his feet, looks back up. His voice suddenly soft, he says, "Holly, you have to be honest with yourself. Walter ... he's right. You have changed. That shit back in Vegas, you never would have done that before."

"Another one of my fucking little crusades, right?"

"Holly—"

"Why do you do it, Nova?"

"Why do I do what?"

"The work you do."

His gaze steady on mine, he says, "Work is work."

"It's that simple?"

"Why do people become accountants? Why do they become bank tellers? Why do they become CEOs of fucking oil companies? They have to do something. And me, well, I have to do something too."

"But why killing?"

"Our work is more than just killing."

"Answer the question."

He stares at me, his eyes still intense. Finally he looks away, shakes his head.

"No," he says. "It's none of your goddamned business."

"That's what I thought. People like us, we're driven to do this work. Something in our past makes us who we are."

"What the fuck are you now, a shrink? Of course something in our past makes us who we are. It's the same for everybody."

"But we kill people."

"We do more than that."

"Do you want to know why I do it?"

"Why?"

"To save lives."

Nova just smiles. He takes a swig of the Cuervo, tilts his head back and gargles it like mouthwash before swallowing.

"I'm serious, Nova."

"I'm sure you are."

"That's how I've always rationalized it. We kill the bad guys so the good guys keep living."

"And what's changed now?"

"Apparently I'm on a gradual decline." My voice seethes with sarcasm. "*Have* been on a gradual decline."

Nova says, "What is this really about? Is this about Scooter? You feel guilty now and you're having a fucking pity party for yourself?"

"It's not like that."

"Isn't it?"

"I don't know what you and Walter are talking about. I haven't changed at all."

Nova barks out a loud laugh. "That's a good one. Got anymore?"

"Fuck you."

"You want the truth, Holly?" He takes three quick strides until he's standing in front of me, his face right in front of my own. "You've become reckless. You've become irresponsible. You don't give a shit about anybody else except yourself. And the worst part about that? I don't even think you like yourself very much."

He hasn't shaved in the past two days and his face is full of stubble. Normally he looks very good—hence his name, Casanova—but now his eyes are bloodshot, his face haggard.

My voice low and steady, I say, "You don't know anything about me."

"Yes, I do. I know more than I fucking want to."

"You don't know shit."

"Oh, fuck you." He turns away, takes another swig of the Cuervo. His back to me, he says, "Quit being a cunt, Holly," and I'm moving before I even know it.

I come up behind him and kick at the back of his knees. He loses his balance and falls down, dropping the bottle, and with the heel of my hand I punch him in the ribs. He groans, tries to reach for me, and I grab his arm, twist it up behind his back.

"Call me a cunt one more time."

"Cunt," he spits.

I twist his arm even more, right to the point it's ready to dislocate.

"Go ahead, Nova, say it again."

But he doesn't say it again. He's drunk off his ass and he weighs one hundred pounds more than me, but he's not stupid, not when he's in this position.

"I'm in control of my own life," I whisper into his ear. "Got it? And there's nothing fucking wrong with me."

In one quick motion I let go of his arm and stand back up, step out of his reach. It doesn't matter. He just stays on the ground, his face against the stones, groaning softly as he moves his arm back in place. I stand there watching him for another moment, then turn and start toward the roof door we'd left propped open with a broken piece of brick. I only stop when Nova calls my name.

"You go ahead and tell yourself that," he says. "But ask yourself this—had the Vegas mission taken place two years ago, would you have gone out to that ranch? Would Scooter still be alive?"

I continue walking, right to the door. I grab the brick and open the door and then toss the brick out on the rooftop, letting the door close loudly and lock in place.

TWENTY-ONE

Total silence.

They say there's no such thing except in space, but there are moments when I'm alone in my apartment with the windows closed that I sit or stand very still and it's like the world doesn't exist anymore, that such things as screams and gunfire and crying are just a distant dream.

It's well past midnight and I lie in bed and stare at the ceiling and think about total silence. It's so quiet that if a mote of dust was to float down and land on the floor it would be as loud as a firework popping.

Over the years I've come to crave total silence. There's something peaceful about it, something so soothing that it almost helps me forget all the bad shit there is in the world.

It's like a black hole, a void I can crawl into and curl up and just fall asleep. No pain. No suffering. No murder.

A car horn sounds outside, shattering the silence.

I blink, take a breath.

I imagine Zane lying in the bed next to me. He stares up at the same spot of ceiling I'm staring at. I want to turn to him, snuggle into his embrace, hold on to him and never let him go.

Before him I'd felt empty, insecure, unloved. He'd helped open my eyes to the world. Helped me understand that behind every façade, every smiling face, there is an evil just ready to make its move.

I imagine him lying beside me and asking, What's wrong, Holly?

I fucked up royally this time.

Why?

Scooter's dead.

And it was your fault?

Yes.

No, it wasn't. Stop blaming yourself.

But I'm scared.

Scared about what?

But I can't answer him, because before I do I take my eyes off that spot of ceiling and turn my head and find his side of the bed empty. A tear hatches from the corner of my eye and starts to slither down my cheek. I don't bother wiping it away.

The silence returns and I stare back up at the ceiling.

I think about a lot of different things.

About murder and death and how they're wedded together, a perfect union.

About two years ago, down in Miami, on that drug lord's yacht, a fire having already broken out, a number of the bodyguards dead, and my father and I finding the drug lord cowering below deck.

About taking the entire bottle of Valium concealed behind the bathroom mirror.

About dragging the drug lord up to the deck and aiming my gun at him and my dad turning to me and raising his own gun at my head.

About Karen and what she confided in me.

About floating in my tub filled with warm water and slicing the veins along my arms.

About Zane stepping out of nowhere, shouting for my dad to stop, and my dad turning his gun and firing three rounds at Zane's chest, the bullets forcing Zane to stumble back and fall over the edge and into the water.

About going to the roof of my apartment and stepping up onto the edge and just letting gravity do its magic.

About the dry Iraqi desert.

About shooting my own father, one two three four five times in the chest, screaming as I do it, stepping closer and closer, and then while he lies flat on the deck moving in even closer for the kill shot.

About taking one of my many pistols hiding scattered throughout the apartment and placing the barrel in my mouth.

About the stench of the porta potty, the urine and shit mingled together.

About standing there with my gun aimed at my father's face and wanting more than anything to pull the trigger, to watch his head explode.

About turning on the oven and sticking my head in like Sylvia Plath.

About opening the porta potty door and knowing who would be on the other side and ducking the punch coming for my face.

About watching my father already lying there covered in blood and knowing that the yacht would soon sink and deciding that for the moment there had already been enough killing.

About just lying here in bed and staring at the ceiling and letting days and nights pass and not getting up, not eating, not drinking, just letting my body waste away until there is nothing left.

About shaking my head at my father before turning and running away, stepping up onto the edge and diving into the water toward the place where Nova was waiting in the powerboat.

About all the people I've killed and all the people I've saved because of the people I've killed.

About the first man I killed, the two of us alone under the clear Iraqi night sky.

About swimming toward Nova as he came toward me and being underneath the water for a few moments at a time, hearing nothing at all, floating in a void.

About Scooter dying in my arms.

About my mother and my sister and her husband and the boys.

About Casey and David, Marilyn and Walter.

About Karen again.

About all the people I've killed and all the people I've saved because of the people I've killed.

About Nova helping me up out of the water just as the fire on the yacht finally reached the gas tank and the entire thing went up, momentarily lighting the night, and how he was shouting above the explosion, asking what happened, what the fuck just happened.

About two weeks later learning I was pregnant.

About knowing I couldn't keep it.

About taking myself to the abortion clinic and then driving myself home.

About nobody ever knowing, not even Tina.

About Karen, saying in her deep southern accent, Can you keep a secret?

And about how sometimes when I'm in total silence, in the dark void, my unborn child is with me and we curl up together to keep ourselves warm and then just float there, mother and child, safe from everything that is evil.

TWENTY-TWO

"Holly, Holly, look at that elephant!"

"David," I say reproachfully, giving him a look.

His smile fades a moment as he works the translation in his head. Then, in a slow, stunted voice, he says, "*Regardez … l'éléphant?*"

"*Très bon,*" I say with a nod.

Casey tugs at my shorts. "Can we go see the sea lions?"

She doesn't ask the question in French, and before I have the chance to give her the same reproach I just gave her brother, David points and says, "Hey, that's not fair!"

I place a hand to my forehead, try strangling this migraine before it grows any stronger. Another night of little sleep and I didn't do any running, any exercises, which I know I should have done this morning but which I put off anyway and now here I am with the kids at the Smithsonian's National Zoo even though the sky is overcast and threatening rain.

"Holly," David says, stressing my name in two syllables, "how come I have to speak stupid French and she doesn't?"

One of my few nannily duties is teaching the kids French, Spanish, and Japanese. Tuesday we try to speak French as much as possible; Wednesday it's Spanish; Thursday, Japanese. As can be expected, Casey and David have never been thrilled with the task, but they do pretty well, especially Casey who seems to be picking up the languages very quickly.

But today I don't feel like fighting with them.

David starts to whine again but I turn and lean down and extend my finger so it's right in his face.

"I'm not in the mood, David," I say, my voice low and hard.

His face goes serious. He nods slowly.

"If you two don't want to speak French today, then I don't care. It's for your benefit anyway."

I stand up straight and turn away. I start walking toward the Seals and Sea Lion exhibit. I don't bother glancing back to see if the kids are following me; I know they are because I can hear the scuff of their sneakers on the macadam.

We've been to this zoo enough times that I practically have the entire layout memorized. At least once a month, if not twice, we take the metro up to the zoo. Today their vote was to come here even though they're calling for rain—and as can be expected the place is pretty much deserted. Still, it's summer and there are families here who drove from out of state, even day campers, and a few adults walking around with cameras and brochures.

By the time we get to the Seals and Sea Lion exhibit, David and Casey have caught up and are matching my pace. Casey reaches up and takes my hand; David just walks beside me, his arms swinging.

We're quiet for a long time as we watch the sea lions. A brown pelican walks around behind the thick glass, opening and closing its massive beak.

After a while, I clear my throat.

"David, I'm sorry for snapping at you. I've just … it's been a bad couple days."

"Is it because Jenny is getting married and you aren't?"

Jenny is Blondie.

"No, kiddo, it's not that."

"But you don't have a boyfriend or anything."

I look down at him and grin. "What are you saying—you want to be my boyfriend?"

"Yuck," he says, crinkling his nose. "Girls are gross."

Casey says, "We are not!"

"Guys," I say.

"You are too!"

"Enough," I say, my voice so loud it causes the pelican to stop its walking, for a couple of the sea lions to glance our way, not to mention a handful of people standing around us. "If you two keep it up you'll be speaking French all day."

Both stay quiet.

My cell phone rings.

I dig it out of my purse, see it's my sister calling.

"Yeah, Tina, what's up?"

"Tomorrow afternoon, one o'clock sharp. You'll be meeting with Sandra Price. She'll want your résumé and a completed application, but the application is just for their records, so don't sweat it. Do you know what you're going to wear?"

I'm quiet for a moment, not having any idea what the hell it is she's talking about.

Then it hits me and I say, "I'm watching the kids all day tomorrow."

"I know that," Tina says. "David and Casey have played with the boys before. I figure I'll take them to a movie during the interview. They won't even know you're gone."

I glance down at David and Casey, both who are looking up at me.

"I don't know what I have to wear," I say.

"I'll help you with that."

"I don't even have a résumé."

Tina says she'll stop over at my apartment later with the boys to raid my closet. Later, they'll take me back to their house where she'll make dinner and Ryan will help me with my résumé and walk me through what is expected of me at an interview.

The kids are still watching me, so I say, "Sounds good, Tina, I'll see you then," and end the call.

I must be smiling, because David says, "Guess the week's looking better, huh?"

TWENTY-THREE

It's already raining by the time we make it back to the house. I park beside Walter's car and David throws off his seat belt, opens his door, and bolts toward the back porch. By then I'm already getting out of the car, shouting at him, "Thanks for being a gentleman and waiting," and then I hurry around the car and open up the door for Casey who has already unclipped her seat belt. On the drive, there had been lightning, and Casey hates lightning, absolutely hates it, and for this reason alone she wants me to carry her.

"Thanks, Holly," Casey says simply, kicking her feet so I will let her down once we're inside.

I set her down and she scampers away, the lightning suddenly forgotten. The only evidence that David has been through here is his wet sneakers lying scattered on the floor.

I enter the kitchen to find Sylvia cooking something on the stove. Baron lies off in the corner, watching me, his tail thumping.

"Smells good."

Sylvia smiles at me. "Why look at you, Miss Holly—completely soaked."

Now that the kids are home, I don't have to worry about them anymore. They'll plant themselves in front of the TV for the next hour or so until Marilyn comes home.

I grab some paper towels by the sink, start drying my hair.

Sylvia has two large pots going at once. She stirs one of them, stirs the other, then turns to me and says, "Mr. Hadden said he'd like to see you when you came in."

"Was he in a good mood or a bad mood?"

"Child, that man only has one mood: serious."

On the way to Walter's study I check in on the kids. They're both on the couch, their attention glued to a rerun of *Blue's Clues*. That works for me. I continue on and then stand outside the study door. I still have the paper towels in hand, now damp, and I stare at them thinking about what I should say to Walter, whether I should tell him about my job interview and how soon I will no longer be watching his children. Then I wonder whether I'm being selfish, that Casey and David are innocents in this, and that it's been my job for the past two years to watch over and protect them, and that so far I've done a good job and they've come to like me a lot, even love me, just as much as I love them, and now I'm going to turn my back on them and leave them forever?

I knock once and then enter the study. As usual Walter has hardly any lights on, just the small desk lamp that throws a soft yellow glow on the clutter of papers beside the laptop.

He tells me to shut the door, and I shut the door. He tells me to take a seat, and I take a seat. Then he sorts through the clutter of papers and comes away with a large surveillance photograph and hands it to me asking if I know who that is.

I look at it only for a moment before I say, "That's Roland Delano's assistant."

The photo is one Nova must have taken last week, because it shows her and Delano coming out of the Luxor.

"That's right," Walter says, nodding slowly. Today must not

have been a Pentagon day, because he's wearing khakis and a dress shirt, the top two buttons undone. "Do you remember her name?"

"Alayna something."

"Alayna Gramont."

"Right. So what about her?"

"We've just gotten word that she is continuing with Delano's work. In three days she will be selling Delano's code."

"His what?"

Walter opens his mouth but thinks twice and shuts it. He glances down at the clutter of papers, takes a breath, then looks back up at me.

"Remember Delano's flash drive?"

I nod.

"Well, it's impossible for us—for anyone—to access it without a code. That's the way Delano designed it. The encryption is unlike anything we've ever seen."

"So nobody knows what's on it."

"That's right."

"Who says there's anything important on it at all? Could be the guy's grocery list."

"Could be," Walter says. "But for practical purposes, let's stay with the idea that it's not."

"Okay. For practical purposes what's on that flash drive is a matter of national security."

"No, no"—Walter holds up a finger, shaking his head—"a matter of global security."

"Fine. A matter of global security. And nobody can access the information on that flash drive without a code."

"Yes."

"A code that this Alayna Gramont is going to sell in three days."

"That's right."

"But that doesn't make sense."

"No, it doesn't."

"Why would anyone want to buy the code for something they don't even have?"

"That," Walter says, "is a very good question."

For a moment neither one of us speaks as the rain outside continues, unabated.

I think of something and lean forward in my seat. "Be honest with me here. Is the U.S. one of the buyers?"

Walter's face stays impassive. He gives a quick shake of his head and says, "No, it isn't. From our intel, the buyers appear to be the same buyers Delano was meeting in Vegas."

"So even though they don't have the flash drive, they want to buy the code."

"It appears that way."

"And why are you telling me this?"

Walter doesn't answer.

"I thought you said I was done."

"I say a lot of things."

"You said I've been on a gradual decline."

"You have been. But unfortunately all I have right now are you and Nova, and I can't send Nova into this by himself."

"Where?"

"Paris."

Another moment of silence passes, the two of us staring back at one another.

"Don't send me," I say finally.

"Why not?"

"You were right before. I've become ... reckless. Irresponsible. I can't be trusted."

"This doesn't sound like the Holly Lin I know."

"The Holly Lin you know has changed."

"Has she?"

"I'm through with it, Walter. I'm getting out."

He stares at me for another moment, his dark eyes intense.

Then he leans back in his chair, starts sorting through the clutter of papers again. Not looking at me, he says, "Fine. You want out, you're out. But at least do me this one favor first."

"Walter—"

"Do you still blame yourself for Scooter?" He glances up at me. "Do you? Because as far as I'm concerned, as far as the United States of America is concerned, as far as Scooter's memory is concerned, the Vegas job is unfinished. The only way to finish it is go to Paris and stop the buy."

"You want me to take out this Alayna Gramont?"

"If you have to. But at the moment she isn't a threat. The code, however, is."

"How so?"

"I don't know. But that code cannot fall into the wrong hands."

"What does it matter if it does? They can't do anything without the flash drive."

"At this point we're not taking the risk."

"But—"

"Tomorrow night you'll fly to Paris. Nova will already be there. You will meet up with a team of foreign agents who have been watching Delano for the past two years. They already have surveillance on Gramont. The task here is to wait to see who the buyers are, then take them out if need be and secure the code. Understand?"

"How do you know there aren't copies of this stuff? Whatever Delano had on that flash drive he probably has on one of his computers. The same with the code."

"Tomorrow night, Holly. You want out, you're out. But first this mission."

I stare back at him, this aging man with his firm face and intense eyes. Always so calm, always so in control. Always giving orders, never taking any.

I wonder for an instant what things might have been like

had I turned down Walter's offer eight years ago when he walked into my prison cell in his uniform and his two general stars flashing gold in the light.

What my life would be like had I said no.

What I would be doing right this instant had I told him to go fuck himself.

TWENTY-FOUR

After a delightful dinner of chicken and steak kabobs, the boys are excused to the living room and Tina starts to clear the table. I stand to help her but she shakes her head and tilts her chin toward Ryan.

"You're going with him."

Ryan leads me into his den, which is nothing more than a spare bedroom filled with bookcases and filing cabinets and a desk with a computer on top. He pulls up a chair beside the one already behind the desk, tells me to sit down.

"Are you nervous about tomorrow?" he asks as he moves the cursor around on the screen and brings up a program.

"No," I tell him, but I don't think I'm very convincing.

"Don't worry, you'll do fine. Just be yourself."

That's easy for you to say, I think. *At least you know who you are.*

"Okay," Ryan says, sitting back and exposing the beginnings of a gut. I've teased Tina about this growing gut, saying how her husband is getting fat. Now for some reason I wish I could go back and keep my mouth shut, instead tell Tina just how lucky she is to have a guy like Ryan in her life. "This right here is an outline of your basic résumé. All we need to do is fill in the information. Like here"—he starts typing—"your full name and address and phone number."

He gets the address and phone number wrong—both off by a couple numbers—so I tell him and he corrects them.

"Now," he says, "we do the objective."

"What's the objective?"

"That you're interested in an entry-level position at a thriving and up-and-coming law firm."

"Thriving and up-and-coming?"

He smiles as he types a paraphrase of what he just said and then he sits back again, folds his hands back over his gut.

"Next are your qualifications for the job."

I take a moment to think it over, a very long moment, then say, "I know how to type."

"Do you know how to type well?"

"I can get by."

"They're going to be expecting at least sixty words a minute. Preferably more."

"I'm pretty sure I can do that."

"What about ten key?"

"What the hell is ten key?"

He nods once, takes a breath. "That's what I was afraid of. Look on the keyboard here—see the square of number keys? That's called the ten key. They'll probably test you on that too."

"I'm going to be *tested*?"

Ryan gives me a long look. After a moment he says, "Holly, are you sure this is what you really want to do?"

Of course it's not what I really want to do. It's the very last thing in the world I want to do. But still I nod and tell him yes.

He studies my face for another moment, then leans forward and places his fingers on the keyboard. He doesn't type anything but just keeps his fingers there, the tips grazing the tops of the keys.

"Qualifications," he says, staring at the computer screen, and it takes me a couple seconds to realize he's waiting for me to list them. I even open my mouth, wanting to start listing off one qualification after another, but the résumé that would make is one Ryan is not prepared to see. Nobody in my family would be prepared to see a résumé that lists hand-to-hand combat and weapons training and expert driving, let alone knowledge in explosives and poisons and how to hot-wire a car and how to break into a safe.

"I have a good personality," I say.

"Let's skip this for now and go to education."

"You mean all the schools I've attended, even in elementary?"

As my dad was moved from army base to army base, I'd been in at least a half-dozen schools before finally settling down just outside of Washington, D.C.

"High school and college is sufficient."

"You know I never went to college."

"Your high school then. We'll even add your four years in the Army. It'll look good."

Right after high school I'd joined the Army and stayed for only four years. Or at least that's what my family believes.

I tell him the name and he types it into the form, then asks me about any clubs or extracurricular activities I'd been involved in.

"None."

He glances at me, almost warily, then says, "Okay. How about relevant experience?"

"Ryan, you don't have to do this."

"What do you mean?"

"This is a waste of time."

"No, it isn't."

But as I stare at the computer screen and the very little typed there, I can see it is. As far as everyone else in the world is concerned, those few words sum up my life. Not how many languages I speak, how many countries I've been to, how many missions I've gone on, or how many people I've killed and hopefully saved. All that matters in the real world are objectives and qualifications and education and experience, and in the real world I have none.

Ryan doesn't move from his place in his chair. He keeps the tips of his fingers on the keys of the keyboard and stares at the screen. I know he's waiting for me but I don't have anything to say so I glance away, up at one of the bookcases that contains a few of his trophies. In high school and college he had played lacrosse, which has always been hard for me to picture, but apparently he was pretty good and had constantly been in training. Now years have passed and he is married with two children and working a nine-to-five. He has let his body go, so much so that the gut he now tries to hide will someday double and then maybe triple and every time he looks at those trophies he'll think about the days when he had his entire future open in front of him. Now after just another dinner with his wife and children he sits in his den with his sister-in-law and tries to help her find work.

"Relevant experience," he says after a long time has passed, after the silence has become so palpable it's like an invisible wall has been erected between the two of us. He continues to stare at the screen. "What relevant experience do you have?"

I open my mouth but then shut it and just shake my head.

We sit there then, both of us silent, both of us allowing that invisible wall to rebuild itself again until a couple minutes pass and my sister comes in, asking us how we're doing.

TWENTY-FIVE

We take the orange line to Metro Center, then get on the red line and take that to Gallery Place-Chinatown. It's almost noontime and the trains are busy, the stations even more so.

Both David and Casey are excited. The movie they're seeing today is the new Pixar; they've been talking about it ever since they first saw the teaser trailer a year ago.

We come up from under the Verizon Center to the movie theater. Tina and the boys are waiting for us.

"I've already got the tickets," my sister says.

Matthew and Max smile and talk with David. Nobody pays attention to little Casey, who stands beside me, holding my hand.

Tina leans forward and smiles at Casey. "Excited about the movie?"

Casey nods.

Tina holds out her hand. "Well, come on then, let's go inside. We'll get some popcorn."

"Popcorn!" the three boys yell at once.

Casey looks at Tina's outstretched hand, looks up at me.

"Go ahead," I say. "Have fun."

Casey is still hesitant. That's just the way she is, even around people she knows.

"Come on, Casey," David says, grabbing her other hand.

She lets go of my hand, allows her brother to drag her toward the boys.

Tina smiles at me. "The natives are restless."

I just nod, sweeping my gaze around at the people walking here and there. I'm wearing one of Tina's old pantsuits—there was nothing suitable in my closet—and it's a little too tight around the shoulders.

"Nervous?"

I nod again.

She reaches out, places a hand on my arm. "Don't worry, Holly. You'll do fine."

I try to smile but it's difficult, almost impossible, and so I just shrug my tightly wrapped shoulders and say nothing.

"Remember what Ryan said. Just relax and be yourself."

"Mom called me this morning."

"She did?"

"She invited me to dinner tonight."

"And you're going?"

"I couldn't think up a good enough excuse in time so I had no choice."

"That's good," Tina says. "You both should talk."

"Oh, shut up."

"Excuse me?"

"It's pretty odd Mom calling me up out of nowhere on the day of a job interview. I could tell she was dying to wish me good luck."

Holding a hand to her chest, looking completely perplexed, Tina says, "And you think *I* had anything to do with it?"

I glance past her to where the kids are congregating, David talking to the boys. He keeps pulling away from his sister but Casey keeps grabbing at his hand, wanting that physical link.

"You better get going," I say.

Tina glances at her watch. "You better get going, too." She leans forward, kisses me on the cheek. "Good luck."

I nod again and then just stand there and watch Tina lead her charges into the lobby, each of the kids glancing back and waving. Casey is the last and it's no surprise when she breaks away from the group and hurries over to me. Her eyes are starting to water.

I crouch down so I'm on her level and she wraps her arms around my neck.

"Why are you leaving us?" she near-sobs.

"I'm not leaving you."

"But you aren't coming with us."

"I'll be right back. When the movie's over, I'll be waiting for you."

She wipes at her eyes, at her nose. For an instant I understand she never acts this way with her mother and a heavy needle pierces my heart.

"Promise?" she asks.

"I promise."

Tina slowly makes her way over to us, asking me with a look if everything's okay.

"You don't want to miss the movie now, do you?" I ask.

Casey wipes again at her eyes, quickly shakes her head.

"Then you better hurry. Especially if you want popcorn."

Tina steps up behind her, leans down and whispers in her ear. Casey stares back at me as she listens and then she nods and takes Tina's hand and walks with Tina toward the boys.

I want to keep standing there, watching them, but I don't want to be late either, so I quickly turn and head back to the station.

I take the red line to Metro Center, switch to the blue line that takes me to McPherson Square. Soon I start up 15th Street, take a left and head west on K Street. Five minutes later

I come to the large glass building that is Ryan's firm and I open the door to enter but pause.

This is it, I think. Through these doors is another life. No more Walter. No more Nova. No more killing. No more Casey and David, either. No more trying to make the world a better place. No more Holly Lin.

TWENTY-SIX

The interview doesn't last long. A glance at my résumé, a few questions asked, and then a handshake and a promise that they'll be in touch.

I wait in the lobby of the movie theater almost an hour before the film lets out. David and the boys lead the pack, David bear-hugging the nearly empty tub of popcorn. Matthew keeps sticking his hand in, keeps shoveling popcorn into his mouth, Max and David laughing and laughing while yellow puffs fall everywhere.

Tina doesn't notice their shenanigans because right now she's busy tending to Casey. Casey's face is red and there are tears in her eyes. She isn't crying now but it's clear she has been.

When the boys see me they head in my direction. Tina follows, holding Casey's hand, and when Casey sees me she lets go and hurries toward me.

"What's wrong?" I ask her, feeling a strange sense of déjà vu, understanding in this moment that I cannot leave this girl, not ever.

Tina answers for Casey. "There was a sad part near the end.

You know, they make you think the hero doesn't make it but she overcomes it and everything is okay."

"Then why are you so sad?" I ask Casey. "Everything turned out good, didn't it?"

Casey mumbles into my shoulder: "Just because everything turned out good doesn't mean it's a happy ending."

How about that—profound thoughts from a four-year-old.

Casey won't let go of me so I pick her up and cradle her in my arm.

Tina asks, "So how did it go?"

I shrug.

"That bad?"

"I don't know. I've never done one of those before."

"Did they have you do a typing test?"

"Nope."

"Oh."

"Yep," I say, making the word pop with my lips. It brings Casey out of her dour mood, enough so that she giggles. "What—you like that?" I ask, and do it again, and again, and again, every time the little girl giggling harder.

Still holding her, I ask, "Ready to head back home?"

Smiling now, she nods.

I force my own smile at Tina. "Thank you."

"Not a problem. Good luck with Mom tonight."

"Yeah, thanks. I'm going to make sure I get you back for that, by the way."

Together we head down into the station. We say our farewells. Tina and the boys get on the red line leading toward Glenmont; David and Casey and I get on the red line leading back toward Metro Center.

We sit on one of the plastic benches, Casey on one side, David on the other.

"So why'd you miss the movie?" David asks.

"I had an appointment."

"With a doctor?"

"Yeah."

"You ain't sick, are you?"

"Don't say ain't."

The buzzer dings and the doors close. The train starts to move.

Casey says, "Can we go to the zoo?"

"We were just there yesterday."

"But we didn't get to see *every*thing."

"What's so special at the zoo that you need to see it again today?"

"She likes the elephants," David says. He has a particular giggle in his voice, something I think Matthew and Max manage to infect him with because every time they get together it's there and David becomes a brat. "She likes them because she's as fat as them."

"I am not fat!" Casey yells. Her soft but high-pitched voice causes everyone on the train to glance our way.

"Enough," I say, my teeth clenched. I reach out and grab a spot on David's thigh, just above his knee. I give it a slight squeeze and the smile vanishes as he takes a quick breath.

Keeping my hand on the pressure point, I lean down and whisper into his ear, "Done?"

He nods.

I let go and sit back. We'll be at our stop any moment now. My heart rate is up, just a little, and somehow I've come back to myself, the true Holly Lin slipping back into the shell that was created when she stepped into the lobby of Ryan's firm. My senses become heightened. I begin to hear every noise, smell every smell, see every little detail there is to see.

So it's no wonder that when the train stops and we get off and head toward the orange line train, I realize we're being followed.

TWENTY-SEVEN

There are certain rules one must follow when properly doing a tail. Keeping a healthy distance, looking as if you're busy, acting as if you belong where you are and that the very last thing you're doing is following someone else. You have to keep your target in sight at all times, while at the same time you have to act like your target barely even exists.

Of course I know all this. I was trained for it. I followed people, had people follow me. I know what to do when I'm working a tail. Likewise, I know what to look for when someone is tailing me.

Which two men are doing right now, following me and the kids toward the orange line train.

They're not together, these men, which may be what makes them even more conspicuous. One is wearing a business suit, carrying a briefcase in one hand while he looks at his cell phone in the other. The other is in blue jeans and a T-shirt, a Nationals cap on his head. He's carrying a copy of the *Post*.

Both men are wearing Bluetooth headsets.

Both are keeping their distance from me as well as from each other.

How do I know for certain these two are following us? I don't. But it's a sense I have, an instinct, one that I've come to trust in the past four years.

These two men are trying too hard to act normal, so much so that I peg them right away.

And instead of heading toward our orange line train, I take us toward the escalators.

"Where are we going?" David asks.

I don't answer. I'm carrying Casey and she kicks one leg freely.

We get on the escalator and ride it to the top level. Washington, D.C. has one of the cleanest metro systems in the country. The stations remind me of those in Europe, with their high arched ceilings, clearly positioned signs, and easily accessible trains.

I glance back and see that Suit is just now stepping onto the escalator. Blue Jeans has fallen back, looking at his newspaper, not dedicating himself to any one train.

"Holly?" David says. "I thought we were going home."

"Change of plans."

As we walk I do a quick sweep of everyone else on this level. A few businesspeople, a few students, but mostly tourists. Nobody else sticks out as being a threat.

We head toward a train that has just arrived. It's a blue line train headed toward L'Enfant Plaza.

"Where are we going?" David says.

"David, do you want to play a game?"

"What kind of game?"

"The silence game."

"That's a stupid game."

"Oh look, you lost."

We wait for the train to clear of its passengers. I glance around us again. Blue Jeans is missing, but Suit is forty yards away. He stands in line for the train but not with everyone else right on the edge of the platform. He's still looking at his phone, and as I look at him, he glances up. It's just for an instant and then he's looking back down at his phone. But it's enough. I've made him and he knows it and now he's stuck. Can't move forward, can't move away. Frozen in place until I make my move.

We get on the train and take our seats. I glance back out the window and see that Suit quickly does the same. He's three cars down.

There's a ding and the doors close and we start moving.

Casey now sits beside me. She's humming something, a tune I don't recognize, maybe something from the movie. David looks around, the start of a scowl on his face, something he inherited from his father.

I place my purse on my lap. My gun isn't inside it. I'd taken it out because of my job interview today. I'd taken it out because in the past two years there has never been any reason to carry it.

The train slows and stops at Federal Triangle. People get off, people get on. From what I can see Suit hasn't left his car.

The doors close, the bell dings, and then we're moving again.

Next stop is the Smithsonian. It'll let us up into the National Mall. A lot of space, a lot of people.

As the train moves, I stand up. I grip the metal rail. My hand is sweating. Strange, it wasn't even sweating during my interview.

When the train starts to slow, I reach out and take Casey's hand. Then the train stops and I lift Casey up into my arms. I motion for David to follow, and we walk out onto the platform.

I don't bother glancing back to see whether Suit has gotten off, too.

We get onto the escalator and ride it up to the top level.

We follow everyone else and take another escalator up to the surface. I walk the kids a good twenty feet away from the exit and then turn around to watch the people coming up.

"Holly"—David again—"what are we *doing*?"

"You lost again, David."

"I don't want to play that game."

"That's probably for the best, because you're not good at it."

"That's not true."

"It's not?"

"No."

"Then prove it."

David crosses his arms and starts to pout, his face growing red.

I keep watching the exit. Watching students and tourists. Watching men and women and children.

Then watching Suit, still holding his briefcase, still holding his phone, rising to the surface.

He doesn't even look once in our direction.

He turns south and starts walking toward Independence Avenue. He waits at the corner for the light to change and then continues forward with everyone else.

"Holly?" Casey says hesitantly.

"There," David says. "She lost."

"She wasn't playing," I say.

"What are we doing?" Casey asks.

"Going for a walk, honey."

We head north over Jefferson Drive and take one of the pathways across the Mall. The sky is clear and blue. A nice breeze rustles the leaves on the trees. Two people are throwing a bright yellow Frisbee, three others are juggling a hacky sack.

I figure we'll enjoy the afternoon and walk a couple blocks uptown to Federal Triangle. There we'll take the orange line train back to our stop.

Only as we cross over the Mall and reach Madison Drive

do I get that sense again, that instinct, that we're being followed.

I pause and glance around us.

The guy in the blue jeans and T-shirt and baseball cap, the *Post* in his hands, the Bluetooth flashing in his ear, is headed our way.

TWENTY-EIGHT

Blue Jeans is crossing the Mall directly behind us, coming up the same pathway we've just walked. He walks casually enough, the paper swinging at his side, his attention on the three juggling the hacky sack.

I glance around quickly, considering my options. The National Museum of American History to our left, the National Museum of Natural History to our right.

"Let's go," I say.

"Where are we *going*?" David says.

"Lost again."

"I'm not playing."

"Look, think of this as a game, okay? We're playing hide and seek."

"Really?"

Casey says, "Who are we playing hide and seek with?"

"Trying to figure that out is half the fun."

As we approach the Museum of Natural History, David starts looking around.

"Don't," I tell him.

"Why not?"

"You don't want to make it obvious that you're playing."

"I don't?"

"No. The idea is to act like everything's normal."

Outside the Smithsonian buses are lined up, off-loading and on-loading day camps. The steps are littered with parents and children and counselors and campers. We weave through the crowd toward the entrance, then wait in the line that takes us to the metal detectors. If Blue Jeans is definitely following us, and if he is packing anything from a gun to a knife, he won't be able to come in here.

We head toward the African elephant display in the lobby. I set Casey down, take her hand and place it in David's.

"Stay right here," I say.

"Where are you going?"

"Not far. You'll be able to see me and I'll be able to see you. Just make sure you stay here and don't let go of each other's hands."

I head back toward the entrance, glancing over my shoulder every few seconds. Casey and David stay right where I told them to, holding hands. Both of them watch me just as I keep watching them.

I'm not too worried about them getting snatched. At least not in here, not with a thousand witnesses. And if anybody did try to make a move on them, it would take me less than five seconds to make it back to their location. And even with witnesses, the sorry son of a bitch who tried laying a finger on those kids would be lucky if I didn't break his neck.

My only purpose now is seeing what's become of Blue Jeans.

And I guess I'm not surprised to find that he's outside, waiting in line, almost ready to enter the main doors.

I turn back around, quickly return to the spot I'd left the kids. I pick Casey up and motion for David to follow me.

We head toward the back where the stairs are located. I realize much too late that I've drawn us into a box. Not that I expect anything to go down here, but the only way out—the only public way—is back the way we came.

Which gives me pause, because if that's the case, Blue Jeans wouldn't have to come in after us. He could just wait outside, sit on a bench and act like he's reading the *Post* until we appeared.

So why is he coming in?

We take the stairs to the second floor. I glance over the banister and see that Blue Jeans is just standing there in the lobby. I survey the rest of the lobby, all those people and kids, and then I spot a couple museum employees, at least one security guard.

"Okay, let's go."

We turn away from the stairs toward the closest bank of elevators. I can tell David wants to ask again where we're going but he manages to keep silent. We wait along with two mothers and their strollers and then we all squeeze into the elevator.

The elevator lets us off on the first floor. A museum employee is standing nearby. I walk over and set Casey down, make her hold David's hand again, then step closer.

"Excuse me. Can I talk to you for a minute?"

She nods.

"See that guy over there, the one in the Nationals hat?"

She nods again.

I lean in close and whisper, "My boy over there said that man was watching him while he was in the bathroom."

The woman raises her eyebrows.

Now it's me who nods, gravely, keeping a straight face.

The woman stares at me another moment, then glances at David, then turns her attention back to where Blue Jeans is standing in the lobby, all those kids running around him. She unclips a walkie-talkie from her belt, starts speaking into it.

I turn away and walk back to the kids. I pick Casey up and start toward the exit.

"Miss, you need to stay here," the employee says.

"I can't."

"But—"

Up ahead, two male security guards have converged on Blue Jeans. They step up close to him. One of the guards even puts a hand on the guy's arm.

"What's this about?" Blue Jeans asks, looking back and forth at the guards. As we walk past his gaze shifts to meet mine. I smile and wink at him and then we're headed through the exit doors.

I scope out the steps, the sidewalks, even the street. All looks well. But then we reach the sidewalk and I can see Suit farther down the block, on the corner of 12th and Madison. He has his hand to his ear, listening to something (probably the guards asking his partner why he was in the bathroom looking at boys), and then he spots us.

He starts forward immediately.

Still holding Casey, I tell David to move it and turn left and we start walking.

As we walk, David can't help but look back over his shoulder. I don't bother telling him not to.

"The guy in the suit?" he asks.

"Yeah."

"He's coming pretty fast."

I increase my speed. David does too. We reach the end of the block and turn left up 9th. Just after we make the turn I set Casey down and once again put her hand in David's.

"Take your sister halfway up the block. Stop when you get there. And don't turn around until I tell you to."

"What are you going to do?"

"Go, David."

Casey starts crying. "Holly, what's happening?"

"Go!"

David starts pulling his sister forward. She cries harder now and people are looking and David once again becoming the good big brother tries to pick her up and carry her.

I don't see how far they get.

I don't because I can hear Suit coming, his shoes slapping the sidewalk.

I don't because I'm pushing myself up against the wall right next to the corner, flattening myself.

I start counting, going one two three four, and then he appears, jogging now, and I step forward, throw my elbow into his face. The briefcase hits the sidewalk a second before he does. Both hands fly to his face, holding in the blood. I pick up the briefcase, grip it in two hands, bring it down on his stomach.

"Stop," he says, or tries to say.

I bring the briefcase down again. I don't think about the people watching us, about David and Casey behind me. I think about this man and his partner and about what it is they want to do with the kids and how I'm not going to let that happen.

The man takes his hands away from his face. I've busted his nose and more blood squirts out. He holds one hand up to block another blow as he reaches into his suit jacket with his other hand.

"Keep your hands where I can see them," I shout.

The man tries speaking but blood streams into his mouth, goes down the back of his throat. He coughs and only manages to say, "Me-eye."

"I will smash your face in with this," I tell him, holding the briefcase up over my head, and the man pauses in trying to reach for whatever it is in his jacket.

He opens one eye, looks up at me. Coughs again and force-fully enunciates, "F—B—I."

"What?"

"Me ... and my partner ... we're FBI," he says, and judging that I won't smash his face in with the briefcase, he pulls out his badge and holds it up.

And yep, there it is in big blue letters: FB-fucking-I.

TWENTY-NINE

"What do you want me to say?"

"I want a good goddamned reason."

"And what makes you think you deserve one? They're my children, Holly. Like I told you before you took this job, my kids are the most important thing in the world to me. I will never let anything harm them."

"And all of a sudden I'm not good enough to watch them myself?"

Walter doesn't answer, at least not immediately. A long moment of silence passes. I'm out in the driveway, the kids inside with Sylvia, and I'm pacing around my car, my cell phone to my ear, Walter off in whatever secret corner of Washington he's hidden himself today.

"You said yourself you wanted out. Didn't you?"

"You were the one that said I've been on a gradual decline."

"Holly—"

"I would never let *anything* happen to your children. You know that."

"Yes, I do know that. Consciously, you would never let anything happen to them. But unconsciously ..."

"What the hell does that mean?"

"Your heart's not in it anymore."

"Why would you say that?"

"Again, you told me you wanted out."

"You made it sound like I didn't have a choice."

"The last couple days have been tense for all of us. We may have said things we didn't mean."

"Oh, so now you're taking back what you said?"

"You're going to Paris tonight."

"You know what I mean."

"One thing I've always asked of you is honesty."

"I've never lied to you."

"No? Then how was your job interview?"

I've been pacing, circling the car, but now I stop and just stand there. I don't speak. I can't speak.

"Remember, Holly, my family is the most important thing to me. I make it my mission to ensure their constant safety. And so yes, after our little spat the other day, I talked to one of my friends over at the FBI and requested a surveillance team be put on my children."

"How did you know about my interview?"

"How do I know anything, Holly? How do I know when Islamic terrorists are planning to make a hit, or there's a three-car pileup along an obscure highway just outside of Munich?"

"You have my phone tapped?"

"Holly, if you want to resign your position as my children's nanny, that's your choice. But I ask that you stay until we've found a suitable replacement."

"What—another undercover assassin?"

"Let's just say someone more dedicated."

"Fuck you, Walter. I'm more dedicated to those kids than you are. I love them like they're my own."

"That's a little too overdramatic, even for you. Besides,

what are you trying to say? Are you saying you love them so much you wouldn't leave them alone with your sister while you went to a job interview at your brother-in-law's firm?"

"They were in no danger and you know it."

"No, Holly, what I know is that all of us are in danger. In one way or another, each and every one of us needs a guardian. And right now my focus is making sure my children do not lose theirs."

"But you're going to replace me."

"If it comes to it."

"So I'm fired?"

"It's not that easy, Holly. Really, we should talk about this in person."

"And what about Marilyn? What convenient lie will you tell her this time?"

"I've never lied to my wife. She knows about your background. She knows that's the reason I picked you."

I ask sardonically, "So she knows the whole truth and nothing but the truth?"

"She knows as much as she needs to know to be happy." He pauses. "By the way, I've changed your flight for tonight."

"What?"

"You'll be hitching a ride on a cargo jet going to Europe. Completely under the radar. You won't even need a passport."

"Why so secretive?"

"Because after the trouble in Vegas I wouldn't be surprised if Alayna Gramont now has your face on file. She'll probably have a bulletin out at all the airports for a single Asian woman of your age flying alone."

"You think she can actually do that?"

"You really have no idea how powerful Roland Delano was, do you?"

"Okay, so now what?"

"Now we terminate this call. I have a meeting in five minutes, and you need to ensure my children remain safe. Do you think you can handle that?"

THIRTY

My mother doesn't feel like cooking. She doesn't feel like going out either, so we order pizza from a place nearby. Medium pie, half mushroom, half pepperoni. The mushrooms are for my mother; the pepperoni for me.

We sit at the kitchen table and eat our slices in silence. My mother doesn't even turn on the stereo in the living room, which is odd. The only sounds besides our chewing are the clock ticking and the refrigerator occasionally kicking on and off.

Finally, after five minutes of this unnerving quiet, I say, "Go ahead and ask."

"Ask what?"

"How the interview went."

"How did it go?"

"Pretty sucky."

My mother doesn't respond. She continues working on her already half-eaten slice, holding it up to her mouth with two hands, taking almost petite bites. She has a thoughtful look on her face but doesn't speak, doesn't even look at me, until she's finished the slice and sets the crust down on the side of her plate and then dabs her mouth with a napkin.

"I'm very proud of you, you know."

"Mom, please don't."

"Why can't a mother tell her daughter she's proud of her?"

"For starters, the mother in question never once told her daughter that before."

My mother's expression is one I'd expect to see had I just slapped her across the face. "That is not true."

"Oh really? Then when—when have you ever said those exact words to me?"

She stares at me for a long moment, just stares, and then slowly she lets her gaze fall to the table. In a soft voice, she says, "I never did tell you girls about the camps."

Now it's like I've been slapped—my entire body goes rigid for an instant, the blood draining from my face. In all my twenty-eight years my mother has never once talked about her time in the internment camps, even when Tina and I had begged her, because we felt it was something she should talk about, something to help exorcise those terrible demons.

I don't speak and just watch her, listening to the clock ticking, to the refrigerator once again shutting itself off.

"You have to keep in mind I was just a child at the time, only two years old. I don't even remember what it was like."

My mother's parents came to the United States in 1939. My mother was born just a year later, making her a legal American citizen. This little I know.

"But my parents remembered. They could never force themselves to forget. Growing up, it was one of those things I knew they thought about but would refuse to speak of."

After World War II, my grandparents wanted to change my mother's name to something more American. But by that time my mother was eight, still an only child but at an age where she could make her own decisions, and she stubbornly made them keep it. This little I also know.

"The War may have been over, but people didn't forget. People ... they never forget. Even though everything was over, even though I was an American, they treated us like ... like trash. They treated us like we were ..."

"Less than human?"

She looks up at me, like she's surprised I'm still here in the kitchen with her. Her eyes have begun to water. She stares at me and then nods.

"Yes, like we were less than human. It's not an easy thing to live through, especially as a little girl. And though the years passed and people supposedly forgave and forgot, I could still see it in their eyes. Not every person, mind you, but walking down the street, or standing on line at the grocery store, there would be this flicker behind some people's eyes, like they ... they didn't trust me. Like they thought I was still the enemy. I know your father felt the same way, even though he hadn't been alive then."

My father had been eleven years younger than my mother. Tina and I had always speculated the reason why but had never learned the truth.

"You still miss him, don't you?"

"Of course," my mother says. "Every day. Don't you?"

I think of him shooting Zane, the darkness in his eyes when he pulled the trigger. I think about shooting him and then him staring up at me, waiting for me to finish him off.

"Yes," I whisper. "I miss him too."

"I always felt my life had no meaning, that it was ... purposeless, until your father. He ... he somehow made me forget the distrust in other people. He made me ... happy."

"Why did you and Dad get married so late in life?"

My mother looks at me again, her face at first blank, then

filling with a mischievous sort of grin. "If I tell you this, you must swear to never tell your sister. Do I have your word?"

"Yes."

"I was previously married before your father. To a white man. He was half-Irish, half-German. He worked as a mechanic. I was a senior in high school. It was such a foolish thing for me to do, but I started seeing him behind my parents' back. They wanted me to only date and eventually marry a man from Japan. But then I got pregnant and, well, we had no choice but to get married. I had just turned eighteen three months before. We went away for a while, found an apartment in Chicago. We lived there for seven weeks before we were forced to come back home, face the music as they say, and as you can imagine my parents wanted nothing to do with me. Even when I told them I was pregnant with their grandchild, they turned their backs."

"Do I have another sibling?"

My mother shakes her head slowly, her eyes brimming now with tears. "No, dear, I had a miscarriage. And, well, that pregnancy was the only thing keeping us together. After the miscarriage, our marriage crumbled. We didn't even last six months. I had no choice but to return to my parents."

"And they took you back?"

"My father didn't want to, but my mother persuaded him. He … he called me a few names I'm sure you can imagine. But as the years passed he seemed to welcome me back as his daughter. Other men, however, other suitors, would not come near me. They had heard what happened. They knew I was … tainted."

The tears have finally sprung free; a few race down her cheeks. She wipes them away, shakes her head even more slowly.

"I tried killing myself once. I took an entire bottle of pills. My mother found me in time and I was rushed to the hospital.

I spent two weeks there. And after I came out I needed a job, something to fill my time. But it was difficult finding a respectable job without a high school diploma. First I had to return to high school and finish my classes. Even then many places told me they weren't hiring. But apparently the Army would hire almost anyone. I didn't enlist, of course, but was hired as a civilian. It was there that I met your father, who was a soldier. Yes, he was eleven years younger than me, and he was Chinese, which obviously would not go over well with my parents, but … well, he asked me out and I accepted and here you and I are today."

She wipes a few more tears away, grabs a new napkin to blow her nose.

"Your father, he was just so sweet. He brought me a rose every time he came to see me. He wanted to marry me, but then the Vietnam War broke out and he had to go fight in that … it was hard waiting, you know? Thinking that every day that passed was the day he would die. It tore me up inside. But he would write letters, sometimes even poems. He served three tours of duty, and after the last one we got married."

From what I know of my father it's hard to picture him as a man who brought roses and wrote poetry. From what I know of my father I see him slitting throats and breaking necks.

"Did he know about your first husband?"

"Yes, he did. I confessed it to him the week before our wedding. I wanted him to know the truth and to understand I had been irresponsible then, almost reckless."

I say, "When Tina started dating Ryan, did you …"

"Have reservations? No. I'd decided long ago that I wasn't going to become my parents."

A silence falls between us. My mother picks up another slice, eats two bites, sets it back down. I have a couple bites of my own slice and then glance at the clock. In less than two hours I'll be taking off in a cargo jet headed across the Atlantic.

My mother clears her throat. "Holly, I apologize if you think I expect too much from you. It's just ... I see so much of my younger self in you, and I remember how unhappy I was at your age. How I felt ... like I was just floating aimlessly through life. I want better for you. I want you to be happy."

"I am happy, Mom."

"Really?" She reaches across the table, takes my hand in hers. "Are you truly?"

"Yes," I say, but it's after a moment of hesitation, enough for both of us to catch it and understand the importance.

"Despite what you think," my mother says, "I am proud of you and Tina. I love you both very, very much. But Tina ... the direction of her life has already been set. She's married. She has the boys. She paints when she can. But you, Holly, I see the future wide open for you. I see you doing so many different things, and then ... then I open my eyes and I see you are still here, living less than twenty minutes away from me. I want more for you. I want you to live life."

"I am living life."

"Are you?"

"I guess we all live life differently."

"I guess."

My mother retracts her hand, takes another bite of her slice. I just stare at mine, no longer having any appetite.

"As long as this life is the life you want," she says, "then I'm happy for you. I can't say I won't try to push you again, but if I do please understand why I'm doing it. If you're happy, I'm happy."

"Yes, Mom, I'm very happy," I say, and this time I don't hesitate at all.

THIRTY-ONE

For some reason I expect Nova to be the one who picks me up. Instead, it's a small man with a shaven head and a pointy nose who introduces himself simply as Philippe. He wears a long brown raincoat and holds an umbrella.

"Please, please"—motioning me toward a gray sedan parked on the edge of the runway—"let us get out of the rain."

The cargo jet did not land in Paris but at an airstrip located fifteen miles south of the city. The entire area is surrounded by farmland. Cows that haven't been ushered into barns lie on the ground beneath trees and watch us dully.

Once we load into the sedan, Philippe asks, "How was the flight?"

"Eight hours with no real seat, no toilet, and no service carts—how do you think it was?"

We start driving past farms. Eventually we get on a highway called the N12. Philippe doesn't play the radio, he doesn't talk. After eight hours of listening to myself think, the silence becomes much too unnerving.

"So are you a company man or do you work off the books like me?"

Philippe moves his jaw around, like he's chewing something, before answering. "I'm an operator with the *Recherche Assistance Intervention Dissuasion*. It's a—"

"Counterterrorism unit of the French National Police." I smile at him. "I'm not as stupid as I look."

"Yes, well, that is what I am officially."

"And what are you unofficially?"

He gives me a sideways grin. "Why are you in this line of work?"

I think briefly of Nova when I say, "Work is work."

"I don't believe you."

"Is that so?"

"You have a fire in your eyes. You have a passion."

"If you're trying to get in my pants, you're going to have to do better than that."

He holds up his left hand, just long enough for the headlights of an oncoming car to illuminate his silver wedding band. "Married now fifteen years, have a beautiful wife and three children at home."

"Good for you."

"Yes," he says, nodding slowly, his voice suddenly somber. "Yes, well, I do what I do to keep them safe. But it's never enough. When I work officially I have to deal with the law. But *un*officially …"

Staring out my window, watching the quickly passing buildings and lights drenched in rain, I say, "Laws are meant to be broken."

Philippe goes silent for another minute. He has a thoughtful yet conflicted look on his face. Finally he clears his throat.

"There is a man very well known around Paris. He is a bad man much like Roland Delano was before he was killed. Speaking of which, I'm told we have you to thank for that."

"I do what I can."

"Well, the world is better off without him, trust me on that. But now this other man, I fear he plans to take Roland's place. He already has his hand in drugs, pornography, weapons, and money laundering. We know all of this, but of course we cannot touch him. That's the law for you. It protects the worst of the criminals."

We drive for another minute in silence. After we merge onto the A12, I speak.

"What did he do to you?"

"Excuse me?"

"You said I had a fire in my eyes, a passion, that that's what makes me do this work. It's the same for you, only when you speak of this man there's a darkness in your voice."

"He was responsible for the death of my parents."

"How?"

Philippe shakes his head. "It doesn't matter."

"What's his name?"

"Why—do you plan to kill him just as you killed Roland?"

"If I have the time."

"Let's stop talking about him. Our worry right now is Alayna Gramont."

"Who else is here?"

"You mean besides your associate Nova?"

"Yes."

"Two agents from England, both MI6, and an agent from Russia who's FSB. Tell me—do you know what is on Roland's flash drive?"

"No, and to be honest, I don't care."

"You should. Because if the flash drive and the code fall into the wrong hands ..." He shakes his head. "I don't even want to imagine the consequences."

"Let me guess—the end of the world as we know it?"

He glances at me, and in the dark I can see that his face has actually paled. "That would be the very least of our worries."

THIRTY-TWO

Our safe house is a two-bedroom flat in a tall and ornate building overlooking the Seine. Apparently it's one of the places rented out by Philippe's unit for covert operations such as this.

Nova is the only one waiting inside. He has a Beretta in his hand, and he has it aimed at the door when we let ourselves in. Then, once the door is closed and locked, he lowers the pistol and smiles at me.

"There's my girl," he says, in that cheerful way of his. He even steps closer and places his hand on my shoulder, making me think that he's not too sore after our little spat earlier in the week. "How was the flight?"

"Do you know what Walter had me fly in on?"

Grinning now, he nods.

"You're an asshole."

"Among other things." He turns toward Philippe, his face suddenly serious. "Boylan left twenty minutes ago to relieve Reed."

Philippe glances at his watch. "Very good."

I say, "And who exactly are Boylan and Reed?"

"The MI6 guys," Nova says. "Boris is the Russian and he's stationed on top of the building across from Gramont's place."

"His name is actually Boris?"

Philippe says to Nova, "Want to get her situated? I have to use the restroom."

"My pleasure." Nova motions for me to follow him as Philippe leaves us. We come into one of the bedrooms where tables have been set up with computers and papers and surveillance photos. He grabs one of the photos and hands it to me. "Remember her?"

"Yeah, that's Alayna."

"If you remember back in Vegas, she didn't have any guards on her. The only protection she had was when she was with Delano and his men."

"And should I assume she has guards now?"

"You should."

"How many?"

"Three."

I glance back down at the photograph, the slim woman in the smart pantsuit, blond hair and sunglasses. Around her is an entourage of at least two men in suits, also wearing shades.

"You said before she used to be some kind of model, right?"

"That's right."

"Why did she quit?"

"From what I'm told she got too old and somehow fell in with Delano."

"How old is too old?"

Nova grins. "Twenty-eight."

Philippe enters the room. He has two bottles of Evian and hands one of them to me.

"How much have you informed her?" he asks.

"Just about the guards," Nova says. "At least the guards we know of right now."

Philippe takes a swallow of his water, nods slowly. "I wouldn't be surprised if more show up tomorrow."

"Do we know where the buy's going to be?" I ask.

Philippe shakes his head. "Just that it's at noon. We'll have to follow her from her place to God knows where. It's my guess it'll be somewhere in the city."

"Where is her place?"

"Technically it's Delano's place. And it's not a place so much as a mansion. It sits right along the Avenue La Motte Picquet and overlooks the Parc du Champs de Mars, which is where—"

"The Eiffel Tower is located," I finish for him. "Sounds like pretty snazzy digs."

"The rest of the team has been watching her for the past three days," Philippe says. "After Delano's memorial, she hasn't left the mansion once."

"There was a memorial for that guy?"

"Believe it or not"—Philippe makes a sour face—"that monster had many friends."

I think briefly of the man Philippe mentioned on the ride here, the one who might take over in Delano's place.

"What about the code?" I ask.

Nova says, "What about it?"

"It doesn't make sense. Why would someone want to buy the code without the flash drive?"

Both men look at each other, look back at me, and like that an extra piece of the puzzle falls into place.

"Unless," I say, "they plan to get their hands on the flash drive."

"Impossible," Philippe says. "Your government has that sealed more tightly than your nuclear weapons. What we have been speculating is whether there is more than one flash drive."

"But I thought Delano wore the only one."

"You don't think he would have a copy?"

I turn and walk to the window and stare down at the traffic below us. I think about that night in Vegas, at the party, the man greeting me with the flash drive around his neck, the gold glinting in the light.

"Actually no, I don't. If he had more than one copy, why would he go to such lengths to protect the flash drive he wore?"

"If he wanted it truly protected," Philippe says, "he would have put it in a safe."

Turning back around, I say, "But safes can be broken into. They're not one hundred percent secure. Keeping the flash drive around his neck at all times was his own personal form of security. He believed nothing could touch him, hence nothing could get at the flash drive."

Nova says, "Let's not waste time going back and forth on this. The facts are clear. Someone is coming to Paris to buy the code, and it's our job to figure out who that someone is." He turns to me. "I'm assuming you didn't get much sleep on the flight over here."

"You would be assuming right."

"There are a handful of cots in the other bedroom. Go lie down and try to get some rest. Tomorrow's going to be a long day."

THIRTY-THREE

But I can't sleep. The cot is too uncomfortable. Nova and Philippe continue to talk in the next room. After a while, someone else arrives—one of the MI6 guys—and a third voice is added to the mix.

I toss and turn. I hold my breath, try to asphyxiate myself into sleep. I regret not bringing sleeping pills.

Eventually I get up and join the men out in the flat. The new man is Reed. It's clear he's MI6: broad shoulders, strong face, piercing eyes.

Nova takes me aside, asks if I'm okay.

"I can't sleep."

"Why not?"

"Jet lag," I say, but it's a sorry excuse. The truth is I keep thinking about what my mother told me during our dinner. Never once has she opened up like that before, and now she had to go do it and mention my father and for some reason that's all I've been thinking about. Not the man I knew—the coldhearted killer—but the man who brought roses and wrote poetry.

Philippe and Reed sit off in the corner conferencing about something. I stand with Nova on the other side of the room.

I whisper to him, "Do you buy his theory that the flash drive is really that secure?"

"I don't see why not."

"Then why are we here, Nova? Why would someone want to buy the code if they can't even use it?"

He stands there, rubbing his fingers over the stubble on his chin. Finally he shrugs and says, "I guess we'll find out tomorrow."

I wander into the bedroom with the tables and computers. I sort through the surveillance photos, the reports. Everything is written in French. Daily reports on Delano's residence, on Alayna Gramont's movements.

I sit down at one of the computers and pull up Google. I put in Roland Delano's name. Over one hundred thousand hits come up. One site gives his background: a man born in Egypt but raised in America, a rich man who gave huge amounts of money to charities. Another site paints a darker picture: the arms dealer, the ties to known terrorists, the murderer.

Many of the sites refer to his death in Las Vegas. A mob hit, one site claims, while another points the finger at a competing arms dealer.

I bring up the website for *Le Monde*, one of Paris's top newspapers. I search Delano's name. The names that are associated I scribble down on a notepad beside me.

I try the same thing at another Paris newspaper site, then another. I keep scribbling down names. Out of the handful I have listed, only one sticks out.

I start searching the name. Looking at the sites that come up. Reading over the information posted.

At one point I yawn and rub my eyes. I look at the time in the corner of the screen and am surprised to see that two hours have passed.

I stand up, stretch, tilt my neck back and forth. My entire body aches.

I go out into the rest of the apartment and find only Philippe. He sits in a chair with a book opened on his lap. He has reading glasses on, and when he looks up at me he shifts the glasses down on his nose so he can look over the rims.

"I'm on watch," he says. "Reed and Nova went in to sleep."

"I found out his name."

"Whose?"

"Xerxes."

Philippe curls his lip, shakes his head. "That's not even his real name."

"No, it's not. But that's what he calls himself and what the rest of the world knows him as."

"You look tired."

"I know why he had your parents killed."

"Go in and try to sleep for a few hours."

"Your mother was a witness. She was going to testify."

"Please, I don't want to talk about this."

"Of course Xerxes couldn't have your mom testify, so he had her and your dad killed. Made it look like a random drive-by shooting, like they were just collateral damage. It was too obvious and the police took him in for questioning. But they had no evidence on him, nothing to charge him with. They had no choice but to let him go."

Philippe slams the book shut. His face is red. Glaring up at me, he says, "That's right. The man is untouchable."

"Nobody's untouchable."

"Why do you care, anyway?"

"I'm just curious."

Philippe continues to glare back at me. A long moment passes. Finally he takes a breath, shakes his head, and opens the book.

I leave him and slip into the bedroom with the cots. Both Nova and Reed are asleep, their snoring loud. Fucking great.

I lie down anyway. I stare at the ceiling. I try not to think about anything. I try to clear my mind. But somehow Karen slips into that empty void.

And then I'm asleep and dreaming and back in Iraq. Karen has already killed herself. I'm left with what she told me. I've already talked to my father. I've made my decision. And then I'm waiting in the porta potty, just waiting, and when I open the door I suddenly stop because it's not the monster I'm expecting.

No, this is a completely different monster.

My father smiles and says, Surprise.

THIRTY-FOUR

"She's on the move."

These are the very first words I've heard Boris speak, and as they come across the radio his heavy Russian accent is unmistakable.

Next is Philippe's voice: "Reed, do you have a visual?"

"Affirmative."

Nova is with Reed in a car parked two blocks down from Delano's mansion. Boris is still on top of the building across the street. I'm nowhere close but still I can visualize it in my mind: Boris peering over the roof with binoculars, keeping Alayna Gramont and her entourage of guards in sight as they get into a car. The car will be something flashy, just like the mansion, if not a limo then maybe a Bentley. Once she is inside the car with her guards, they will be on the move. It's eleven thirty and the buy is supposed to be in a half hour. Reed and Nova will follow in their car for at least three or four blocks, depending on Gramont's direction, then they will pass it off to either Philippe or Boylan and myself.

Boris: "They're getting into a black Mercedes SUV."

Damn, I was somewhat close.

Boylan hasn't spoken the entire hour we've been in the car. Just like his counterpart, he has broad shoulders and a strong face. In fact, they could be brothers if it wasn't for Boylan's reddish hair and green eyes.

Reed's voice comes through the radio: "They've just turned onto Boulevard de Grenelle, headed southeast."

"Keep on them," Philippe says. "Boylan, get ready."

Philippe is positioned ten blocks to the north, while we're positioned ten blocks to the south. At Philippe's word, Boylan starts the engine, glances once over his shoulder, and shoots us out into traffic.

Philippe: "Reed, status."

"They're taking their time, definitely in no hurry. Right now we're turning onto Boulevard Pasteur."

"Boylan?"

"Almost there," Boylan says beside me. His hands are tight around the steering wheel as he maneuvers us around a slower-moving vehicle. Buildings and parked cars and pedestrians whip past us. I want to tell him to slow down but this isn't my show; Nova and I are along for the ride, here just in case additional backup is needed.

Speeding past a hospital, Boylan says, "We're coming up on the corner of Rue de Vaugirard and Boulevard Pasteur. Reed, your location?"

"Still headed down Pasteur. The target appears to be turning left onto Vaugirard."

"When?"

"Less than ten seconds."

Thankfully the light changes at the intersection and we're forced to stop. As people cross in front of us, we watch the cars turning left onto Vaugirard. We both make the black Mercedes SUV as it turns. Philippe and Nova continue down Pasteur. I see Nova in the passenger seat, making a furtive glance our way.

Reed: "They're all yours."

"Copy," Boylan says, and once the light changes, he presses down on the gas and we shoot through the intersection.

The SUV hasn't gotten far in the time the light cost us. We catch up to it within seconds, then follow as it makes the turn onto Avenue du Maine.

Philippe: "Boylan, your location?"

"Headed south down du Maine."

"Copy that."

Right now Philippe is speeding through the city, headed in our direction. Reed and Nova have fallen back but are keeping pace a block or two away.

After a couple blocks, Philippe has managed to catch up and he takes over the tail as we turn off. Philippe follows them the entire way down the Boulevard Saint-Jacques until they come to Place d'Italie.

"Shit," Philippe mutters in all of our earpieces.

Place d'Italie is a traffic circle that interconnects eight streets. At least this is what Boylan tells me.

Philippe: "The SUV's stopping."

By now our car and Reed and Nova's car have converged on the location. We're just within a block.

Philippe: "Gramont is exiting the vehicle with two bodyguards. They're headed toward the fountain."

Beside me, Boylan murmurs a curse. He shakes his head. When I give him a questioning look, he says, "They're hiding in plain sight."

THIRTY-FIVE

Alayna Gramont stands with her back to the fountain, watching traffic. She wears one of her smart pantsuits today, something that probably costs half a year's rent for me. Her blond hair is pulled up in a French braid, which I think is a little too cliché. Because it's almost noon and it's clear and sunny, she wears designer sunglasses, probably worth more than my car.

Beside her are two of her guards, both dressed in suits, both wearing shades. Even though I can't see weapons on them, I know they're packing.

Alayna stands completely straight with her hands clasped in front of her. She holds a briefcase. In that briefcase, presumably, is the code.

I'm positioned on the southern end of the circle, Nova on the northern end. Reed dropped him off just as Boylan dropped me off. After all, we couldn't keep circling around the fountain until the buyer made his move. So here we are, each at separate spots, trying our best to blend in with the rest of the people walking the streets.

Only it's hard to blend in when you're stationary.

Because Alayna might be on the lookout for me, I'm wearing a baseball cap and sunglasses.

Philippe's voice in my earpiece: "Anything yet?"

Nova responds. "Nothing."

That's right. For fifteen minutes now nothing has happened. She's just been standing there, holding the briefcase, watching the traffic. If she was the target and all that was needed was her assassination, the job would already be done. Leaving herself out in the open like this, completely vulnerable, all someone would need to do is drive around the circle, lean out, place two in her head. Or take a position on one of the rooftops with a sniper rifle.

But Alayna knows she's in no danger. The target is not her life, but rather the code she has inside the briefcase.

Another five minutes pass and still nothing happens. Philippe and Reed and Boylan have all parked somewhere close by or are circling around a nearby block. If something goes down, they'll be here in less than thirty seconds. Which, when you think about it, is an eternity.

Nova clears his throat. "I've got movement."

From my position, a few trees by the fountain are in my way, but yes, I can see someone approaching Alayna Gramont and her pair of guards. Someone small. Someone that looks like…

"It's a kid," I say.

Philippe: "Repeat?"

Nova: "Holly's right. A boy, no older than ten, is approaching the target."

The kid is dressed in baggy jeans and an extra large T-shirt that drapes down to his knees. He has on a red baseball cap that's tilted toward the side. He looks like a punk, like a poser, and it makes no sense why he's approaching Alayna now, or why Alayna turns to him.

The two guards haven't moved at all. They watch the boy who stands only a couple feet away, saying something.

Philippe: "What's happening?"

Nova: "The target and the boy are talking."

"Repeat?"

"It looks like they're having a fucking conversation."

The boy turns away slightly, jerks his thumb at something over his shoulder. Alayna nods. She speaks. She steps closer, extends her hand, and fuck me if the boy doesn't take it and they shake like they're finishing a business transaction. Then all of a sudden the briefcase is in the boy's possession and he's turning away and walking quickly toward the metro entrance.

"The briefcase has switched hands," Nova says. "I repeat: the briefcase has switched hands."

Alayna Gramont and her two guards have turned away. They now walk to the edge of the circle where the black Mercedes SUV pulls up. One of the guards opens the back door. Alayna disappears inside. Then the two guards climb in and the SUV screeches away.

The boy has already disappeared down into the station entrance.

I'm moving before I even know it. Tires screech. Horns blare. People shout. I barely notice as I sprint across the street toward the circle, toward the metro entrance. I can see Nova on the other side, doing the very same thing.

"I'm headed after the second target," I say to no one in particular because I'm certain right now all three cars are speeding toward this location right this instant.

I have to fight past people coming up the steps. I reach into my pocket for the few euros Philippe provided me. I feed them into the machine and get my ticket. I hurry through the turn-stile without even glancing back to see if Nova is keeping up.

The platforms are packed. People everywhere, but I can't see the boy in the red cap. I hurry as inconspicuously as I can, weaving in and out of the throng, looking for him.

In my ear, Nova says, "Holly, do you see him?"

I don't answer. I just keep walking, keep looking. Thinking that maybe he's hiding somewhere. Thinking that maybe he's passed the briefcase off to somebody else.

Then I spot him.

Standing thirty yards away, right on the edge of the platform for the M6 train. Holding the briefcase in his hand like it belongs to him. Just standing there, waiting along with everyone else. He's tapping his shoe, bouncing his head, and it's not until I get closer do I see he's wearing earbuds.

"I've got him," I say just as somewhere down the tunnel comes the sound of the approaching train.

Philippe: "Do not lose him."

No shit, I think.

I turn toward the platform, waiting for the train. Keeping a visual on the boy from the corner of my eye.

The train arrives. The doors open and people pile out, then the crowd on the platform piles in. I pause to make sure the boy heads into this train—he's two cars down—and he does. I consider heading in that direction, maybe slipping into his car in case there's someone waiting there for him. But then there's a ding, and an electronic voice speaks in French, and I hurry into the nearest car.

The doors shut. The train starts to move.

A crackle sounds in my ear, probably Philippe, but because of the thick concrete all I hear is static.

The train makes a stop at Nationale. I get off along with everyone else, keeping an eye out in case the boy appears. He doesn't, so I slip into the next car.

As the doors close and the train starts moving again, Nova speaks.

"You still have him?"

The car is full of people. I don't want to look like a complete wacko, so I turn away and say yes into my shoulder, hoping it's enough for Nova to hear.

"Holly, do you still have him?"

I decide to ignore Nova and wait for the train to stop again. This time it's at Chevaleret.

I get out along with a few other people, keeping an eye on the boy's car. He doesn't appear. A sinking feeling hits me and I start to take a step toward the car when someone grabs my shoulder. I turn back around, already reaching for my weapon, but stop when I see it's Nova.

"Where's the boy?" he says.

I turn away from him and hurry to the next car. I make it in time before the doors close. Nova doesn't. He smacks the glass as the train pulls away. I turn around and take a deep breath, like I just ran to catch the train in time. Nobody looks at me. Not even the boy, sitting over in the corner of the car, the briefcase between his legs. He's still bouncing his head to the music, completely oblivious. He doesn't even seem to know anybody's around him until the train slows again and then he stands up and starts toward the door.

He leaves the briefcase.

This stop is the Quai de la Gare. Almost everyone gets off, including the boy. He just walks right past me, bouncing his head, lost in the music. I consider grabbing him but then realize it's just me and that the main objective here is the briefcase.

I let him go untouched, then turn around. Stare at the briefcase. Maybe the kid left it for someone else. Maybe someone will pick it up at the next stop. But that doesn't make sense because right now it's open game and anybody can take it.

Shit, I think, I'm anybody, so I weave my way through the

people toward the briefcase. I sit down. I look around, see nobody watching me. I lean forward, pick up the briefcase.

Thinking good, finally, the code is secure.

Then thinking, shit, what if it's a bomb?

What I should do is wait for the next stop, get off the train, go to the surface, and try to hail the team.

What I should do is leave the briefcase alone until everyone else is there.

I consider it, I really do, but then I set the briefcase down on my lap. I undo the clasps. Then, as the train streaks through the tunnel toward yet another station, I open the case to see what's inside.

THIRTY-SIX

A flash drive.

That is what's inside the briefcase, protected by foam padding. Just like the one Roland Delano had hanging around his neck, only this one is silver.

Philippe asks, "Shall we see what secrets this holds?"

We're all standing in the main living area, everyone except Boris who is still on the rooftop watching the mansion. Apparently after leaving Place d'Italie, Alayna Gramont returned home with her guards. She hasn't left since.

Philippe takes the flash drive from the briefcase and carries it into the bedroom with the tables and computers. He sits down at one of the computers. He takes off the flash drive's cap, reaches behind the computer. It takes him a couple seconds, but then he has the flash drive inserted.

And like that, the screen starts to flicker.

Nova steps forward. "What the hell?"

The flickering gets worse.

"Pull it out," I say.

The flickering is a hodgepodge of a million scattered pixels swirling about.

"Pull it out!"

Philippe reaches behind the computer, jerks the flash drive out. But it's already too late. Whatever virus installed on the flash drive has already stormed its way into the computer, conquering data boards and chips and whatever else, corrupting everything. And on the screen the flickering scattered pixels begin pausing in place, dots filling black, until an image starts to form.

Seconds later the image is complete.

A security camera shot taken from the Bellagio, showing me in my schoolgirl outfit. The image is fuzzy because of the angle and my body movement—I must have been running at that point—but still there's a good shot of my face.

A couple seconds of silence passes. Philippe still has the flash drive in his hand. He looks down at it. Looks at the screen. Looks up at me.

Suddenly my image fades away, replaced by another image: a gigantic mushroom cloud, frozen in time as it works to rise higher and higher into the sky.

Still more silence.

Then, materializing over the mushroom cloud, these four words:

THE CLOCK IS TICKING

THIRTY-SEVEN

Because Nova and I are responsible for Roland Delano's demise, Philippe, Reed, and Boylan take turns buying us drinks.

We sit in the back corner of some bar in the southern part of the city. It's what Philippe calls a "safe place."

When the fourth round comes, Philippe holds up his beer and says, "To Holly and Nova!"

Reed and Boylan echo the toast and we all clink glasses, take large gulps of beer. I'm feeling a little toasty but that's okay. The soonest Walter can get us out of Paris is at ten o'clock tonight. When he learned we'd gotten the runaround, he decided to stop wasting our time and bring us back home. Our flight is another cargo jet leaving from the same airstrip on which I entered the country. I'm not looking forward to it but at least now I know what to expect.

Nova had asked me earlier if I feel okay about what was on the flash drive—which did in fact destroy the entire hard drive of the computer. I had just shrugged and told him I felt fine. But it was a lie. I do feel uneasy. Not that my image appeared on the screen along with that frozen mushroom cloud and those words, but the fact that Alayna Gramont or whoever else made the virus knew that I would be involved and would see the message. After all, it was a message for me, wasn't it?

Then again, maybe I'm overthinking it. Maybe I'm being paranoid. Yes, they included my image, but that's simply because I was responsible for eliminating Delano. There was no possible way Gramont or whoever could know I would be involved in the surveillance of the code buy. Right?

"Holly?"

I blink, look up to see Reed grinning at me. Both he and Boylan have definitely relaxed over the past six or seven hours. No longer the uptight agents who never smile, now alcohol has done its magic and helped them loosen up.

"What's that?" I ask.

"Can you tell us about it? How you took out Roland?"

For a Friday evening at eight o'clock, this bar is surprisingly empty. Only a few people lined up on stools at the bar, a few other people scattered around the tables. Nobody close enough to overhear us, not if we keep our voices down, and besides, the music pulsing from the speakers is a healthy rock beat and will help drown out my voice.

Still, I wonder, should I tell them?

I glance at Nova. He's watching me. His look is almost cautious. He has his large hand wrapped around his beer glass and is rubbing his thumb up and down the side. It's such a small thing I don't think he even knows he's doing it.

I know I shouldn't. My work is classified, even if it is unsanctioned. But nobody has ever asked me to tell stories before. Sure, I've described things to Nova and Scooter, even Walter, but that was more or less a simple debriefing of the events. Not storytelling simply for amusement.

"Well?" Boylan says. His eyebrows are raised, his lips curled in a smile. I notice he's wearing a wedding band now—he hadn't earlier during the surveillance—and I wonder about his family. Whether he has any children, and if so, how he treats them when he's home. About what he tells his wife when he comes home from work, what he might say to her on the phone if he hasn't seen her in weeks.

I glance at Nova one more time, see the caution still in his eyes, and then I lean forward and say, "Delano was having a party at this casino …"

The story doesn't take long to tell. Five, maybe ten minutes pass. When I'm done, I finish off my beer and sit back and cross my arms. I can't stop smiling. I don't know why, exactly, but the look on the guys' faces, the one of complete awe, is something I've never had aimed at me before.

Beside me, Nova takes a sip of his beer, looks away. He doesn't say anything.

Finally Reed says, "And then what happened? You just … went home?"

I told the story up to the part where I returned to the garage. Where Nova and Scooter confronted me about Rosalina. Where Rosalina told me about the ranch.

I lower my eyes, thinking now about Scooter. Remembering how he saved me even though I shouldn't have been there in the first place.

I think about him chewing his Bazooka Joe bubblegum. About him aiming his cell phone, ready to take a picture of me in the schoolgirl outfit.

He's gone now, having died in my arms, and today may have been my very last mission.

"Yeah," I say, my voice soft, "then I went home."

Nova glances at me, glances back down at his beer. His hand is still wrapped around the glass and his thumb keeps rubbing the side.

"Did you say anything to him?" Boylan asks.

"Who?"

"Delano. Before you shot him. Did you say anything?"

I find it a strange question, an unlikely question, in fact, coming from a guy like Boylan. As far as I can tell, he's a professional. And saying something to the target before you kill him, that's just too ... Hollywood.

"No," I say.

"That's a pity." Something dark enters Boylan's eyes. "If it had been me, I would have said something."

"Like what?"

"I would have reminded him about Abraham and Kenneth. Made him think about their deaths in the instant before he died."

The mood has shifted. The music continues around the bar, people talk and laugh, but it's like a glass partition has suddenly appeared, cutting us off from the rest of the world.

Boylan has gone silent, now staring down into his beer. Reed glances at him, then glances at Philippe. Finally he looks at me.

"Abraham and Kenneth were part of our team two years ago. Roland Delano had them killed."

"How so?" I ask.

"Delano had men come after them. Actually, he had men come after all of us. We were the team assigned to keep constant surveillance on the man and his dealings. Delano somehow found out about it. He didn't like it and sent men to scare us off."

"He really thought doing that would work?"

"The thing about men like Delano is they don't think. They just act. And so he sent men and ..." Reed looks down, swallows, shakes his head.

Philippe clears his throat. "One of the main reasons Boris isn't with us now, why he's still up on the rooftop watching the mansion, is that he was shot in the leg that night by Delano's men. They almost killed him. He now has to use a cane to get around."

Boylan looks up at me, his face even darker. "They shot me, too. Right here." He taps his left shoulder with a finger.

I glance at Reed. "What about you?"

"Me?" He shakes his head. "I happened to be taking a piss at the time. Wasn't in the room when Delano's men stormed in. There were four of them. Abraham and Kenneth were closest to the door so they were killed first. We returned fire and managed to take two of them out, and the other two …"

He shakes his head again. Nobody speaks for the longest time. That invisible glass partition is still around us, keeping out the rest of the world.

Finally, Boylan shakes his head. "On second thought, I wouldn't have said anything to him before I pulled the trigger. I would have just shot him five or ten times. Then I would have walked right up to him and spit in his face. Either that or pulled out my dick and pissed all over him."

A beat passes, then another. Reed smiles first. Then Philippe. Then Nova. Then Boylan. I'm the one who laughs first though, and it starts the rest of them off, all of us laughing, contained in that invisible glass partition that ensures nobody else in the world knows the joke.

THIRTY-EIGHT

By the time we leave the bar it's nine o'clock and it has already started raining. Philippe's sedan is parked two blocks away in one direction, Reed and Boylan's car parked three blocks away in another direction. We say our goodbyes on the sidewalk, shaking hands, patting shoulders, nodding heads. Knowing that we did everything we could today to try to save the world but sometimes your best just isn't good enough.

The three of us walk quickly toward the sedan. As we near it, Philippe reaches into his pocket for the keys. I hurry my step, snatch the keys from his hand, and tell him I'll drive. Before he can protest, I hit the button to unlock the car and slide into the driver's seat.

Reluctant, Philippe gets into the passenger seat. Nova sits in the back.

Philippe says, "Do you even know where you're going?"

"I've driven in Paris before."

"That doesn't answer the question."

I put the car in gear and wait for an opening in traffic before I pull out into the street. The sedan handles better than I thought it would, the engine powerful, and it takes me a minute to adjust.

The rain picks up. One of the wipers is obstinate and doesn't clear the windshield properly.

I drive up one street, down another. I stop at traffic lights, stop signs. I know what I'm looking for but start to wonder whether it's worth the risk. As much as I'm dreading the flight back home on the cargo jet, I don't want to miss it.

Finally I find the street I'm looking for. As I make the turn, Philippe starts to notice what section of the city we're in. His body tenses. He sits up straight in his seat. He looks at me, just stares, before speaking.

"What are you doing?"

I spot the club two blocks up. It's almost impossible not to, what with the bright flashing lights and the large neon sign that in French proudly proclaims Xerxes's Palace.

There's a vacant spot along the curb. I park the sedan, shut off the engine.

"Holly," Philippe says, his voice stern. "Just what the fuck do you think you're doing?"

"Being reckless and irresponsible," I say, undoing my seat belt and reaching for the door handle.

Philippe grabs my arm.

Nova, just as fast, leans over the seat, grabs Philippe's hand, and pulls it back off. He says, "What the hell is going on here?"

Philippe ignores him, keeps staring at me. "You can't go in there."

"Why not?"

"What do you expect to accomplish?"

"I just want to see him."

"There's no guarantee he's inside."

Nova says, "What the fuck are you two talking about?"

Philippe jerks his hand out of Nova's grip. "The man who

owns that club was an associate of Roland Delano. It now appears he's planning to take Delano's place."

Nova closes his eyes, lets out a breath. He says my name, starts to say more, but I open the door and step out.

"I'm not going to do anything. I just want to see him for myself."

"What about your flight?" Philippe asks.

"I'll be back in ten minutes."

Nova says, "And if you're not?"

I smile at him. "Then you know what to do."

Even with the rain there's a line outside the club. Thankfully a canopy has been set up and I find shelter underneath it.

The line moves fast. I don't have identification on me but the bouncer likes my smile and lets me in anyway. I'm forced to pay a cover charge. Then I enter a dark atmosphere of head-pounding music and flashing lights. A corridor past a small bar leads into the club. It's a wide open space with four levels. The middle is open with a large dance floor on the first floor. The place is packed.

I move along the first level, past booths and tables, past waitresses dressed in skimpy outfits. I take the stairs to the second level, where the booths and tables have been replaced with plush beds. People lounge on these beds, drinks in their hands. I walk to the balcony and stare down at the dance floor, then glance up at the ceiling which is a mirror reflecting the flashing lights.

I start to head up to the third floor but decide to go back downstairs instead. If Xerxes is here, he's in a VIP room or another level I'm not able to access.

I make it to the first level without any problems. A guy wearing too much cologne and too much gel in his hair approaches me. He has a drink in each hand. He hands me one, asks if I'd like to dance.

"No thanks," I say, handing him back his drink.

He calls after me, his voice rising above the head-pounding music, asking what's wrong, baby, don't I want to party? I keep walking. Past the tables, past the booths, past those skimpily clad waitresses. Down the corridor past the bar, twenty feet from the exit, fifteen feet, ten feet, when suddenly two men in suits place themselves in my path.

"Excuse me," says one of the men in English. "If you wouldn't mind, please come with us."

In French I tell them I don't speak English. I tell them I was just leaving.

The man steps closer. "Don't make this difficult on yourself, Miss Lin. Mr. Xerxes would like to have a word."

In French I tell them again I don't speak English. I raise my voice, hoping to draw attention.

The other man, the one who hasn't spoken yet, places his hand inside his suit jacket. He pulls it out, only slightly, to reveal the butt of his gun.

I glance past them at the exit, only ten feet away. I think about Nova and Philippe waiting outside in the sedan. I think about witnesses. I think about how many seconds it would take the man to fully bring out his gun and what all I could do in that time. I think about my reason for coming here, how I wanted to see Xerxes, to glimpse him, and how now I've just been given a personal invitation into his quarters.

I smile and in English say, "All right then, fellas, lead the way."

THIRTY-NINE

A private elevator takes us up to the fifth floor. The suit who showed me the butt of his gun was the one who frisked me. He'd spent a little too much time around my ass and crotch and breasts and when I told him that would be twenty dollars he muttered fuck off.

Now when the elevator doors open he's the one who steps out first and motions me forward.

The first thing I notice is that the room is large and sparse. A few potted plants, a bar in the corner, and in the middle of the room three plush chairs. Sitting in one of those chairs, right in the middle, is a black man in his forties. He has a handsome face with a sharp goatee.

The second thing I notice as I'm pushed from behind by the other suit is that the floor is glass. No carpet, no wood, no concrete, but glass. It's broken up in square segments by the steel frames keeping this level supported, and as I walk I remember looking up and seeing only a mirror that reflected the flashing lights and the images of the people on the dance floor.

Despite the head-pounding music playing downstairs, it's

quiet up here. The only sounds are our footsteps on the glass as we approach Xerxes. He watches, a drink in his hand. It doesn't appear like he's going to say anything, so I decide to break the silence.

"Nice two-way mirror," I say, looking down at the club below. "I didn't take you for a voyeur, but I guess it's not surprising."

He wears black dress pants and a pink collared shirt. Not many men can pull off pink, but he manages it swimmingly.

Xerxes keeps watching me for another moment, then smiles. When he speaks, I'm surprised to find he has a British accent.

"I'm glad you approve. I hope my men weren't unprofessional when they stopped you on your way out."

Besides the two suits behind me, three other men are stationed around the room. All keep their eyes trained on me.

I jerk my thumb back at the suit behind my left shoulder. "This asshole was a little too fresh when he patted me down. Just so you know, if he ever does it again, I'll break his fucking nose."

Xerxes smiles. He glances at the man and raises an eyebrow. "Do you think she has the ability to break your fucking nose, Richard?"

"Who," the man says, "her?" and as he steps forward and touches my arm, I spin around and jam the heel of my hand into his nose. My intention is not to kill him, so I don't hit him with my hand raised up which might send bone particles into his brain. Instead, I keep the hand straight, popping him just enough to break the cartilage, and then he's down on the ground, his hands to his face, blood running down his suit and spreading on the floor.

Already the three men stationed around the room move forward. The suit to my right grabs me.

"You *cunt!*" the suit on the ground shouts, his mouth full of blood. He starts to stand, reach for his weapon.

"Enough," Xerxes says loudly. "Richard, she gave you fair warning. You were stupid enough to test her. Now get out of here. You're making a mess."

The man keeps one hand to his face, glaring back at me. I can tell he wants to ignore his boss, pull out his weapon, shoot me in the head. I can tell he even considers the idea.

Then, with another curse, he turns and stalks out of the room, leaving a trail of blood in his wake.

Xerxes sighs, rattles the ice in his glass. He motions for me to sit in the chair beside him.

"Would you care for a drink?"

The chair is some large modern piece of shit that threatens to swallow me whole. Not very comfortable at all but it's not like I'm going to complain.

"No thanks."

"May I ask you, Holly—may I call you Holly?"

"Right now you can call me whatever you want."

"Okay then, Holly it is. May I ask you what it was you expected to accomplish by coming to my club tonight?"

"I actually thought this was a karaoke bar."

"Did you?"

"Yes. I've been having the urge to sing some Gwen Stefani lately."

"Then why did Philippe and your American friend stay in the car?"

"They don't care much for my singing."

Xerxes's smile is thin. "What did you think of the message?"

"What message?"

"Don't play coy. After all, you were the one who eventually ended up with the briefcase, no? It seems almost appropriate when you think about it."

"To be honest, I thought it was a little overdramatic. It just felt too … hack."

Two women enter the room with paper towels and bottles of cleaner. They get down on their hands and knees, start spraying and wiping the floor.

Xerxes says, "Roland was a close friend of mine."

"So I've heard."

"He was like a mentor to me."

"That's sweet."

"He taught me everything I know."

"Does that include sucking cock?"

The women pause in their cleaning, stay motionless for a second or two, start cleaning again.

Xerxes says, "You are a very arrogant woman."

"That's what people tell me."

"You should have taken your plane ride back to America. You should have walked away."

"Like I told you, I thought this was a karaoke bar." Thinking, how does he know I'm already supposed to be headed back to the States?

The women are quick and concise. In less than two minutes they've cleaned up the blood, gathered their things, and exited.

"How is Philippe, anyway?" Xerxes asks.

"He still blames you for his parents."

"Pathetic. I had nothing to do with his parents' passing."

"Of course you didn't."

"I wasn't even in the city when it happened."

"No, you're much smarter than that."

"Just as I won't be anywhere close by for your unfortunate death tonight. Not that anyone would suspect me."

"Of course they wouldn't. You're a model citizen. Drugs, weapons, whores—I'm surprised they haven't given you the Nobel Peace Prize yet."

"Again, you are very arrogant. Aren't you afraid to die?"

"Not really."

He leans forward. "What about me—do I scare you?"

"What scares me is your breath. Seriously, have a Mentos or a Tic Tac or something."

He's faster than I take him for. He slaps me once across the face, then leans back and takes a sip of his drink.

I sit there a moment, trying not to give him anything. A couple seconds pass and I shift my gaze down at the glass beneath my feet. I can see the dance floor. I can see the people moving frantically about. And I can see Nova moving through those people, moving with purpose.

Xerxes says, "What is it like?"

"What is what like?"

"Being a murderer."

"I'm not a murderer."

"No? Then what is it you call yourself? You kill people for a living, no? You take their lives away. The last I checked that was called murder."

"Work is work."

"So you're just a drone then, is that it? A puppet who waits for her strings to be pulled?"

"What I do is try to keep the world safe."

He smiles, actually chuckles. "Oh, come off it."

"People like your father figure are evil fucks that don't deserve to live."

"Hmm, that's interesting. You believe Roland was evil. You believe, I assume, that I am evil too."

"Among other things."

"And so in your mind if you eradicate Roland and me and the rest of the evil men and women in the world … what—the world will suddenly be a better place?"

He waits for me to respond, and when I don't, he grins.

"I'll let you in on a little secret, Holly. Everyone's evil. Even you. And not considering yourself a murderer is simply naïve. After all, killing is killing. Don't you agree?"

He's wrong, of course. I do consider myself a murderer. I'm not proud of the fact, but murdering people is what I do. And I'm good at it. One of the best. And I'll be damned if I have some pink-shirt-wearing-ice-rattling-cocksucker tell me otherwise.

"Are you in denial, then?" I ask.

"About what?"

"About being a terrorist."

"*Terrorist?*" He laughs, shakes his head. "I am no terrorist."

"Then what would you call yourself?"

"What I call myself already. Xerxes, which means—"

"Douchebag?"

He takes another sip of his drink, again rattles the ice around in the glass.

"Terrorists for the most part want to destroy the world. But that's not my ultimate goal."

"What is your ultimate goal?"

He looks at me like the answer should be obvious. "Why, to rule the world, of course."

He leans forward, places his lips to my ear.

"Roland was my friend," he whispers, "and I loved him like a brother. And while I mourn his death, I can't help but also be happy. Because now I have the chance to advance. Now I have the chance to take his place. And it's all thanks to you, Holly Lin. Not like you knew what you were doing at the time—after all, you're just a drone, aren't you?—but you helped secure my place in history and … well, I just want to say thank you."

He leans back, takes another sip of his drink. He stares at me, waiting for me to speak.

I say, "Did someone really buy the code today?"

"This morning, yes. It was done electronically."

"And the boy?"

"One of my runners."

"So the entire thing was meant to be a huge waste of time."

"Not entirely. We still wanted to send you a message."

"How did you know I would even be here?"

He smiles again. "You can't even begin to imagine how much I know."

I glance around at the men watching us. I think about options, possibilities, causes and effects. I think about Nova somewhere downstairs, trying to find me. I think about Philippe somewhere close by too, either outside or in.

"So now what?"

"Now I'm afraid we part ways." He sets his glass aside, stands up. "It was a pleasure finally meeting you. You are a very attractive woman and I wish we could have met under different circumstances."

"Yeah," I say, standing, "like you would ever have a chance."

"Perhaps." Xerxes smiles again. "But what you have to remember about men like me, Holly, is that we always get what we want."

Three men approach. Two of them take my arms, turn me around. They steer me toward the elevator that's already standing open. They push me into it. The doors slide shut and we start to descend. I think about options again, about possibilities. The men haven't let go of my arms. Their grip is tight. They may not know my entire background, everything I can do, but they witnessed me take out one of their own so they know I'm capable.

I think about struggling but know it's not worth it. It would just waste time, burn energy, and right now I want to save up as much strength as I can.

We pass the first floor, continue down to the basement. The doors open, revealing a parking garage. A car is parked in front of us. Reed and Boylan stand beside it. Reed has a Glock 17 in his hand, Boylan a plastic zip tie.

"Thank you, boys," Reed says. "We'll take it from here."

FORTY

They force me to put my hands behind my back. Then they put the plastic zip tie around my wrists. Next thing I know I'm being shoved into the backseat next to a large man with a double chin and a cane who smells like cheap cologne.

He doesn't look at me.

Reed and Boylan get into the car. Reed slides into the driver's seat, starts the engine, and then we start driving though the garage.

"Boris?" I ask.

He turns his head slightly, looking at me out of the corner of his eye. He says nothing.

"Where are you and Rocky and Bullwinkle taking me?"

Still no answer.

"You know, you're a lot fatter than I pictured."

He's much faster than he looks. One moment his hand is on the tip of his cane, the next it flies up to backhand me across the face. Then it's back on the tip of the cane, like it never moved at all.

Boylan shifts in his seat to glance back at me. "Just shut the fuck up, Holly."

We drive up the ramp to the exit. Reed pauses for the gate to open.

As it does, I play around with the zip tie. When they placed it around my wrists I'd balled my hands into fists and kept them together. Boylan hadn't seemed too worried about it because otherwise he would have noticed this gives me more room when I move my hands so the wrists are touching. It doesn't give me a lot of room, but it gives me some, enough to start working the zip tie.

The gate opened completely, we drive out into the rain.

"So where are we going?"

Nobody answers.

"You seriously don't think Philippe isn't going to figure this out?"

Still no answer.

I think about it a moment, then say, "Unless Philippe is in this with you guys, too."

Then I shake my head, say, "No, he wouldn't be that corrupt."

I say, "Philippe is a good guy. A true good guy. Not a poser like you fucks."

Boris does his lightning-quick handwork again. This time I'm ready for it and turn my head away. His backhand hits me in the ear. And because it hits me in the ear, he grunts with frustration and punches me in the ribs.

We turn down one street, turn down another. I have no idea where they're taking me. All I know is that when we get there they're going to kill me.

I keep working at the zip tie behind my back.

"At least tell me what the appeal is. From what I could see, Xerxes isn't all that charming. Why would you guys want to be in his pocket?"

Reed brings the car to a stop at a traffic light. He flicks the turn signal on.

I stare out my window, at the cars parked along the street, at the lights in the stores. "Abraham and Kenneth. Delano never had anything to do with them. At least, he never had men try to come in and kill you all."

The light changes. Reed presses his foot down on the gas, bringing us into motion again.

"By that point Delano had already gotten to you. He'd made a deal. Probably offered you money."

The windshield wipers screech back and forth.

"He probably offered you a lot of money. And maybe you didn't want to split it between five people. Or maybe you knew Abraham and Kenneth would never go for it in the first place."

Up in the passenger seat, Boylan tilts his head from the left to the right, from the right to the left. In the heavy silence the pops are like gunshots.

"Yeah, you knew they wouldn't flip, that they would be good until the end. So you had to take them out. You had to kill them. Yourselves. Except ... except Boris and Boylan were shot in the process. And so were Delano's men ... or were they even his men?"

Boris shifts beside me in his seat. I pause in trying to free my wrists, ready for another blow. One doesn't come.

"So you had men standing in as Delano's men. You killed them, only after you killed Abraham and Kenneth. And then ... what—did you guys draw straws or something to figure out who would get shot and who wouldn't?"

The windshield wipers: back and forth, back and forth.

"You sick fucks. You did draw straws, didn't you?"

My wrists working the zip tie: back and forth, back and forth.

"And Reed managed to luck out. He was the one who would walk away without a scratch."

The windshield wipers and my wrists: back and forth, back and forth.

"All so you could be the ones who ran surveillance on Delano. Philippe doesn't know. He might suspect, but he doesn't know. And taking him out of the equation is too risky. Raises too many questions."

One wrist, almost free.

"So you keep him around. You keep him around because you don't want to kill him. Or because by killing him you would bring in more people. And right now you guys like it the way it is. You like it just being the three of you and Philippe."

One wrist, moving back and forth, almost free.

"But one of these days Philippe is going figure it out. And if he doesn't, someone else will. Because dumb fucks like you always mess up. And while Delano may have liked you, who says Xerxes will feel the same way? Who says he won't get tired of your bullshit and decide to take you all out instead?"

The zip tie bites into my skin, drawing blood.

I turn to Boris, lean in close.

"What do you think? What do you and your chinny-chin-chins think of that?"

His face scrunches up. He grits his teeth. He grunts as he raises his cane, swings it awkwardly at my head.

But my hands are now free and I grab the cane, twist it out of Boris's grip. I turn the cane around, so the tip's pointed at his face, and I jam it right into his eye.

Boylan is already in motion. He has his seat belt flung off, is reaching into his jacket for the Glock.

I pull the cane back out of Boris's eye, swing it toward Boylan.

That's when the car behind us speeds forward and smacks us in the rear.

FORTY-ONE

Boylan drops the Glock. I drop the cane. Before either of us can try to reach for our respective weapons, the car behind us bumps us again.

Boylan's gun is knocked forward to the footwell. He turns and bends down, scrambles for the gun, but by the time he comes back up with it I have the cane in my hands again, the bloody tip pointed at his face.

Like I did with Boris, I aim for one of Boylan's eyes. But Reed swerves the car, trying to outpace the car behind us, and the tip of the cane grazes Boylan's ear.

He fires wildly, shooting into the roof. Reed swerves the car again. The car behind us comes on faster, tries to bump us a third time. I lean forward and smack the gun out of Boylan's hand, then I elbow Boylan in the face, one two three times right in the nose.

One hand on the wheel, Reed uses his other hand to reach for his gun. He pulls it out, raises it upside down and starts firing over his shoulder.

I duck down as the rear windshield shatters. A hand reaches for me. At first I think it's Boylan, but it's Boris.

The Russian is alive despite losing one eye and he's trying to grab me, strangle me, break my neck, but the car behind us rams us again and our car jerks forward and Reed keeps shooting despite the sudden rocking and his aim gets thrown off, a couple bullets ripping into Boris's chest.

Up ahead is an intersection and a pileup of cars. Reed drops the gun in his lap, grabs at the wheel with both hands. He veers us into the opposite lane where a truck barrels toward us, flashing its high beams and blaring its horn, and then we're up over the curb onto the sidewalk, riding it to the end of the block while the few people out in the rain run or dive out of the way.

Boylan regains his composure, regains the Glock. He turns to shoot at me again, but I grab for the gun, grip onto his wrist, try to push it away while he tries to push it toward my face.

The car bounces again as we make it back onto the main street. Only it's a one-way street and we're headed in the wrong direction.

Reed doesn't seem dissuaded by this, though; he grips the steering wheel tight and takes us forward, playing chicken with the oncoming cars that quickly realize they're dealing with a psychopath and swerve out of the way.

Boylan grits his teeth, says something underneath his breath. He's still trying to fight me with the gun and decides to let off a couple more rounds. They shatter the rear door window—my window—and the shots are deafening and the stench of cordite is bitter and I swear that it felt like one of those bullets took out the tips of my hair, just a couple, and I grit my own teeth and push his arm again, push it hard, and he fires again just as I push it down and a bullet tears into Reed's face.

Despite his seat belt, Reed's body leans forward over the

wheel. His foot hasn't lifted from the gas pedal, has in fact been pushed down harder, and the car begins to accelerate.

The street curves up ahead, cars parked along both sides. I see what's going to happen next and jump back, grab my seat belt, snap it in.

Boylan doesn't have a chance.

Three seconds later we smash into a car parked along the street. Boylan, not wearing his seat belt, flies through the windshield. An explosion of glass. I quickly smell smoke, gasoline.

The seat belt kept me secure, but it hurts like a motherfucker. I move slowly at first, making sure nothing's broken or strained. I unclip the seat belt, glance first at Boris to make sure he's dead, then try to open my door.

But I can't, no matter how hard I try. The edges of the door have been crumbled from the crash and I can't get it open far enough for me to get out.

I decide to escape through the rear windshield. I have to be careful not to cut myself on the shards of glass still sticking up.

The rain feels like it's coming down even harder, trying to wash away the world.

Drivers have stopped their cars, stepped out into the rain. A woman calls out in French, asking me if I'm okay.

I don't answer her. I crawl through the window, over the trunk, and down onto the ground.

Off in the distance I can hear the oncoming rush of sirens.

At first I figure I'll just wait here for them. Philippe is technically still police, so he'll be able to bail me out.

Then I wonder what if Philippe is in this, too.

What if he's just as dirty as these three dead bastards?

The sirens are closer now, maybe two or three blocks away. I start walking in one direction but stop when I remember the car that rammed us and figure yes, that was Philippe, coming to my aid, trying to save the damsel in distress.

Wasn't it?

I start walking.

That same woman calls out again, asking me to stop. Others pick up the chorus.

My walk picks up into a jog.

The sirens are a block away. Their flashing lights reflect off the buildings ahead.

My jog turns into a sprint.

As it's a one-way street, I can't help but pass the first police car coming toward me. Out of the corner of my eye I see the two cops inside turn their heads as they try to track where I'm going.

I reach the end of the block by the time the second car arrives. It screeches to a halt, reverses, darts in my direction.

I sprint down one block, down another. The cruiser stays with me.

I spot an alleyway across the street. I keep sprinting on this side of the sidewalk though, pumping my arms and legs, until I've reached the end of the block and then I stop, pivot, start sprinting back the way I came.

The cruiser streaks past me, its siren still blaring. It screeches to a halt, starts to reverse just as I cross the street and run into the alleyway.

Which happens to be a dead end.

A dumpster is set up at the end of the alleyway. A few trashcans are scattered about, all of them overflowing.

A fire escape hangs off one of the buildings. I jump for it but the ladder is too high for me to reach.

I grab one of the trashcans, dump it out, place it upside down directly underneath the ladder. I climb up onto the trashcan as the cruiser pulls into the alleyway, its high beams splashing me.

I grip the first rung and pull myself up. Reach for the second rung, then the third.

The cruiser below me has screeched to a halt again. Both

doors open. One of the cops shouts in French for me to stop. The other pulls out his gun, aims, and fires at the top of the ladder.

He doesn't hit me. What he hits is the steel, enough to send a massive vibration to pass into my hands, through my arms, and into the rest of my body.

I let go of the ladder.

The fall is maybe ten feet. Not too high, but enough to knock the wind out of me when I hit the ground. My body has already been dealing with enough pain, it doesn't need this, and when I try to sit up, try to move, it's like my body has gone on strike and refuses to do anything before it's been given a raise.

The two cops approach me. Both have their weapons held at their sides.

One of the cops says in French, "I can't believe we found her. Just our luck."

The other says, "What did Xerxes say he wanted done with her?"

"Taken out."

"Shit."

"I know."

There's a silence, and then the second cop asks, "So how do you want to do this?"

The first cop shrugs. "I don't know. Nothing was ever said to me about killing."

"You're being paid, aren't you?"

"Yeah. So are you."

Still lying on the wet ground, showered by rain, trash all around me, I try to move. But my arms, my legs, even my head, don't want to move.

"All right," the second cop says. "If you're too chickenshit to kill her, I'll do it."

He steps forward.

I look up, catch only a glimpse of his face.

He grimaces as he raises his gun, aims it at my head.

I don't close my eyes.

The shots aren't as deafening as they were in the car, though they echo in the narrow alleyway.

The cop standing over me jerks. His mouth falls open. His fingers relax, dropping the pistol. It clatters to the ground just as he falls to his knees.

The first cop spins around, raising his weapon, but he's shot, too—*bang bang*—and then falls to the ground, dead.

The rain keeps falling. It doesn't let up.

My hair is soaked. My clothes are soaked. My entire being is soaked.

Slowly, so very slowly, I push myself up into a sitting position. It isn't easy. The pain is intense. Rain drips into my eyes, forcing me to blink them away.

A figure stands behind the police cruiser. The lights keep flashing, playing red and white patterns off his dark overcoat, off his black mask and black fedora.

I can barely see his eyes.

He raises his gun, aims it right in my direction. Even though there are ten yards between us, I know the barrel is centered at my face.

The moment stretches on. The rain continues to fall.

The man keeps the gun aimed for another couple seconds before he lowers it, turns, and hurries away.

I lie back down on the ground. I close my eyes. Raindrops cover my face. Run into my mouth. They taste like tears.

PART THREE

WHAT GOES AROUND, COMES AROUND

FORTY-TWO

When I make the turn onto Arbor Drive Monday morning, I notice a black sedan parked across the street from the Haddens' house. In the car are two men, both sitting in the front. I get only a glimpse, but it's enough for me to see that one of the men wears a white bandage over his nose.

Inside, Sylvia greets me as she always does, asking if I'd like breakfast. She knows I'll want coffee and already has a cup waiting, handing it to me with a smile. But the smile is short-lived when she gets a good look at my face, at the bruises that I haven't been able to conceal. I know she wants to ask if I'm okay, but I just smile and take the cup of coffee with a quiet thank you.

I continue toward the kitchen table where Marilyn sits with the children. She has today's *Post* open before her and is busy scanning an article. Without glancing up at me, she smiles and says, "Good morning, Holly. How was your trip?"

As usual my absence is explained by some sort of trip—visiting friends, family, whatever. Walter almost never clues me in on specific details and so when asked a general question about a trip I give a general answer.

"It was good, thanks."

She smiles again, turns the page. "Glad to hear it."

Casey and David both wave and say hello. Their smiles fade when they see my face. In all honesty, the bruising isn't terrible. From a distance you can barely tell it's there. But up close, with the kids less than ten feet away, they can see it and at once worry clouds their faces.

I look at both of them, look at them hard, and quickly shake my head. I can deal with the kids later, but right now I don't want to deal with Marilyn. She won't be as discreet as Sylvia. She won't accept a simple answer of it being an accident. She'll worry, ask questions, maybe even call the police on my behalf. She's a good woman who means well, but right now she's the last person I want to deal with.

"Hey, kiddos," I say, taking a sip of my coffee. "You guys ready for a fun day?"

"Yeah," they answer together, though the enthusiasm they usually share at this time in the morning has been diminished by their worry.

I don't bother asking Marilyn if her husband is home. I don't bother making a silly excuse to leave the kitchen. Two years now I've been working for this family, giving me the right to have the run of the house when I want it, and so I continue past them through the house all the way to Walter's office.

I don't bother knocking. I open the door and walk in and then stand there, holding the coffee.

Apparently today is a Pentagon day. Walter sits behind his desk wearing his uniform, his three stars aglow from the artificial light of the computer screen. He looks away from the monitor, stares at me for a moment, and says, "Christ, you look like hell."

"It's good to see you too, Walter."

"Nova told me it was bad, but … Christ."

"You really know how to lift a girl's spirits."

He doesn't say anything, just watches me.

"I see you have the FBI still chaperoning us."

He shrugs. "For the time being it makes sense."

"Which means what exactly—how much longer before you replace me?"

"That's not—"

"I don't want to be replaced."

"Holly—"

I take a step closer, lower my voice. "I don't want to be taken off the team. This is what I do. This is what I'm good at. I can't ... I can't do anything else."

Walter doesn't say anything.

"If the issue is about me being reckless and irresponsible, I can change that. I can be better."

Walter shakes his head. "No, you can't. That gradual decline you're on, it's too steep. You'll never get back to where you were before."

His words, they're like a slap in my face. In a soft, stunted voice, I say, "That's not true."

"Isn't it? I'd assumed after what happened to Scooter you would learn your lesson and not knowingly put your team members in danger. But from what I understand, you walked into Xerxes's club just because you wanted to see the man." He snorts a disgusted laugh. "Just how stupid are you?"

I look away from him. "What happened to Philippe?"

"What do you think happened? He just found out his entire team has been working as double agents. He's under investigation, and will probably never return to that detail again."

"That's not fair. He's a good man."

"His superiors feel otherwise. And quite frankly, I can't say I blame them. After all, Philippe has been making this thing against Xerxes personal. His feelings got in the way of rational thought."

I didn't get a chance to talk with Philippe about what happened. Nova was the one who had found me. He was the one who drove me to the airstrip and got me on the cargo jet out of the country. He even rode with me, holding me most of the flight. And when we had landed he took me home, fed me and put me to bed where I slept almost the whole day.

"Something's troubling you," Walter says. "What is it?"

"That man in the alleyway. The one who saved my life."

"What about him?"

I fix my gaze on Walter's. "He held his gun right at my face, like he was going to shoot me. But he didn't."

"Yes, I'm aware. We still don't know who he is."

"It's not just that. It's ... I had the sense he didn't even intend on killing me. But he wanted me to see that he had the opportunity. He wanted me to understand in that instant he had the power of deciding whether or not I lived."

"And that scares you?"

I nod.

"Why?"

"That's exactly it. Why? *Why* did he save me from those cops? *Why* did he decide to let me live?"

I glance down at the carpet, glance back up. Shake my head.

"Just what am I to him, anyway?"

FORTY-THREE

The agents' names are Colin and Mitchell. Mitchell's nose is the one I broke. It's clear they don't like me much—I have to admit, after what I put them through, I wouldn't like me much either—but their assignment is to keep an eye on us and so that's what they do.

I have to let the kids know about them. There's no getting around it. Their combined ages might equal ten, but they're not stupid. They remember what happened last Wednesday. They remember the faces of those two men. And now those two men will be following us everywhere, and so I explain to them that they're FBI agents and that they'll be following us today and maybe tomorrow and maybe for the rest of the week.

David says yeah, they already know about the FBI guys. He says Daddy told him and Casey. He says Daddy asked them to keep it a secret from Mommy and Miss Sylvia, and if they keep that promise, they'll both get a present.

"A really *big* present," Casey says, a huge smile on her face.

We make our usual trip to the community pool. Brunette and Redhead are lounging in the shade of their favorite tree. Blondie is nowhere in sight.

I don't want to bother with the girls—not with my face the way it is today—but Redhead spots me and points me out to Brunette, who stands up and waves me over with both hands flapping wildly.

The kids are already suited up. They race into the kiddie pool. David makes his way over to his friends. Casey, who has trouble making friends, stands off to the side. She watches everyone, bending slightly so she can graze the tips of her fingers in the cool water.

Colin and Mitchell station themselves by the entrance. They wear jeans and polo shirts. They wear sunglasses that scream they're police.

When I reach the girls, Brunette says frantically, "Holly, you won't believe—oh my God, what *happened*?"

She reaches out, touches my tender face. It takes everything I have not to flinch.

"I'm fine," I say.

Redhead approaches, her mouth open and her eyes wide. "Holy crap, are you okay?"

"Really, I'm fine."

"Was it him?" Brunette says, meaning I guess my fictional boyfriend. "Did that bastard do this to you?"

I hesitate, trying to think up all the different ways this could go. Finally I lower my head and nod and murmur, "Yes."

"Oh, poor dear," Redhead says. She steps forward, gives me a hug.

"I'm through with him," I say, thanking God I'm wearing sunglasses and don't have to fake tears. "I told him if he ever comes around me again, I'll call the police."

"Good for you," Brunette says, like I'm a two-year-old who just used the potty by myself for the first time.

"But really, don't worry about it," I tell them. "It's all over with. What were you going to tell me? What won't I believe?"

And suddenly it's like my own horror story isn't news

anymore and they start telling me about what happened to Blondie, both of them talking over one another in their excited, breathless voices.

"She found out he's cheating—"

"—has been cheating—"

"—and that one of the girls he's been cheating with—"

"—like, one of her best friends—"

"—and she's not the only one either—"

"—yeah, there's been like three or four other girls—"

"—and when she called me she could barely talk she was crying so hard—"

"—she told me she threw her ring at him, hit him right in the eye—"

"—she should have kept the thing, tried to pawn it or something—"

"—so terrible—"

"—yes, so terrible."

They fall silent at the same time, staring at me, probably waiting for me to start up the chorus where they left off. I even open my mouth but then close it. I don't want to tell them what I'm thinking. How I'm happy this happened. How I've listened to Blondie talk about her boyfriend all this time and how they gushed over the ring and the wedding details and how they left me out and how if anybody in the world should be happy it's me.

It's a terrible, selfish thing for me to think, but I can't help it.

I shake my head and echo their chorus: "Terrible."

Before the girls can start up again, I hear Casey's voice rising among the rest of the voices shouting out around the pool.

I turn and see that she's being splashed again. They might be the same kids as before but they might not. Regardless, two of them are splashing her while the lifeguard once again has his attention focused on something else. David is off on the other side of the pool, playing with his friends. He doesn't hear his sister, or if he does, he's ignoring her.

I tell the girls I'll be right back, and start toward the kiddie pool.

David reaches the two brats before I do. I'm forty feet away when his sister's cries finally burrow into his brain. I'm thirty feet away when he turns and breaks away from his friends. I'm twenty feet away when he starts hurrying through the water, then ten feet away when he reaches the two brats.

I slip off my sandals and step into the water when David grabs the closest brat on the shoulder, turns him around, and punches him in the gut.

I reach them a second later. The brat that's just gotten punched cries out, and of course his shout catches the attention of the waste-of-space lifeguard. The lifeguard jumps to his feet, blows his whistle, hurries into the water. A woman's voice rises up among the rest. It's the voice of the brat's mother, and she's screaming as she runs to the kiddie pool.

I grab David and pull him back. He tries fighting me, looks up at me like I'm crazy, like I should let him punch the kid again.

Casey is crying. The brat is crying. The lifeguard reaches us, asking what the matter is. And the mother is now standing on the edge of the pool, her hands to her mouth. She screams like a banshee, drawing everyone's attention, screaming like her boy is being murdered in front of her eyes.

FORTY-FOUR

"What the hell were you thinking?"

"He was picking on Casey."

"That doesn't give you the right to punch the kid."

"But he was *hurting* her."

We're out in the parking lot, grouped around my car. Casey is standing with the agents while I crouch down to look David in the eye.

"Again, that doesn't give you the right to punch him."

"Why not? You punched him," David says and points at Mitchell.

I glance back at Mitchell and see the agent shaking his head, looking off toward the fence and the pool beyond. I turn my attention back to David.

"That was different."

"How?" he asks. "How was that different?"

"The point is what you did was wrong. You should never hit anyone."

"But you hit *him*," David says, pointing again.

"That's right, I did, and do you know what? I was wrong. If I could go back, I wouldn't have done it."

David looks down at his feet. He smiles when he says, "You really kicked his butt."

"David."

"Do you know kung fu and ninja stuff?" He looks up, his eyes hopeful. "Can you teach me?"

I glance over at the agents and catch them grinning. Casey stands between them, holding tightly onto her towel, looking down at the ground. I want to go to her, hug her, tell her that everything is all right. I want to give her a reason why people are mean and how she can avoid those people for the rest of her life.

I say to David, "What I know how to do is protect myself. That's the purpose of karate: self-defense. You should never use it to attack another person."

"Can you show me?" His eyes and smile growing even larger. "Huh? Can you? Can you please?"

I stand up straight, reach into my purse for the keys. "Not today."

"Oh, come on—*please?*" Now holding his hands flat together. "Pretty please?"

One of the agents chuckles.

"You're being a real brat, David," I say.

He keeps his hands flat together, pouting his lips, looking so very un-David-like that I can't help but smile.

I open the car, throw in my bag, then glance back at the agents. I decide Mitchell has had it a little too rough lately so I motion Colin to come forward. He glances at his counterpart, glances at me, shrugs and walks over to us.

I gesture for Colin to stand behind David and take him from behind. Colin does just this, quickly grabbing David's right arm and pulling it back as the agent wraps his other arm around David's neck.

"Now this, David," I say as the boy starts to struggle, "is

called a sleeper hold. Do you know why it's called a sleeper hold?"

David keeps fighting, trying to squirm and wiggle his way out of Colin's grasp. Colin grins at me, the sun reflecting off his shades, and behind me Mitchell doesn't stifle his chuckle this time. He lets out a full-fledged laugh. Even Casey giggles.

I lean down close to David. "Stop struggling. That's your first lesson. The more you struggle, the more you'll wear yourself out."

David is reluctant at first, but he stops struggling. His chest heaves.

"Okay, good. Now what you want to do next is—"

"I know what to do next," David says, and with his free arm he lifts his elbow and brings it right back down on Colin's crotch.

Mitchell lets out a great roar of laughter as Colin groans and releases David and turns away. Even Casey giggles again.

David smiles at me triumphantly. "Like that, right?"

"No, you dummy, not like that."

I start toward him, meaning to grab him by the ear and lead him to the car, when my cell phone rings. Thinking it might be Walter, I reach into the car and grab the phone from my bag. I don't recognize the number but answer anyway.

"Hello, is this Holly?" a female voice asks.

"Yes."

"Holly, this is Gloria Stevens from Markham & Davis. How are you today?"

I frown. Markham & Davis is Ryan's firm. I interviewed there last week.

"I'm fine, thanks. How are you?"

As the woman tells me she's doing fabulous, thank you, I motion to Mitchell and Colin that we're leaving.

Colin has righted himself again but he's wincing, breathing

through his teeth. Mitchell walks up behind him, claps him once on the back.

"The reason I'm calling, Holly, is that I'd like to schedule you to come back for a second interview."

With the phone to my ear, I manage to get Casey into her child's seat. She watches me click in the harness when I say, "Really?"

"Yes. I'm sorry we rushed your interview last week, but there was a funeral I had to attend, and ... well, regardless, I would like you to come back in so you can take a typing test and so we can discuss the job in more detail."

I stand up and glance over the roof, watch Colin and Mitchell heading to their car. Mitchell is still laughing; Colin shakes his head and gives him the finger.

"Holly? Are you there?"

"Yes, I'm here."

"So can I schedule you to come in sometime this week?"

I glance down at Casey in the child's seat, at David who has opened the opposite rear door and climbed in and slammed it shut.

"I ... um ... I'm not actually interested anymore."

"Excuse me?"

"In the job. I gave it a lot of thought, and I don't think it's a good match for me."

"Oh," the woman says. "Okay. Well, that's no problem at all. I, um, wish you luck with your other endeavors."

Endeavors. The word makes me want to roll my eyes. "Thank you. And thank you for calling."

"My pleasure. Have a good day."

"You too," I say and immediately hit the button to disconnect.

"Who was that?" Casey asks. She kicks her legs hanging over the child's seat back and forth.

"Wrong number," I say, smiling at her, and shut the door.

I start around the car to the driver's side when the phone rings again. I don't recognize this number either, and after dealing with Miss Endeavor I don't feel like dealing with anymore asinine bullshit, so I answer with a tired and irritated hello.

"Hello, Miss Lin," a man says. He has a Spanish accent. "How are you today?"

I open my door but don't get in just yet. "I'm sorry, who's this?"

"How much do you care for the welfare of those two precious children?"

A red light starts flashing in my head. My body tenses. I don't move, though, don't give the caller the satisfaction of knowing his words have had the desired effect. After all, judging by the way he posed the question, how he called right after I was done with my previous call, he's no doubt watching me.

"Miss Lin."

"Who is this?"

"Would you die to keep the boy and the girl safe?"

I close the door. Turn away from the car. Breathe into the phone, "Who the fuck is this?"

"I don't much care for your tone, Miss Lin."

"Yeah, well, fuck you."

The man sighs. "Very well. If you do not wish to take this situation seriously, then that is up to you."

"And what situation is that?"

Colin and Mitchell pull up in the sedan.

"If you want the children to stay alive, do not end this call for any reason. Do you understand me? As long as you stay on the line, the better chance they have of survival."

I start to take a step toward the sedan, but stop. I think about this caller and how he's watching me right now and what might happen if I approach the agents.

"What do you want?"

"First, I would like you to wave to the two FBI agents."

"Why?"

"Do as I say."

I raise my free hand, slowly, and wave it back and forth at Mitchell and Colin. They frown, glance at each other.

"There, I waved to them. Now what?"

"Now say goodbye."

The shots are instantaneous. One shot at Colin, one shot at Mitchell. The windshield spiderwebs, blood spraying the inside of the car.

"And now for the second part," the man says. "Drive."

FORTY-FIVE

I'm in the car and have the engine started before I even realize it. The phone to my ear, I throw the car in reverse and glance over my shoulder as I screech out of the parking space.

Behind me, David says, "What's happening? What's going on? Did those guys ... are they ..." while Casey starts crying in her seat.

"Where?" I say into the phone, and the man on the other end simply says, "To the exit."

Five seconds have passed since Colin and Mitchell were killed. The shots came from the direction of the pool entrance. It had to have been done with a sniper rifle, some kind of silencer attached. I hadn't heard a thing except for the popping of the windshield as it broke.

I speed through the parking lot, up one lane and down the next. I try not to hit the few parents and children leaving or entering the pool. Already people have seen the black sedan, the dead bodies. They're either on their phones, calling 911, or they're trying to track where I'm going. After all, only a guilty person flees from the scene of a crime.

At the exit, I say, "Now where?"

"Take a left and keep driving straight until I tell you otherwise."

I wait for a break in traffic and then pull out onto the road. Even though I don't want to, I ignore Casey behind me, still crying, just as I ignore David who has started to mumble his questions of what's going on and what's happening.

I keep glancing at the rearview mirror, not sure what I expect to see. The voice on the other end doesn't say anything. I have to pull the phone away, check the screen, to make sure we haven't been disconnected.

After a mile, the voice says, "At the upcoming intersection, make a right."

The intersection in question is less than three hundred yards away. I flick on my turn signal. I don't know how this man sees me—as far as I can tell I'm not being followed—but right now I don't question it.

The traffic light is red. We stop behind a minivan with a bumper sticker that says WHAT'S YOUR BEEPING HURRY?

Casey is still crying. David has started crying too. I glance at the phone again, hit the mute button, place the phone back against my ear and quickly look back over my shoulder.

"Everything's okay."

David wipes at his face. "What—what—what's happening?"

"Just don't think about it, okay?"

It's a stupid thing to say but I don't know what else to tell them.

The light turns green and traffic starts moving and once I make the turn the voice says, "Now, Miss Lin, tell me again— would you die to keep the boy and girl safe?"

"Yes."

A pause.

"Miss Lin?"

"I said yes, goddamn it!"

Another pause.

"Very well, Miss Lin. If you do not wish to answer me, then—"

I remember the mute button is engaged and quickly click it off. "Yes!" I shout. "Yes, I would die for them!"

The pause this time lasts almost five seconds. It feels like five minutes. The traffic is going at a fairly reasonable speed, yet it seems like we're barely moving five miles per hour.

The man says, "That is very good to hear, Miss Lin."

"What do you want?"

"We will be discussing that matter soon. Now at the upcoming intersection, make a left."

I glance behind me at the kids, then back at the road. At the intersection I turn left and drive for another half mile until the voice speaks again.

"At the next intersection, turn right."

I make the turn. I drive for another half mile. We've left the main strip with all the restaurants and businesses and car dealerships and are now in a residential area.

My hands are sweaty against the wheel. Blood beats heavy in my ears. Not even five minutes have passed since we left the pool, and all I can think about is the safety of the two children in the backseat.

A stop sign looms ahead.

The man says, "At the upcoming intersection, stop the car and turn off the engine."

I glance again at the rearview mirror. Both Casey and David have managed to cry themselves out. Now they're sniffling, wiping away their tears.

At the intersection I stop the car and turn off the engine.

"Now step out of the car."

"What?"

"Step out of the car."

I want to say something to the kids. Tell them I'll be right back. Tell them I love them. But I don't want to waste any time either, so I open the door and step out.

"Close the door."

I close the door.

"Place the keys on the roof."

I place the keys on the roof.

"Now walk across the intersection to the other side."

I hesitate. I don't want to leave the kids. But I can't stop thinking about how Colin and Mitchell were taken out so quickly, so efficiently.

"What about the children?"

"The children will be safe as long as you follow directions."

I walk across the intersection. It's deserted. The entire neighborhood is deserted.

At the other end of the intersection, I stop and turn around. The car is less than fifty feet away. It seems like a mile.

I can see the children in the back, crying again. David starts to undo his seat belt, starts to reach for the door.

I shake my head, wanting to yell at him to stop it, to stay put. But right then comes the screeching of tires and the angry roar of an engine.

A red Porsche pulls up next to the car. Its windows are tinted. The passenger-side door opens and a Hispanic man steps out. He wears a black suit and sunglasses. He opens David's door, bends down and says something, then leans back and slams the door shut. He glances at me for only an instant before he takes the keys off the roof, gets in, starts the engine, and pulls out into the intersection.

He drives right at me.

I step aside. I watch helpless as he passes me in my own car, the Porsche following. David is the closest to me, and as they pass, he places his hand flat against the window, holds it there, tears all over his face.

I want to do something but can't think of anything to do. I refuse to wave goodbye because it's too final, too concrete, and I plan on seeing them again. When and how, I'm not sure, but I plan on seeing them again.

In my ear, the man says, "Now that the children are gone, are you ready to get them back?"

"Yes."

"Good. I believe it is now time for us to meet."

He disconnects the call.

I look at the phone, start to redial the number, when a black Lincoln Town Car appears down the street. It too has tinted windows. It stops right beside me.

The back door opens.

I step inside.

FORTY-SIX

There are three men in the Town Car. The driver, of course, and a man in the passenger seat who once I slip into the car turns around and aims a gun at me. The third man sits in the back. He looks to be in his late-forties. He has jet-black hair and dark skin and has an odd attractiveness like Marc Antony. He smiles at me and says, "Good afternoon."

I don't say anything.

My door closed, the Town Car starts in motion again.

For a long time there is silence. The man beside me stares out his window. The man in the passenger seat stays turned in his seat, the gun aimed. His eyes are deep and brown and don't leave me for a second.

For an instant I have that sense of déjà vu, being back in Paris, riding in the car with Reed and Boylan and Boris. At that time I hadn't really cared what happened to me. I didn't mind talking bullshit. I didn't have anybody to worry about but myself.

Finally the man says, "Do you know who I am, Miss Lin?" He continues staring out his window. "My name is Javier Diaz.

My father is Ernesto Diaz. You caused us some very serious trouble recently."

"I apologize."

The man looks away from the window, smiles at me. "Is that so?"

"Whatever trouble I've caused you and your father, I'm sorry. You can do whatever you want to me, but please, don't involve those two kids."

"It's more complicated than that, Miss Lin. If it were up to me and my father, you would already be dead. But there are other parties involved. Parties that have requested we spare your life for the time being."

"What are you talking about?"

"Though this is odd to say, my father and I are grateful for what you did. Not that it lessens our anger in any way, but your ... attack helped give us new perspective in certain areas of our business."

"What business?"

"Are you really that stupid, Miss Lin?" The man pauses, shakes his head. "No, I suppose you are not. I suppose you cause so much trouble you cannot keep all the events separate."

We're out of the residential area now, driving back along the main strip.

"As you seem to be lost right now," Javier Diaz says, "the trouble to which I am referring happened in Las Vegas."

"The ranch."

"Yes, the ranch."

"You're in charge of it."

"Technically, no. My father and I have no *legal* ties to the place at all."

"Of course not."

Javier Diaz keeps staring out his window. "The man who was in charge of our Las Vegas operation, what you could call a manager, was becoming much too lax. He was skimming the money for security into his own pocket. And the men he had looking after the girls … well, if they were able to be taken out by you and you alone, what does it say about them?"

"They were under-trained."

Javier smiles at his window. "Perhaps, yes. Regardless, the man in question has been dealt with. So have the rest of the men in that operation. We have been forced to relocate, find new girls, start from scratch. But, as I said, you have helped give us new perspective. And not just in Las Vegas, but in all our operations."

"I'm glad I could be of some service."

We are now on the expressway. The man in the passenger seat hasn't moved an inch. The gun hasn't either.

"Just so you know," Javier says, "she did not die quickly."

"Who?"

"Rosalina." Shaking his head. "A pretty name for such an ugly whore."

I close my eyes. Picture her striking Jerold over the head with the phone. Picture her cowering in the bathtub. Picture her standing beside the car while I loaded my weapons.

"You found her?"

"It wasn't difficult. She barely got twenty miles before one of my men tracked her down. From what I understand, she wouldn't talk, not at first. She needed … convincing."

Javier shifts in his seat to look at me.

"They sent me several photographs. Parts of her body that they cut off. Even some areas where they sliced off her skin. Would you like to see them?"

I don't answer.

"No, I suppose that might be too gruesome, even for you. Regardless, she did eventually break. She told my men all about you and the two men you were with. The information didn't help us, not right then, but shortly afterward we were contacted by an outside party."

The driver veers off to the next exit. We take it to the top of the ramp, stop for the traffic light.

"This party apparently lost something of theirs, something they believed you were also responsible for. This party somehow knew you had been responsible for both incidents. And this party promised to reimburse us for everything we lost and even more if we were to bring you in."

We turn right at the light and start down the road and immediately I know where we're going. I've had an idea since we started driving, but now I'm certain.

"This party," Javier says, "expects something out of you. To be honest, I don't know what it is, nor do I care to know. I only care that my father and I have been wronged, and that worst of all we were wronged by a fucking *puta*."

Down one street, down another. Into another residential area. The houses growing larger. The cars in the driveways becoming more expensive.

"Just so we're clear, Miss Lin, despite what may happen between you and this other party, things are not done between us."

The driver turns down a familiar street, past familiar houses and trees and mailboxes.

"Do you understand me, Miss Lin? Do you understand how you have shamed me and my family?"

Swallowing, my throat suddenly dry, I say, "Yes, I do."

"Are you sorry?"

"Yes, I am."

"Why do I not believe you?"

I don't answer him. I don't answer him because we've arrived.

The driver slows. He makes the turn into the driveway. He pulls to a stop in front of the garage. He places the Town Car in park, gets out.

"Now it is time for us to part ways, Miss Lin. Just

remember what I told you. Remember what we did to Rosalina."

The driver opens my door. I get out. The man in the passenger seat, the man with the deep brown eyes and the gun, gets out too. He has the weapon concealed but it's clear he no longer needs it. I know it just as well as he does. I'm not going to fight them.

They take me to the back porch. They take me inside.

The kitchen is a mess. It's clear a struggle took place. Some pots and pans are strewn across the floor. A chair is tipped over.

We walk out of the kitchen and into the living room.

Here Sylvia lies on the couch. Her wrists and ankles have been tied. Duct tape covers her mouth. There's some dried blood on her forehead. She hears us enter the living room and opens her eyes and watches us as we pass through the living room and into the hallway.

Blood soaks the carpet outside of Walter's office. What's left of Baron lies beside it.

I close my eyes, take a deep breath, and step inside.

Someone is sitting at Walter's desk. They're in the chair, turned away from me so they can stare out into the backyard.

One of the wooden kitchen chairs has been brought into the room. It's placed in front of the desk.

The men force me to sit down on it. With plastic ties they strap my ankles and wrists to the chair. The driver slaps duct tape over my mouth.

The entire thing takes less than ten seconds, and then they're gone and it's just me and the person in the chair.

After a moment, the chair swivels around and I find myself staring at a ghost.

"Hey, Holly," Zane says. "Been a while, hasn't it?"

FORTY-SEVEN

"I guess you're surprised to see me, which is understandable. After all, it's been two years and … well, it's complicated."

Zane leans back in Walter's chair, raises his arms and puts his hands behind his head.

"I wish this didn't have to happen. I really do. But it was unavoidable."

The last time I saw Zane he was on a yacht and had just been shot by my father. He had brown curly hair then. He had a silver ring hanging from his left ear.

"I'm sure you're asking yourself a lot of questions right now. I wish I could answer those questions. I wish I could tell you this is all a dream. But it's not. I'm just as real as you are. As real as"—he leans forward, raps his knuckles on the desktop—"this desk."

Now his head is shaved to a crew cut. His face wears a couple days of growth. The silver earring is gone.

"Let me cut to the chase. The job you guys pulled in Las Vegas—that really fucked us over. That meeting Delano had scheduled for the next day, that was with my employer. He was going to purchase the flash drive."

He pushes away from the desk, stands up. He appears taller than I remember, but I know that's ridiculous. He's the same size he's always been; in my mind's eye he's just grown smaller.

"We need that flash drive, Holly."

I sit there, staring back at him. I don't move. I don't make a sound.

Zane walks around the desk, taking his time, letting his finger graze along the side of the oak finishing. He comes to stand in front of me, leans back on the desk, crosses his arms.

"Now we know you have nothing to do with the flash drive. For you it was just a mission. You made your hit, grabbed your prize, and then you left. Only you didn't leave, did you? You did an attack on that place out in the desert."

He's wearing baggy jeans and a gray shirt. He has a nice, healthy tan.

"The Diaz Family wants you dead. I can't say I blame them. You made them all look like fucking idiots. Trust me, word has gotten around. Everyone knows one of the Diaz places was taken down by one person. Worse, that one person was a woman. It just doesn't look good."

His eyes are robin-egg blue.

"But I'm sure Javier explained that to you. He may even have explained how we contacted him. Like I said, Holly, the family wants you dead. Actually, they want you tortured and then dead. But we managed to persuade them otherwise. We managed to extend your life."

He has a small cleft in his chin; jokingly I always referred to it has his little baby's butt.

"Trust me when I say we wouldn't do this for just anybody. But you … well, believe it or not, I do still love and care for you."

I'd seen him shot in the chest by my father. I'd seen the blood.

"You're going to be my messenger, Holly. You're going to tell Walter what we want in return for his children."

I'd seen him fall over the side. I'd heard the splash his body made when it struck the water.

"It's not going to be easy for Walter. We're aware of this. It's not like the United States government will simply hand over the flash drive to him so he can hand it over to us. But I'm sure he'll do his best to get it back. Don't you agree?"

He turns away from me, turns back around with a syringe in his hands. He inspects it closely, tapping the sides to release the air bubbles as he pushes the plunger.

"I'm not going to be melodramatic about this. I'm not going to set a deadline. If he wants his children back, he'll get us the flash drive as soon as possible. It's that simple."

He moves to the side, to my right, and stands beside me.

"We'll be watching everything. We'll know what he's thinking. We're more powerful than he cares to admit. Just remind him of that, okay?"

The aftershave he wears is the same he wore two years ago. I can close my eyes and picture the two of us naked in bed. I can close my eyes and almost taste his sweat.

"This right here, Holly, this is only a sedative. It'll knock you out for a couple hours. By that time Walter should be here."

With his free hand he twists my arm, looking for a vein.

"He'll want to know what happened. And you'll tell him. You'll tell him everything."

He finds a vein and keeps it in place with his thumb, then places the needle on the vein.

"You're the only one we can trust now, Holly. We know how you feel about those kids. We know you'll do your best to get them back safely. Won't you?"

He pushes the plunger down with his thumb.

"By the way, I heard about what happened to Stuttering

Scooter. Can't say I'm surprised. The guy was always out of his element."

The syringe empty, he pulls out the needle and stands back.

"It should only take about a minute or two. Are you feeling anything yet?"

I glare at him.

"Don't judge me, Holly. I'm not going to give you some bullshit excuse for standing here right now. I picked this path and I'm happy with the decision."

His face starts to blurs. The room starts to go in and out of focus.

"It's starting to take effect, isn't it?"

My eyelids grow heavy. My head grows heavy too, so heavy that I drop it and then quickly try to bring it back up.

"Remember, Holly—if Walter wants his children back, he'll get that flash drive."

Zane leans forward, and as I look up at him, his face begins swirling toward the vortex of his nose.

"Also tell him no bullshit. We'll be watching. We'll know everything."

The world tilts, starts to go gray.

"For the children's sake, Holly," Zane says, "don't fuck this up."

The last thing I know before the gray turns to black is Zane kissing me on the forehead.

FORTY-EIGHT

At some point I open my eyes. A whiteness stares back at me. I think that this is it—this is death. There is no heaven. There is no hell. All that waits for us at the end is nothing. We're taken back to the place we began, to a womb of whiteness, and here we stay for eternity, staring at that numbing white and thinking about everything we could have done better in our lives, every misstep and every mistake, and never any of the good stuff, no matter how much there was.

Someone clears his throat.

When I look away from the whiteness—what I quickly realize is a ceiling, the ceiling of the Haddens' guest bedroom— I have to do it slowly because the world's largest department store has set up shop in my head, a hundred thousand cash registers going *ka-ching, ka-ching, ka-ching* all at once.

A man in an Army uniform stands in the doorway.

"How are you feeling?"

I open my mouth but close it. My throat is dry.

"Do you need something to drink?"

I nod.

He walks out of the room, leaving the door open. I take a

moment to look around the guest bedroom. I've stayed here
before, the few times I needed to spend the night. It's one of
Marilyn's pet projects. An actual spinning wheel sits in the
corner. A handcrafted quilt hangs from the wall. This room is
meant to give the impression of a simpler time. A time where
evil was mostly superstition.

When the soldier returns with a glass of water he isn't
alone. Walter is with him, still wearing his uniform, only the
top couple buttons have been undone. His face is strained,
making him look ten years older.

The soldier sets the glass of water on the bedside table. He
helps me sit up. It takes a while because my head is still
pounding and because my body is still sore. When I'm at the
right position, the soldier hands me the glass. He doesn't let go,
though, and helps guide the glass to my lips, keeps his hands
there as I take a sip, then another.

Walter thanks him, tells him he can leave. Then he pulls up
an antique rocking chair beside the bed and sits down.

"Are you okay?"

I nod.

"Can you talk?"

I swallow, clear my throat. In a weak voice, I say, "Yes."

"Good. Now tell me who did this."

"It was"—I have to clear my throat again—"Zane."

Nothing changes in Walter's face. No surprise. No
confusion.

"Walter, did you hear me? I said it was Zane."

"What does he want?"

"Walter"—I sit up even straighter—"how can that be possible? Zane … is dead."

He leans forward. "What does he want?"

"The flash drive."

Walter closes his eyes. He places his fingers to the bridge of
his nose.

"They have Casey and David. They're going to kill them if you don't give them the flash drive."

Again he doesn't react when I use the plural form. Nothing surprises this man. He no doubt heard Sylvia's story already, about the men in suits … that is, if Sylvia is still alive.

"How's Sylvia?"

"What?" Walter looks up, blinks at me. "She's fine. Shook up, but she's fine."

I think briefly of the bloody carpet, the lump of fur. "And Baron?"

Staring at me, Walter shakes his head.

"How is this possible, Walter? Zane … he's supposed to be dead."

"Take me through everything that happened this morning. Every single detail."

"Walter—"

"Goddamn it, Holly, tell me what happened."

I tell him what happened. From the moment we left the house today, to the pool, to the kids picking on Casey, to David coming to her rescue. To my lesson to David in the parking lot, to my first call, to my second call, to watching Colin and Mitchell die, then to getting in the car and taking off and meeting up with Javier Diaz and then to where they tied me up in Walter's study.

"How many would you say there are, in total?" Walter asks.

"At least six. Zane, Javier and the two in the car, the guy who took the kids, the Porsche's driver, and the shooter back at the pool."

Walter nods, as if this is what he's thinking too.

"There's probably more, though," I say.

"Probably."

"How is Marilyn taking it?"

His eyes stare at me for an instant, quickly shift away.

"Jesus Christ, Walter. You haven't told her yet?"

"She's had meetings all day."

"Then call her."

"Not yet. Not until I decide what needs done."

The hundred thousand cash registers have gone silent. The only sound now is the blood beating away in my ears.

"What needs done," I say, swinging my feet off the bed and onto the floor, "is getting your kids back."

"You don't think I know that?"

"You don't seem to care."

"You have no idea how I'm feeling right now."

"They're your kids, Walter."

"I understand that. I fucking understand that. But what they're asking for in return is something … *fuck*."

He throws his arm aside, knocking the glass against the wall. The shattered pieces scatter on the carpet.

For a moment there's silence. Walter glares at me, his jaw set, his face red. There are no tears in his eyes. I can't say I'm not surprised. After all, the man has been trained to be like steel. Even when his children's lives are on the line, he shows no emotion.

For the very first time I pity him.

"You need to tell her, Walter."

"My wife is a great woman." Even though he's looking at me, I can tell he's speaking to himself. "She has sacrificed so much for our family. Now … now this."

"You knew this was going to happen, didn't you? That's why you assigned the agents to watch us."

"I'd had an idea they would retaliate. Especially when I found out your father was involved."

A trapdoor opens up beneath my feet. For an instant I'm weightless, falling, falling, falling. Then I steady myself. I close my eyes. Take a breath. Open my eyes again.

"What did you say?"

Walter blinks. "You mean Zane didn't mention him?"

"My father"—I shake my head slowly—"is alive?"

"Don't be naïve, Holly. You saw Zane with your own eyes. If he's alive, your father's alive too."

"But I ... I shot him."

"That's what they wanted you to think."

"There was ... blood ... blood all over him." I pause, glance back up at Walter. "You knew?"

He doesn't respond.

"You fucking bastard. You knew this entire time. Why didn't you ... why didn't you ever tell me?"

"You should go home, Holly. Get some rest. I'll have someone drive you."

"How long have you known?"

Walter shouts out a name, and a moment later the same soldier from before enters the room.

"Rick, please drive Miss Lin home, would you?"

Rick nods and steps forward.

I ignore him. I keep glaring at Walter.

"How long have you known?"

"Go home, Holly. There's nothing else for you to do here."

I close my eyes. Shake my head. Try to hold back the tears. I want to beat this man sitting in front of me right now. I want to kill him. But instead I take a deep breath and open my eyes and turn and walk past Soldier Rick out of the room.

Down the hallway to the stairs, down the stairs to the landing, from the landing through the hallway to the living room, then the kitchen, I pass at least a dozen soldiers, many MPs, looking for evidence, whispering to each other, trying to do everything they can so they don't have to bring the actual police into the situation. After all, this isn't a civilian issue. This is an Army issue, a United States government issue, and they will try to keep it as hush-hush as possible.

Outside there are a half-dozen cars and SUVs parked in the driveway and along the street. I don't know which one to go to.

I wait until Soldier Rick comes out and then I follow him to one of the cars and get in and then just sit there, my arms crossed, staring out the window.

"Where to?" he asks, starting the engine.

I don't answer.

He puts the car in reverse, backs us out of the driveway. We start down the street, the sun shining through the trees that reach up and cover us, casting shadows everywhere. At the end of the block we reach the stop sign. A car coming up Vine Street stops at the same time, its turn signal flashing.

Marilyn. It's five thirty—I now see the time on the dashboard—and she's coming home from her meetings. Soon she'll arrive home and see all the cars and SUVs. She'll enter her house to find that it's become a stranger's. Then Walter will approach her and she'll see it on his face, in his eyes, and she will begin to cry, begin to wail, falling to her knees, pounding Walter with her fists.

I don't know for certain this will happen, but as we pull through the intersection, as we leave Marilyn behind, I hope it's close enough to the truth.

I hope she punches him as many times as she can.

I hope she makes him pay.

FORTY-NINE

It's one of those silly ironies that on the worst day of my life the elevator in my apartment building is working.

I take the stairs anyway. I let myself into my apartment and shut the door. I think about eating something—my stomach is growling—but I don't have an appetite. I take off my sandals, drop them to the floor, and enter the living room to find Nova sitting on the couch.

He doesn't say anything. He just watches me. In his hand, resting in his lap, is a black Beretta pistol.

I sit down in the recliner facing him.

"Were you followed?" he asks.

"No, but it doesn't matter anyway. They know where I live and if they wanted to take me out by now they would have."

Nova doesn't respond.

"How long have you known?"

He keeps watching me.

"Why the fuck did nobody ever tell me?" I shake my head, lean forward in my seat. "I watched them die."

"No"—Nova shakes his head almost imperceptibly—"you watched what they wanted you to watch."

"So you knew?"

"I had my suspicions."

"But why … why didn't you ever tell me?"

"I figured it wasn't my place. Besides, I never knew for certain."

I lean back in the recliner, run my fingers through my hair. "So everybody figured it out except me."

"John was your father. Zane was your lover. After seeing what you did, there was no way you could ever step back and look at it rationally."

"And if I could have stepped back and looked at it rationally, what would I have seen?"

"For starters, I was supposed to be the one who went on that yacht, not you. But John changed the plan before we left. He said he wanted you there instead."

"That doesn't mean anything."

"No, but remember who gave you your guns."

"Zane did."

"That's right."

"That still"—I shake my head again—"that still doesn't mean anything."

"I know you, Holly. I know how particular you are about your weapons. Especially your ammunition. When you can, you like to load your own rounds. You like to make sure you touch each one before you put them in the magazine. But sometimes you'd allow Zane to load your magazines for you. Why? Because out of all of us, he was the one you trusted most."

I think about Zane again, turning around in Walter's chair, Zane who I watched die two years ago.

"Impossible," I whisper.

"They'd loaded blanks in the magazine."

"No, they didn't. I'd used the gun. I'd fired it."

"But had you hit anything?"

I pause a moment, trying to remember. Everything had been happening so quickly.

"Zane and my dad were doing most of the shooting. They went on the yacht first."

Nova nods, watching me closely. He doesn't say anything.

"But I …"

I don't know why I'm doing this to myself. Trying to work it out in my head, how it could possibly have happened that the two men I trusted most in the world played me for a fool.

But I saw Zane with my own eyes today. I heard his voice. I felt his hands on my arm. I felt his lips on my forehead.

"Why?" I ask finally.

"Who knows. There may not even be a reason."

"There has to be a reason. Zane, my father … they were good men."

"Were they?"

My teeth clenched, I get up and stalk into the kitchen. I open the fridge. The light comes on and I look at the little I have in there—the nearly empty container of milk, the V8, the aging cheese—and I wonder if I died who would be the one to clean out this fridge, what they would think, the story these few remaining items would tell.

I close the fridge door, open the cabinet and pull out a glass. I use the tap to fill the glass and I take a long swallow, then another long swallow. I set the glass in the sink and start to turn back toward the living room when the corkboard on the wall by the phone catches my eye.

On the corkboard, in the top right corner, is the Bazooka Joe comic Scooter gave me.

Nova steps into the kitchen, leans against the doorway. The Beretta hangs at his side.

"You should get some sleep," he says.

Still staring at the comic, I say, "Do you know everything that happened today?"

"I know two FBI agents were killed. I know Walter's kids were taken and are being used for ransom for Delano's flash drive."

"Those kids are already dead, aren't they?"

Nova doesn't answer.

I turn around so I can face him. "Answer me, Nova. Do you think Casey and David are dead already? Do you think Zane—do you think my *father*—is capable of killing them?"

"People are capable of all different kinds of things."

"That doesn't answer the question."

"You should go lie down."

"I'm not tired," I say, but it's a lie. I'm exhausted. Whatever Zane gave me is still working its way through my system and I feel more than a little drowsy.

"I'll stay while you take a nap," Nova says.

"Walter's not going to give them the flash drive, is he?"

I don't know why I ask the question. The answer is obvious. Even if Walter wants to, he can't get to the flash drive. It's now in the safekeeping of the United States government, an organization that has always put the many before the few. The lives of two children don't mean a thing to them.

"They're already dead," I whisper. "They were dead the moment I stepped out of the car."

But I know that's not true.

For those two kids—for little Casey and David—they were dead the instant they met me.

FIFTY

I wake to darkness. I'm lying in my bed. The fan in the corner is blowing, set to low. I rub my eyes, start to sit up, but stop when I see that I'm not alone.

Nova sits in a chair beside the door. He has it tipped back on two legs, leaning against the wall. My eyes are adjusted enough to the dark that I can see his eyes are closed.

I sit up straight. I do it slow enough that the frame doesn't squeak. I swing my feet out. I start to stand.

"Who's Karen?"

Nova opens his eyes, stares straight back at me.

I reach out, turn on the lamp beside the bed, sit back down. The frame squeaks loudly like it always does.

"What?"

"You talked in your sleep. You mentioned the name Karen a couple times."

"She's my lesbian lover. There, I'm out of the closet. Happy now?"

His face remains impassive. His gaze stays steady with mine.

I glance at the alarm clock. Almost ten o'clock. I've been asleep for over four hours.

"Do you really want to know who Karen is?"

"Do you really want to tell me?"

I don't answer right away. I'd never planned on telling Nova about Karen. The only two people in the world who knew about her besides Walter were Zane and my father. *Are* Zane and my father, I have to remind myself.

"It has to do with the first person I ever killed."

He leans forward, drops the chair back down on four legs.

"You don't have to tell me about it," he says.

"No, I want to."

"Why?"

"It doesn't matter."

But it does matter. It matters because right now Nova is the only person in the world I trust. He is always there, no matter how much I treat him like shit. I never had an older brother, someone to look out for me, to stand up for me. Nova, despite his arrogance, makes the perfect substitute.

So I tell him about Karen. A shy twenty-one-year-old girl out of Topeka, Kansas. A girl who had blond hair and blue eyes and an accent that grated on your nerves after five seconds. But she had a good heart. She was sweet. She entered the Army because she didn't do well in school. She tried, but no matter how hard she studied, she always received poor grades. The only places that would hire her were fast-food restaurants and the local mom-and-pop grocery store.

But Karen didn't want that. She wanted to make a difference.

We came to Iraq around the same time. We were assigned the same barracks.

Within a minute of arriving Karen introduced herself to me and the rest of the girls. She told each of us her life story. She told us about her boyfriend back home who was a mechanic.

She told us about how he had promised they would get married after her tour of duty. She told us about the house they would buy, the small yard, the back porch, the children they would have (one boy and one girl) and how during the summers they would rent an RV and one year travel to the Atlantic, the next year to the Pacific.

None of the other girls cared much for Karen. They especially hated her accent. She would even say things like "y'all" and "how do." I seemed to be the only one who could stomach her, and because of this we became fast friends.

Karen wasn't afraid of danger. She knew how to handle her weapon. She knew how to fight. She could run a mile in under five minutes. She could do fifty pushups without breaking a sweat. For a small, petite girl out of Topeka, Kansas, she was a true spitfire.

Why I got along with Karen, I still don't know. Sometimes I thought it was because I was so exotic to her. I couldn't imagine there being many Asian Americans in Topeka. And if there were, I couldn't imagine many of them wasting their time with a girl like Karen. But she had her surprises.

At nights I would lie in my bunk and turn on my iPod and listen to music. Tool, Sublime, Radiohead, Linkin Park, Alice in Chains, Rage Against the Machine, Soundgarden, Stone Temple Pilots. Karen asked me once if she could listen. I gave her my earbuds, thinking she wouldn't care for any of the songs. But she closed her eyes and smiled and started bouncing her head to the music. When she took the earbuds out, she asked me what my favorite band was.

I told her it was a toss-up between Tool and Alice in Chains.

"Both are great," she said. "I do love Maynard. He's just so mysterious, you know?"

And she smiled mischievously, something I hadn't expected

from this girl who I thought only listened to Dolly Parton and Travis Tritt and Garth Brooks.

I asked her what her favorite band was. She said she didn't know, she had so many.

"But do you wanna know what my favorite song is? Lemme see your iPod again."

She scrolled through the list and selected a song, handed me the earbuds.

I put them in. There was a moment of silence, and then I heard the pulsing bass and then the heavy guitars and then Zack De La Rocha started up about how the main attraction is distraction. The song was "No Shelter" by Rage Against the Machine.

I asked Karen why she liked it so much. She said she loved that one line, the one about the front line being everywhere and there being no shelter anywhere. She said she thought it applied to the entire world. She said that was the main reason she joined the Army. She wanted to do something important with her life. She wanted to try to make shelter in any way possible. If not for herself, then for her family. For her boyfriend and their future children.

I didn't have the heart to tell her the truth about the song. How it was really about commercialism and the mass media doing everything it can to manipulate people's minds. How it promoted the government or the Army in no way at all.

Three months later she was beaten up and raped.

I pause a moment, waiting to see Nova's reaction. As usual, he doesn't give one.

He says, "Who was responsible?"

"An American soldier."

FIFTY-ONE

Because of our location in the desert, we had no running water. We had to do our business in the porta potties stationed around the base. One night Karen went out to one of those porta potties. She did her business. When she opened the door, someone was waiting for her. He punched her in the nose. He knocked her down. Then he hit her two more times until she was unconscious and raped her.

"Apparently it happened a lot over there," I say. The fan keeps blowing in the corner, making the drapes over the windows sway. "Some women were knocked out and raped and then left there to be raped by whoever else came along."

"What was done about it?"

"At the time? Nothing."

I forced Karen to go to our CO. She hadn't wanted to; she was embarrassed. She said she couldn't even identify the man if she had to. I wasn't there when she spoke to the CO. I only found out later what the CO said. He apologized but asked her what did she expect—we were at war.

I told Karen we would contact someone else, but she told me just to forget it. Her face was pale, her eyes red. The air was so dry in the desert that it dried the sweat off our bodies. It did the same to tears.

"Don't make a big deal about it, okay?" She hugged her knees up to her chest. "I'm just gonna forget it ever happened. You should, too."

But I couldn't forget. Now every male soldier I looked at was a suspect. It was strange; the enemy had suddenly become the ones inside our base.

I started asking around. A few of the girls admitted that they had heard stories of other women being raped in the same way. None ever admitted it was them. But sometimes I could see it in their eyes. A flicker, nothing more than that. It was the same thing I now saw in Karen's eyes. Before there had been an energetic fire, a passion to try to give shelter to the world, undo all the front lines. But that fire had been extinguished. She became withdrawn. Detached. Distant. One time I found her behind our building, punching the wall. She'd held her broken and bloodied hand up to me and said it didn't even hurt.

I called my father. He was stationed somewhere halfway around the world; I never knew the exact location. I told him the situation. I told him what the CO's answer had been. I told him I suspected it was happening to other girls. He was quiet for a long moment. I could hear the static on the line and pictured a giant black hole between us. Then he said, "You're a smart girl, Holly. You know how to make it right."

There was only one way I knew how to make it right, but I refused to consider the option. It was too extreme. It was too … unlike me.

Then Karen became even more detached. One of the girls found her in our building banging her head against the tiles. She was sent to the infirmary. She was given medication. It was decided she should return home.

The day before she left, however, she overdosed.

I thought about what my dad had told me. How I was a smart girl. How I knew how to make it right.

I decided that night—just hours after Karen killed herself —how I was going to do that.

I began making nightly trips to the porta potties. I would wait inside for five minutes. It was stifling hot. The stench was nauseating. I spent the time counting how long I could hold my breath.

When I opened the door I expected someone on the other side, someone who would try to punch me in the nose, push me down, knock me unconscious.

But there was never anybody there.

A week passed. Then another week. I was beginning to lose hope. I was beginning to look at the rest of the male soldiers during the day with hate. They were all guilty. They were all hiding something.

Finally one night during the third week someone was waiting for me. I heard his boots crunching the dirt outside the porta potties. He was being too sloppy. He was getting away with too much and his ego had grown too big.

When I opened the door he threw a punch at my face, but I ducked it and kicked him in the balls. He grunted, fell to his knees. While he was momentarily stunned, I withdrew my knife and shoved the blade into his chest. I kept it there and didn't take it out until he'd stopped breathing. His body went limp. I pulled the knife out, let him drop to the ground.

There was nobody around. The night was silent. The sky was clear.

And at once a series of impulses began to race through my mind like a line of dominoes: I wanted to kick him; I wanted to stab him one hundred more times; I wanted to cut off his dick and stuff it in his mouth and leave him out for the rest of his brothers-in-rape to see (this last thought so gruesome and unlike me that for a moment I actually questioned my own sanity).

In the end, I buried his body out by the generators. I kept his dog tags. His name was Michael Blair. I'd seen him around. I remembered him as one of the few men who had tried talking to Karen when she first arrived. He had a baby face. He had large hands.

Nobody saw me. I returned to my bunk with a great sense of disappointment. I'd wanted more. I'd wanted to keep him alive longer. At least until I'd tortured him. Until I'd gotten some names, other men who played the same game. Maybe he wouldn't have known anybody else, but that wouldn't have mattered. I would have tortured him until he made up a few.

The next day he was reported missing. Two days later his body was found. The entire base was searched. I hadn't had time to move his dog tags. I'd placed them in the corner of my locker.

I don't know why I kept them, or why I didn't hide them better. I think by that point I just didn't care anymore. Before, I hadn't minded fighting in this war; now I didn't see the point. We were fighting against one type of evil while another type hid behind their uniforms. It reminded me exactly of what Karen had said about the front line being everywhere. It was true: there was no shelter.

As soon as they found the dog tags, I was taken into custody. I was placed in a room with a table and a chair. Two MPs came in and shouted at me. They said things about prison. They called me a bitch and a cunt and a traitor. They said the death penalty would be too good for me. Then they left. I was alone for hours. When the door opened again, it wasn't the MPs who entered the room. It was Walter.

At this point Nova allows a small smile. He says, "He offered you a job, didn't he?"

I nod. I wonder what situation Nova had found himself in that caused Walter to walk in and bail him out.

"He said he knew my father. He said he knew exactly what happened. He said he understood. Then he asked me if I regretted what I had done. I considered lying, telling him I regretted it deeply. But I didn't. I told him what I regretted most was that I had killed him too fast. I told him I'd wanted to make him to suffer first."

I don't bother telling Nova the rest. Not about how Walter told me he could use my services. Not about how he would make it appear I would be taken into custody. Not about my year of intense training. Nova already knew about that; he had been through it himself.

"You can go now," I say.

"Are you sure?"

"Yes."

"Are you hungry? We can order pizza."

"I appreciate everything, Nova, but right now I just want to be alone. Really alone, okay?"

He watches me closely, considering it. I just told him a story about a woman who killed herself. There is no way for Nova to know I am suicidal too. Or maybe there is. Maybe I am more transparent than I care to admit.

"Okay." He stands up. Looks down at the Beretta in his hand. Looks back up at me. "Want me to leave this with you?"

"I have plenty."

He grins. "I'm sure you do. You could probably fill an Easter egg basket with all the weapons you have hidden in this place."

"Goodbye, Nova."

"Yeah, yeah, yeah. Goodbye."

And like that he's gone.

I wait until I hear the apartment door close before I stand up. I need some water. I need some food. I need to pee.

I start toward the bathroom when the phone rings. It's the main line, as my cell has disappeared. I hurry into the kitchen, thinking it's Walter with some good news, then thinking it's Walter with some bad news.

I pause with my hand extended. My eyes once again focus on the Bazooka Joe comic pinned to the corkboard.

I answer the phone.

Zane says, "What—you're not fucking Nova now, are you?"

FIFTY-TWO

A long moment of silence passes before Zane says, "Are you there, Holly?"

"What do you want?"

"Just to talk." His voice grows soft, almost thoughtful. "Remember the nights when we spent hours on the phone just talking about nothing?"

I glance quickly around the kitchen, at all the different places I have weapons stashed. I think about the rest of the weapons—the guns, the knives, even a machete—hidden around the apartment.

"To be honest," I say, "it barely crosses my mind."

"Oh now, come on. That's not fair. I hurt you a long time ago and now you're trying to hurt me."

If I wanted to hurt him I would tell him about our aborted child. But I don't. It's none of his fucking business, and even if it was, I still wouldn't tell him.

"As far as I'm concerned, Zane, you're still dead."

He drops the soft, thoughtful tone. "It doesn't look like Walter is going to come through in time."

Unfortunately this is a corded phone. I don't even know

why I still own it. It was here when I moved in and I always figured it would be here when I moved out. Now I wish I'd broken down and bought a stupid cordless so I could move freely around the apartment.

"It's not that he doesn't want his kids back," Zane says. "I know he does. I know he's fighting to get them back."

He's outside. I know he's outside. How else could he have known I was with Nova unless he watched him leave?

"Anyway," he says, "it doesn't look like Walter is going to make the deadline."

"You said there wasn't any deadline."

"Don't be an idiot, Holly. There is always a deadline."

"So why are you calling me?"

"Because you've now become the wild card. Why else do you think your old man saved your life in Paris?"

I close my eyes and remember the alleyway. I remember the rain and the patterns the red and white lights played against the brick walls. I remember the two officers and how they died. I remember the man who had killed them raising his gun and pointing it at my face like I had once done to someone else two years ago.

"We always knew you would be the key. Ever since that shit went down in Vegas and we realized it was you guys, we knew you would be the one who would come through and help us get the flash drive back."

"Fuck you. Fuck you and my father."

"Now, now, Holly. That's not very ladylike."

"You're a real asshole, Zane, you know that?"

"Yet you still let me sleep with you."

"That was only because I felt sorry for you. You and your small dick."

A moment passes where Zane doesn't say anything, and I start to smile thinking I've had the last word. Then that moment passes and I remember what's at stake. I can't let my emotions overtake me. I can't let my anger blur my focus.

"We could talk shit all night, Holly, but quite frankly we don't have the time. Or I should say the children don't have the time."

"You wouldn't hurt them."

"Wouldn't I?"

I open my mouth to respond but nothing comes out.

"I guess it's safe to assume there are two Hollys now. The Holly of Yesterday and the Holly of Today. Does the Holly of Today, now knowing everything she does, think I wouldn't kill these kids if I didn't get what I wanted?"

"I don't know. But the Holly of Tomorrow has something she wants to say to you. She says that when she sees you next, she's going to shoot you in the fucking face."

"Fuck this," Zane says. "Just remember—the children's blood is now on your hands."

"Let me talk to them."

"What?"

"The children. I want to hear their voices."

"And then?"

"Then we'll talk."

Zane doesn't answer. He doesn't make a sound. I think for a moment that the line has gone dead when I hear a sniveling voice say hello.

"Casey?"

"Holly? Holly, is that you?"

"Casey, it's okay, baby. I'm—"

"Holly, why—"

Her voice fades away and then it's David's voice I hear, David's frightened six-year-old voice quickly saying, "Mommy? Daddy? Hello? Hello?"

I start to say David's name but his voice fades away too and then it's Zane back on the line, clearing his throat.

"Satisfied?"

"What do you want from me?"

"The flash drive."

"I don't have it."

"No, but you can get it. And you will if you want these children to live."

I don't bother questioning him. I know he's serious. I know he'd snap one of the kid's necks just to hear the sound it makes. That's the type of person Zane has become.

"How?"

"Your car is parked three blocks away at the gas station on Vicker Street. Do you know the one I'm talking about?"

"Yes."

"The car is presently unlocked. The keys are in the glove box, along with a cell phone. When you get there I'll call to give you further instructions. Oh, and Holly? No more being a bitch. Any flippant comment made to me will result in one of the children's fingers being broken. Understand?"

"Yes."

"Good. Now you have exactly five minutes to get to the car before I call the cell phone. I will let it ring only five times before I hang up and kill one of the children. Do you understand that?"

When I say I do, he says, "The clock is ticking."

FIFTY-THREE

The clock is ticking, all right. The moment I slam the phone in the receiver, I start the countdown in my head.

One—sprint through the kitchen—*two*—sprint to my bedroom—*three*—open the bottom dresser drawer—*four*—pull out my guns—*five*—strap the Kimber Micro 9 to my ankle —*six*—throw on a pair of jeans and a sweatshirt—*seven*—stick the remaining gun in the back of my jeans—*eight*—run back out into the apartment—*nine*—slip on my sneakers—*ten*— bolt for the door.

My body has gone into overdrive. I have the vaguest sense that I'm moving faster than any human body should ever move.

Out the door, down the hallway, down the stairs, through the lobby, crash through the main doors, and into the night.

Two minutes.

I sprint down the first block.

Two and a half minutes.

I sprint down the second.

Three minutes.

The third block.

Three and a half minutes and I make it to the gas station, my body still in overdrive, the rest of the world a blur, and crowded around my car are three punks in long T-shirts and baseball caps tilted to the side.

When I approach them, the one wearing a Red Sox cap says, "Yo, baby, what's the hurry?"

"Get the fuck off the car."

"Say what?"

I step up close to him, breathing hard, the granules of sand in the hourglass of my head almost expired.

"Fuck off."

He stands up straight. Looks at his boys. Looks back at me and lifts up his T-shirt to reveal the piece he has tucked into the waistband. It's a dinky .38 Special revolver.

I snatch the revolver from his pants, jam the barrel right into his balls.

"Leave," I say.

His eyes wide, he stutter-nods and then backs away, waving his confused boys to follow him.

I tear open the car door. The phone is already ringing. I throw the revolver on the passenger seat, open the glove box, and pull out the cell phone.

"Just in time," Zane says. "One more ring and either little Casey or David would have had their throat cut."

I'm silent, still trying to catch my breath. Finally I say, "I made it. Now what?"

"Notice the GPS system installed on your dashboard?"

I hadn't, not with trying to beat the clock, but now I see the small screen sitting on the dash.

"What about it?"

"An address has already been keyed in for you. It will take you to the home of Atticus Caine."

"Who's Atticus Caine?"

"Walter still doesn't tell you guys shit, does he?"

"Who is he?"

"He's a guy who knows more than he should. If anybody will know where the flash drive is located, it'll be him."

"What if he doesn't help me?"

"Then it looks like these children are never going to see their parents again."

I close my eyes, try to slow my breathing, my heart rate. Try to take myself to that special place, that little piece of shelter where nothing can hurt me. When I speak, it's like all the oxygen has left my lungs.

"I will get you the flash drive."

"That's my girl. Oh, and Holly? I'm getting impatient. You have until six o'clock tomorrow morning."

I glance at my watch. "That's barely eight hours."

"More than enough time, wouldn't you say?"

"How will I contact you?"

"You won't."

Then he's gone and I'm left sitting there alone in a car that used to be mine but isn't anymore. Not after what happened today. Not after it was used in a kidnapping.

I reach back into the glove box, extract the keys. I start the engine just as my rear windshield shatters.

There are whoops and shouts. The three punks have returned. While the one was packing, the others apparently weren't, and now they're back with metal baseball bats. One hits the rear windshield again. Another takes a shot at my tail-lights. The third—my boyfriend in the Red Sox cap—steps up to the front and shatters my left headlight.

He smiles at me, hawks and spits a loogie. It lands with a plop right on the hood.

I consider getting out of the car. Consider kicking the shit out of these three idiots. It will be good for me, help me relieve the stress, but right now these assholes are just a distraction.

I place the car in reverse and punch the gas. The car jerks

backward. It knocks one of the punks aside. He falls to the ground and once again I consider hurting him more, but instead I maneuver a quick one-eighty and peel out onto the street.

My hands are white around the steering wheel. My arms are shaking. Every single terrible thought and scenario is slithering their way through my brain. I feel like I'm on fire. I feel like my head is going to explode. I scream, as loud and as long as I can until my voice goes raw.

Then I scream some more.

FIFTY-FOUR

The GPS takes me north. Up 495 into Maryland, then west on 190 toward Elmer County. Nearly an hour and a half has passed. It's now almost eleven thirty.

According to the address Garmin gives me, Atticus Caine lives in a farmhouse out in the middle of nowhere. A large metal gate blocks the driveway. To access it one needs a code, which I don't have, and even if I did, I doubt I would be able to make it through the gate and up the long drive to the house at the top of the hill without alerting Caine and possibly the authorities.

I drive a half mile down the road. I find a place to park, enough where I'm properly concealed by passing traffic.

The night is still. The shrill of cicadas fill the air.

I start into the trees. I go at a quick enough pace where I won't trip and twist my ankle. I know the direction is correct, because after ten minutes I come across a chain-link fence. Barbed wire runs across the top of it.

I begin to wonder what kind of farmhouse needs the protection of barbed wire when a twig snaps behind me and I draw my gun as I spin around and aim it right at Nova's face.

He says, "I didn't know you were the hiking type."

I lower the gun. "What the hell are you doing here?"

"I figured somebody would be watching your place. After I left, I circled around and parked two blocks up so I could watch your building. After about five minutes I saw you come out and book down the street. I followed you to the gas station. Say, what'd you do to piss off those kids?"

"Does the name Atticus Caine mean anything to you?"

Nova shakes his head. "This his place?"

"According to Zane."

"Zane told you to come here?"

"He says if anybody would know the location of the flash drive, it'd be this Caine guy."

Nova looks at the fence, at the barbed wire. He brings his arm out from behind his back to show a pair of bolt cutters. "I always knew these would come in handy one day."

It takes Nova a few minutes to cut a big enough hole in the fence. Once we're on the other side, he says, "Now what?"

This side of the fence is completely bare. No trees, no bushes, no cover of any kind. The farmhouse sits less than a quarter mile away. It's a two-story and it seems as if every light on the first floor is burning.

"Now that we're in," I say, "we might as well introduce ourselves."

We head up the long slope of grass. At the porch there are both steps and a ramp. As we approach the door, Nova reaches for his gun. I tell him don't.

"Why the hell not?"

"I have an idea this guy's not an enemy."

"Holly, we just busted through his fence. We're trespassing on his property. Trust me, to him we are now the enemy."

I knock on the door. Wait a couple seconds. Knock again.

Nova says, "Fuck this," and reaches out, turns the knob.

The door opens.

He looks at me, shrugs, and enters the house. I follow him, walking slowly, listening to the heavy silence.

"Hello?" My raised voice sounds odd to me, much too strained. "Mr. Caine?"

Nothing.

Nova now has the Beretta out. He walks just as slowly as I do. The floor is polished oak. Framed photographs line the hallway, what look like Ansel Adams's work.

A stairway is directly in front of us. On the left and right are two open doorways. Nova leans up close against the wall, peeks in the one room, then the other. He looks back at me, shakes his head.

An electronic voice says, "Drop your weapons."

Both of us freeze.

"The police have been called. They will be here momentarily. Drop your weapons now and surrender."

The voice comes from every single room of the house.

I shout, "We are here to speak to Atticus Caine!"

A man appears in the doorway directly ahead of us. He's tall and pale and holds a rifle in his hands.

Nova raises his gun at the man.

The electronic voice says, "Regarding what?"

"The safety of Walter Hadden's children."

Silence. The pale man keeps the rifle aimed at us while Nova keeps his gun aimed at him.

Finally the voice says, "Are you Jian Lin's daughter?"

Nova shoots me a quick look.

I say, "Yes, I am."

"Walter Hadden's children are in danger?"

"Yes."

"Why are you here?"

Staring directly at the man with the rifle, I say, "We need to speak with Atticus Caine."

There is another lengthy pause. Then the voice speaks

again, sans the electronic tone.

"James, lower the rifle."

The pale man lowers the rifle.

"Now please escort our two guests to the basement."

Holding the rifle lowered in one hand, James motions us to follow him with the other.

Nova and I look at each other. I nod at the Beretta, and he lowers it. Then I start forward, toward James, into the kitchen. He moves over to a door, opens it, gestures for me to go first.

I start down the stairs.

At the bottom sits a black man in a wheelchair. He appears to be in his sixties, some gray streaking his full beard.

"So you're Holly Lin." His voice is low and deep. "And this gentleman behind you is Nova Bartkowski, correct?"

The entire basement is filled with electronic equipment. In one corner are two dozen monitors, showing different angles of the interior and exterior of the farmhouse. In every other corner are computer screens.

James has reached the bottom of the stairs. Still keeping the rifle lowered, he walks past us and then turns so he's standing behind the man in the wheelchair.

"We're here about Roland Delano's flash drive," I say.

"Who is Roland Delano?" When neither of us answers, the man shakes his head and says, "I don't have his flash drive. You should know that already."

"But you know where it's located."

"I don't, but even if I did, why would I tell you?"

"Because David and Casey Haddens' lives depend on it."

Atticus Caine shifts his weight in the wheelchair. He glances up at James, turns his attention back to me. "Young lady, do you know what is on that flash drive?"

"No."

"Are you aware of what kind of trouble will happen if that flash drive falls into the wrong hands?"

"I have an idea."

Atticus Caine squints his eyes, studies my face. "You care deeply about these children."

"They're innocent."

Atticus Caine smiles. "You remind me of your father."

"Don't say that."

"Why not?"

"Because he's the reason I'm in this mess right now."

The smile fades on Atticus Caine's face. He nods, slowly, and says, "Yes, I know."

Suddenly an alarm sounds. White strobes flash around the basement.

Nova, still holding the Beretta at his side, steps back, looks around wildly. "What is that?"

Atticus Caine takes a remote from his pocket, presses a button, and the alarm and flashing white strobes stop at once.

"That," he says, "is the police."

FIFTY-FIVE

He tells us to wait down here. He says that if for some reason the officers want to search the house—which they probably will—we should hide behind the metal door in the corner. Then he wheels himself to a lift against the wall, presses a button, and with a mechanical whine it raises him up into the air. James looks at us once, nods, and hurries up the stairs.

On the monitors we can see every angle of the house, both inside and out. A police car has stopped in the driveway. Two officers get out. They hurry up to the front door. Another monitor shows the gate at the bottom of the drive open; apparently the police have the entrance code.

Atticus Caine appears on one of the screens. He comes out of a door. James meets him and pushes him into the hallway, then down to the front door.

The officers don't knock or ring the doorbell. They simply walk in.

"What seems to be the problem?" Atticus asks, microphones stationed around the house picking up his voice perfectly.

One of the officers says, "You tell us. We got a call there was a break-in."

"Yes, yes"—Atticus Caine bows his head in shame—"I'm sorry about that. We were working on the system and it malfunctioned. We couldn't get it to stop."

"So everything's okay?" asks the second officer.

"Yes," Atticus says. "Everything is fine."

Both officers look at each other. Then the first one says, "Mind if we check the house, just in case?"

"Of course, be my guest."

Atticus Caine wheels himself back while the two officers enter deeper into the house, their hands on the butts of their service pistols. Even though these two cops are becoming a pain in my ass, they're simply doing their job. If there's a disturbance, they need to check it out regardless. Just because the homeowner says everything is fine, doesn't mean it's so.

Nova taps my shoulder, points at the metal door.

I'm afraid the door will make noise when we open it. It doesn't. It opens smoothly, without a sound.

A motion sensor turns on the overhead lights.

Nova whispers, "Holy shit."

We've stepped into an arsenal. Colt M4s. Heckler & Koch MP5s. A fucking MG5, not to mention dozens of pistols—the weapons either hang off the wall or are displayed on tables.

Outside the door we can hear footsteps coming down the stairs. It sounds like only one set.

Nova is holding the rifle James set on one of the tables. He places it aside, then steps forward, grips onto the door handle.

I hold my breath.

The footsteps move about the basement. They stop in front of the metal door. We can hear the officer grasp onto the lever. We can hear him try to push, try to pull, but the lever doesn't budge. He stands there another moment, then walks away, starts back up the steps.

We wait what seems like an eternity. Neither of us has moved, and because of this the motion sensor turns the lights off. For a moment I feel alone in the darkness. Something inside of me makes me reach out for Nova, and the lights flash back on.

Just then we can hear the mechanical groan of the lift, another pair of footsteps on the stairs, these much more tentative. Atticus Caine calls, telling us it's safe to come out now.

Nova opens the door. We step out and the first thing Nova says is, "Who *are* you?"

Without a response Atticus wheels over to one of the computers. He pulls the keyboard close to him, starts typing. James wanders over to a corner, stands straight with his hands clasped in front of him.

"You have a fucking machine gun in there," Nova says. "What—you guys run some kind of militia or something?"

Atticus ignores him, typing at the computer.

I say, "Those two kids are going to die if you don't help us."

Atticus pauses. "How do you know they aren't dead already?"

"I don't know. But I have hope that they're not."

"Hope," Atticus Caine echoes, chuckling. "Maybe you're not your father's daughter after all."

"What is that supposed to mean?"

"Jian was not the type of man to place much in the way of hope."

"Only family and close friends ever called him Jian. Everybody else called him John. How did you know my father?"

The man doesn't answer, keeps typing.

"Hey." I take another step forward. "Did you really know my father?"

Atticus Caine pauses. He sighs, glances up at me.

"Of course I knew your father," he says. "I was the one who trained him how to kill."

FIFTY-SIX

"Believe it or not, I wasn't always in this wheelchair. I was a completely different man. I was married. I was successful. I was, as they say, happy. Wasn't I, James?"

In the corner, James only bows his head.

Atticus Caine takes a few more seconds to type on the keyboard before he pushes himself away from the computer.

"Once upon a time I did exactly what Walter Hadden does, only in a different capacity. I never had the type of rank that forced me to have meetings at the Pentagon every other day. The work I did … it never existed, if you know what I mean."

"And you trained my father?"

Atticus nods. "I knew he was a killer the first time I met him. I could see it in his eyes. Even when I shook his hand, I could feel the energy running through his body."

I think about my father, the man I knew growing up. Or only half knew, as he was almost never home, always working.

"Not to say that is a bad thing," Atticus says. "A killer and a murderer are two entirely different beasts. Your father knew what had to be done. He knew what his duty was and he never hesitated on a job."

"When I mentioned him before, how he was involved in this, you didn't even flinch. You already knew he was alive."

Atticus nods again.

"How?"

"When the doctors told me I had muscular dystrophy, I was more or less forced into early retirement. It was better than working behind a desk for the rest of my life. So I left with a very nice pension and the unnerving realization that I couldn't stay retired. For the longest time I had been on the inside, knew all the secrets, where every skeleton was buried and just how deep, and now ... now that wasn't going to be my life anymore. Which turned me into this."

He holds up a hand like a game show host, waving it around the basement like the entire thing is one big grand prize.

"Not that I could do it all by myself, of course. That's where James comes in. He's like an angel. Aren't you, James?"

James bows his head again.

"James lost his voice when he was just a boy. He's never spoken since."

I ignore this, stare straight back at Atticus. "That doesn't answer the question how you knew my father is still alive."

Atticus tilts his head to the side. "Let's just say despite being retired I am still in the game."

"My father is working with a man who used to be on our team. Zane."

"Yes, I'm aware."

"Do you know if they're working by themselves?"

Atticus shakes his head. "There's no way they could."

"Then who do they work for?"

"A man named Gabriel Black."

"And who is he?"

"A white-collar terrorist."

"I didn't know terrorists had class distinctions."

"Where have you been, Holly? Everything has a class distinction."

The monitor he was working on beeps.

He turns to it, says, "Ah, here we are," and wheels himself back to the keyboard.

I glance at Nova. Glance at James in the corner. Glance at a clock hanging on the wall: half past midnight.

"What are you doing?"

Atticus has started typing again. Several of the monitors have blinked on and switched over to what appear to be maps of Washington, D.C.

His attention on his work, Atticus says, "After 9/11, the United States opened its eyes to a new form of warfare. Despite what it wanted to believe, the entire country was vulnerable. *Is* vulnerable still, to be quite frank. The enemy knows exactly where our bases are located. They know exactly where our nuclear weapons are stored. So what did the government decide to do? They went mobile."

Nova and I have drifted over to the computer monitors. Closer now we can see the distinct detail of the maps. Mostly major highways, but some primary and secondary roads, even some national landmarks. And on various spots are a handful of red flashing dots with a series of letters and numbers listed below them.

"What are those?" I ask.

Atticus Caine looks up at us. "What vehicles take up most major highways?"

Nova says, "Tractor-trailers."

"That's right. And out of those thousands and thousands of tractor-trailers on the road daily, do you know what's inside any of them?"

"Hold up," Nova says. "You're saying the government has, what, nuclear weapons riding around in tractor-trailers?"

"Nuclear weapons, no. Nuclear waste, yes. Among many other things."

I clear my throat. "And the flash drive?"

Atticus leans forward. He squints at the screen, types some more. After a moment he points at one of the red flashing dots.

"In that tractor-trailer right there."

The red flashing dot is listed as FGT-927. It means absolutely nothing to me. The only thing it does mean is that, from where it appears on the map, right now it's working its way up I-95.

"It's heading toward Washington," I whisper. Thinking this might be a good thing. Thinking that it's returning because Walter has persuaded whoever it is that needs persuading to give him the flash drive.

"That's just a random circuit it drives," Atticus says. "It might head east, it might keep going north. There's never any set course."

"What kind of security will it have?"

"The driver will be armed. There might be an agent or two in the trailer. It depends on what they're transporting. They'll be armed, too. Not to mention that if any trouble is even sensed, a team is immediately dispatched to take care of the situation."

"Not the police?"

"No. The army would like to keep the lid on their mobilization program as tight as possible."

"What's the team's ETA?"

"It varies." Atticus glances up at me. "I know what you're thinking, and I'm telling you it can't be done. Even if the tractor-trailer needs to pull off for gas, there's absolutely no way you can take it."

I watch the red flashing dot as it slowly moves up the map. I close my eyes and still see the red flashing dot along with the children's faces. Thinking of them, I reach into my pocket and pull out the cell phone.

"Zane called me on this from a blocked number. Is there any way to determine his location when he called?"

"It's possible."

"Can you do it?"

Atticus takes the phone from me. He stares at it, then calls for James. When James approaches him, Atticus gives him the phone.

"Do your best, young man."

James turns away. He goes to one of the computers. His fingers dance madly across the keyboard. He pulls out a wire, inserts something into the phone. He crosses his arms and waits almost a minute before something flashes on the screen and then he steps back, a crooked smile on his face, motioning me to look at the screen.

I walk across the room and stand in front of the screen and murmur, "Son of a bitch."

On the screen is a satellite image of my block. I don't realize until another moment passes and I see the darting motion of traffic that the image is a live feed. A green dot appears along the street, just a block up from my apartment. Without being told I know that was where Zane's call originated from. He called me when he saw Nova leave, and then when I asked to hear the children's voices, he let me hear them, but only for a moment, because they were no doubt tied up and gagged in the van or SUV or truck or whatever had been parked there.

I say it again, louder this time: "Son of a *bitch*."

I look up at James, point at the cell phone wired to the computer. "The next time he calls, can you determine his location?"

Smiling again, James nods.

"How long does it take?"

James glances at Atticus. He moves his hands around quickly and, stupid me, it takes a couple seconds to realize it's American Sign Language.

When James is done, Atticus says, "Should be only a matter of seconds. What he can do is clone the phone you have there, so that when Zane or whoever else calls you, we also get the call."

I take this information in, running it through my mind. Then I march over to the metal door, the arsenal. I open it, step inside, look around at everything that's provided.

When I step back out, I ask Atticus Caine if he has any communication gear.

"Holly," Nova says, "didn't you hear what the man said? There's no way we can stop that trailer."

"I'm also going to need a harness and a lot of nylon rope." I walk back to the computer, stare again at that red flashing dot. "Nova, what are you driving?"

"Holly—"

"What. Are. You. Driving."

He sighs. "A pickup."

"How many cylinders?"

"Eight."

"A large bed?"

Nova looks at me. Looks at the screen. Looks back at me. "You're insane."

I ask Atticus if he thinks it's possible we can get everything together in the next hour.

Before Atticus can respond, Nova says, "Holly, I know the clock is ticking on this, and that a lot's at stake, but we have to be rational here. Tell me you're not being serious. Tell me your plan isn't to try to take out that trailer while it's moving."

I smile at him. "Not exactly."

FIFTY-SEVEN

I believe that there's a moment every night where across the country, across the world, portions of major highways are deserted. It can be as much as a mile, but more likely it's a half mile, or a quarter mile. For a couple seconds no vehicles pass over the asphalt. The highway has a chance to breathe. It has a chance to enjoy, if only for an instant, the calming stillness of silence.

From where I'm positioned overlooking Interstate 95, that moment seems to be now. Almost four o'clock in the morning, I can see a quarter mile south, a quarter mile north. No headlights coming toward me. No taillights fading away from me. In fact, there are no cars coming either east or west over the bridge. It's an instant, only that, when the world feels desolate, destroyed, all life taken out of it except my own.

In my ear, Atticus says, "Three miles."

I'm standing on the Commerce Street Bridge, facing north. Springfield Estates is off to my right; Lynbrook is off to my left. About a mile ahead is the 495 interchange, which is why we decided to set up here on this bridge. Because just like Atticus said, the tractor-trailers run random circuits, and there's no telling whether it will go west or east or keep going north.

Headlights appear over the ridge of the interstate. They're coming from the north. A moment later headlights appear in the other direction. That moment of peace and quiet has passed and it's time for the highway to hold its breath again.

I'm wearing a black jumpsuit. My hair is pulled back into a tight ponytail. I wear target-shooting glasses. I have on thin protective gloves.

The traffic coming in both directions have diverged and are passing each other. The steady hiss of their tires and the groan of their engines shatter the silence of the night.

I have a Glock holstered to my belt. The Kimber Micro 9 is snug in its ankle holster. A switchblade is in my pocket. A coil of nylon rope hangs at my side. I'm fitted in a harness.

More cars appear coming north and south.

Magnetic clamps hang from my belt, already threaded with the rope. A special gun hangs from my belt as well, the one Atticus gave me which is loaded with tranquilizer darts.

In my ear, Atticus says, "Two miles."

The traffic below is speeding at sixty-five, seventy miles an hour. That means the tractor-trailer—that red flashing dot marked FGT-927—is less than two minutes away.

I stand up straight. I cross my left arm over my chest, hold the stretch for a couple beats. I do the same with my right arm. I bend down, touch my toes, keep in that position for thirty seconds before standing up straight again.

I've done the math in my head. I know how many feet there is from the top of the bridge to the asphalt below. I know how tall the top of the tractor-trailer will be. I know how fast it will be going—Atticus is able to pinpoint it to the exact mile per hour—and I know, because I've done the math, just how much time I have to make the landing.

If I miss it by a second, I'm fucked.

"One mile."

Continuing to stretch, moving my head back and forth, I think about Casey and David. I think about Zane and I think about my father and I think about Scooter and I think about Karen and for the very first time I wonder what if it had been me coming out of the porta potty, having no idea, just minding my own business and opening the door and then *bam*, that was it.

A car comes up over the bridge. I don't even glance at the driver as I continue to stretch, acting like it's normal for anybody to be standing on a bridge this time of night with the getup I have on.

"Half a mile, second lane from the left."

A concrete guardrail runs the length of the bridge. I have to climb up, balance myself on the tiny space provided.

My toes are right on the edge. Right on the very lip.

I close my eyes. Try to picture nothing. Try to picture complete darkness.

"Quarter of a mile, still in the second lane from the left."

I start the countdown in my mind, the miles per hour, the seconds. The five-lane highway disappearing beneath the tires. The driver crouched over the wheel in the cab, watching the road.

I open my eyes. Glance back over my shoulder. I can see it coming, right there in the left-hand lane. Completely white. Unmarked. Just like the thousands of other tractor-trailers driving across the country every day.

It's coming, seventy miles an hour, seventy-five, and I think about Casey and David, I think about Zane and my father, I think about Scooter and Karen, and turning back so I'm facing north, my hands squeezed into fists at my sides, I take a deep breath, listen for the sound, the roar, the moment the tractor-trailer's grille appears beneath the bridge.

And I step off the edge.

FIFTY-EIGHT

Half a second, that's all it takes, my body in free fall, the wind whipping at my face, and I come right down on the top of the trailer, just smack, and the entire thing is shaking, vibrating, threatening to buck me off, and my body goes into automatic, grabbing for the magnetic clamps, slamming one down on the left-hand side of the trailer, slamming the second one down on the right-hand side, and then, as if on cue, the driver increases the speed and jerks the trailer just enough that I lose my balance.

I tilt to my left, heading toward the edge, the cold and unforgiving asphalt sixteen feet below me. The rope is already threaded through the clamps, attached to my harness, and as gravity and momentum force me to the left, I reach out with my right hand, grip the taut black nylon rope, and pull myself up straight.

Atticus says something in my ear, but it's lost in the heavy roar of wind. I have my left foot placed just in front of my right, and with both hands on different parts of the rope, the rope that is threaded through the clamps, I'm able to keep my balance no matter how fast the driver wants to take us, no matter how many times he jerks the wheel.

They know I'm here now—or at least they know somebody is here—and right this instant a unit is being dispatched to this location; the only thing the driver and the men inside the trailer need to do is keep me busy until then.

Keeping my knees bent, my hands on the rope, I start to walk backward. I draw out more slack on the rope as I go, the coil only having a length of one hundred feet, which I hope is enough.

When I reach the back of the trailer the driver jerks the wheel again, taking us toward the right, the off-bound ramp, and once again I lose my center of gravity, start to tilt to the left, but I hold on, pull myself forward, keep my feet planted.

I pause a moment, waiting until the tractor-trailer takes us the entire way up to 495, merges with the rest of the traffic. Atticus says something else in my ear I can't hear, but it doesn't matter because I know what it is: if the driver keeps going straight in this direction, we'll reach Andrews Air Force Base within ten minutes.

I take a breath. Take another. Then, gripping both lengths of rope tightly, I lean back and look over my shoulder.

The door isn't a rolltop, where it locks and opens at the bottom and is raised up like a garage door. No, this one is like a barn door, split right down the middle.

I lean forward even more, squint to see whether the door is locked. It isn't. Of course it isn't, not with the level of security riding inside the trailer, one or two or three or more just waiting, weapons already drawn.

I take another step back, so I'm right on the edge. I readjust my grip on the rope. The wind keeps slapping at my face, howling in my ears, the air cold and sharp. And before I know it I take another step back and drop down, extending my arms above my head, still gripping the rope, holding on but not as tight as I go down, down, down, until my feet touch the bumper, maybe a half foot of bumper, but enough so I can put my toes there.

Headlights splash me. I raise my head, thinking the unit has already arrived, wondering how many seconds I have to reach for the holstered Glock before the tractor-trailer's driver jerks the wheel again and sends me flying.

But the car belongs to a civilian, just an average person heading home or heading to work.

I bring both sections of rope together, grip it tight with my left hand, then lean forward, slowly, until my right hand grasps the latch. I jerk it up and pull the door open and immediately jump back as bullets tear into the door and disappear into the night. A half moment passes where I see the car behind us has been hit, white splats marking the windshield, and the driver slams on the brakes, swerves to the right, the cars behind blaring horns as they swerve to get out of the way.

The gunfire is still heavy, unabated, and the tractor-trailer's driver decides right then to jerk the wheel again. This time it's to the left, and the door swings open even wider. Then the driver swerves back to the right and the door I'm using as a shield comes undone and opens and before I know it I'm off the bumper, hanging against the side of the trailer, holding onto the rope as tight as I can while feeling it slither between the thin fabric of my gloves, burning my hands, the highway now racing underneath my feet.

Hanging by the rope on the side of the trailer, I'm aware that the gunfire has stopped. I'm aware light is spilling out onto the highway directly behind us, light coming from inside the trailer, and there are shadows there, at least two of them, standing at the edge.

The driver—who must surely see me dangling behind him on his left—jerks the wheel again, and again, and again. His purpose is to make me lose my grip, send me to the asphalt.

Like Atticus said, they will not stop the tractor-trailer until the threat has been neutralized; even when the unit shows up they won't stop, because they would rather be a moving target than a stationary target.

So the driver is doing everything he can to buck me off. But I don't let go. Instead, I reach with my right hand and grip onto the rope and spin myself so I'm facing the side of the trailer. I plant my feet square against the unmarked side and then start to move, first to the left, then to the right, to the left, to the right, making a pendulum, giving me force, giving me momentum, the wind screaming past me at eighty miles an hour, the tractor-trailer passing cars and trucks, and then I'm as far left as I can go and I move right, move right, move right, and before I know it I push off with my feet and go airborne and soar for an instant, half an instant, a quarter of an instant, the rope growing even more taut in my grip, and I hold on and swing around the door and straight into the brightly lit gaping maw of the trailer.

I come in feet first. An agent is standing there, and I knock him to the ground. I let go of the rope and hit the floor and scramble back to my feet while the other agent steps forward. He shoots at me just as I turn away—the bullet puncturing the side of the trailer—and I turn back and grab his arm as he shoots again. He tries to move the gun toward me, right at my face, and I give him a little leeway and then slam the gun back into his nose, drawing blood, and he falls just as the first agent climbs back to his feet.

I reach for Atticus's special gun. I shoot the first agent in the neck, then turn and shoot the second agent in the neck. One of them tries to take a step toward me but the tranquilizer darts work fast. A few seconds and already the stuff is spreading through their systems. Their eyelids grow heavy. Their heads roll on their necks. Their legs give out from under them. They go down.

I stay in a shooting stance for a moment, just standing there, holding my breath. Slowly, very slowly, I lower the pistol.

Atticus must sense the sudden silence, because he asks, "Holly, are you okay?"

"I'm fine. There were two in the trailer and they've been taken care of."

"How long before you find the flash drive?"

The front end of the trailer is filled with filing cabinets, two rows facing each other. Two desks are positioned against the sides, chairs underneath. A mini-fridge, a large cardboard box full of food, laptop computers set up on the desks.

"I'm not sure. It might be a while."

"You have two minutes, maybe less."

"Until?"

"Until the cavalry arrives. Oh, and Holly? They're coming fast, and they're coming strong."

FIFTY-NINE

I start with the desk on my left, ripping open and dumping drawers, papers and pens and paperclips scattering everywhere. The same with the desk on my right, only difference here are some Pop-Tarts stashed in a far corner of the bottom drawer, an old issue of *Men's Health*.

The driver keeps swerving from one lane to the next. I feel like I'm on a boat on a tumultuous sea, like I'm back on that yacht where I thought I witnessed what I did but obviously did not.

As I start on the first filing cabinet, tearing open the top drawer and sorting through the files, I ask Atticus how much more time.

"A minute, if you're lucky."

Slamming the drawer shut, opening the next one, yelling, "Nova, where are you?"

"Ready when you are."

"Can you slow them down?"

"Not all of them."

"How many?"

"Right now looks like three."

Tearing apart files, throwing out papers, finding guns wrapped in plastic bags, bullets concealed in dime bags, until I come to a drawer that has cell phones and discs and pieces of hard drives—

And flash drives.

"Holly," Atticus says, "you have about thirty seconds."

Quickly sorting through the bagged items, looking for a printed name, a flash of gold, I say, "Nova, do your magic."

"I'm trying, I'm trying."

Nothing in this drawer. I slam it shut, open the next, find even more bagged items. I start whispering a mantra—"Come on, come on, come on"—and then I slam the drawer shut, open the next one.

Nova: "They're right on your tail."

I pause and glance up. Three black BMWs are spread out, each taking a lane.

I reach for the Glock but then stop, realizing that won't work, at least not yet. I hurry forward, stepping over the agent with the broken nose, gripping the one steel desk and pulling and pushing, pulling and pushing, until it starts to move. It weighs a ton but it starts to slide across the floor, and I push it toward the back, the three BMWs gaining ground, I push the desk until I reach the edge and then I push some more and the front two legs drop over the side and I keep pushing until the rest slides over and the desk tumbles front over end to the highway.

The desk hits the asphalt, bounces back up spinning in the air. The middle BMW tries to swerve out of the way, but all the driver does is jerk the wheel too hard and the spinning desk lands right where the turning wheel is and jams there and causes the car to flip.

Nova, his voice loud and hurried: "What the hell was that?"

The two remaining BMWs continue on like nothing's happened, taking up the space the third left behind, keeping pace with each other as they come even closer. Both passenger side windows lower. The upper parts of bodies pop out, submachine guns in hand.

I pull the Glock, aim not at the men or the windshields but at the BMWs' grilles, at their front tires. I pop off a half-dozen rounds, enough to give me some time, and I turn back around, run to the other desk, pull it from the wall and then flip it over just as the men in the BMWs open fire.

Crouched behind the desk, feeling the vibration of every bullet, I yell as loud as I can: "Nova, get your ass up here and take care of these cars!"

"What do you want me to do?"

"I don't give a shit! Just don't let them kill me!"

There's a lull in the gunfire. I look around at the two tranquilized agents, both still knocked out cold.

Keeping low, I crawl back toward the nose of the trailer, to the filing cabinet with the bagged electronic items. I start sorting through them, tossing out bags, tossing out more bags, until I slam the drawer shut and go to the next cabinet.

Nova says, "I'm going to be so pissed off at you if I get killed doing this," and then I hear the steady staccato of gunfire.

I pause to peek over the desk. Nova's pickup trails the BMWs, Nova leaning out his window, gun in hand, shooting at one of the cars.

The tractor-trailer swerves again, from left to right, and gravity finally has its way and sends me falling to the ground. I knock my head on one of the filing cabinets, see white for a moment, and then I crawl forward again, open up the next drawer, start sorting through it.

"Holly," Nova yells. "I'm taking on gunfire!"

I peek over the desk again. The two men with the submachine guns have shifted positions and are now firing back at Nova.

Springing to my feet, I tell Nova to get ready.

"Ready? Ready for what?"

I crouch down at the desk, plant my feet, and start push-ing. This desk moves a whole hell of a lot easier than the last, moving like it's on ice, and then it's at the edge and it tips over and crashes down to the ground and slams right into the grille of the one BMW.

Nova's pickup swerves behind the BMW as it comes to a sudden halt, coming right around it, and the agent with the submachine gun in the last car swings back, starts firing at me.

I dive back into the trailer, crawl up to the filing cabinet, just start tearing things out. More files, more papers, more bagged items of discs and cell phones and flash drives and—

Holy shit, there it is.

Wrapped in a plastic bag just like all the rest.

A golden flash drive, one of a kind.

When I speak, my voice is barely a whisper. "I got it." I have to say it again. "I got it." And again. "I got it!"

"About time," Nova says. He's back there behind the BMW, swerving from lane to lane, trying to stay directly behind the car while the passenger keeps firing at him. "You ready to make your exit?"

I stuff the flash drive in my pocket, pat it once to make sure it's secure. Then I work my way forward, grab onto the rope, pull it until it grows taut.

"Yeah, I'm ready whenever you are."

"What side?"

"The left-hand side."

"My left or your left?"

"Your left, Nova! Now come on, I'll cover you."

With both strands of the rope in one hand, I grab my gun and fire at the BMW. Again I don't try to hit the passenger or the driver but I want to slow them down, force them to swerve away, give Nova enough time to swing around them.

Which he does, the black Dodge Ram coming on strong, speeding directly at me, and as the truck comes right up to the trailer I hear Nova's voice in my ear—"Do it now!"—and I fire off one more round and drop the gun and reach for the knife in my pocket.

I start running, sprinting as fast as I can, until I reach the doors and, gripping the rope as tight as ever, I jump out and swing toward the last BMW, the rope catching at the top and the momentum forcing me again like a pendulum toward the left-hand side of the tractor-trailer, where Nova is now, riding as close as possible, making sure I have enough space, and with one deft motion I flick my wrist and extend the switchblade and slice the rope until nothing more is keeping me up and I fall.

SIXTY

The Dodge Ram has a nice open bed. Normally it's empty, but just an hour ago Nova went to Walmart and stocked up on every single pillow and comforter they had. He loaded up the pillows in back of the pickup and placed the comforters on top of them, and while it's not the most ideal thing to land on when just jumping out of a speeding tractor-trailer, it does the trick.

I lie staring at the empty sky for a couple seconds. My heart is pounding. My body is shaking. I'm half-aware that both of those things have been going on this entire time, but what matters is that I realize it now and that I'm happy to be alive.

The Dodge Ram has a partition on the cab's rear window. Nova slides it open and shouts out at me, "You okay?"

I open my mouth to answer but can't speak. I try again and realize that I'm holding my breath, that I've *been* holding my breath. I release the breath and take a few large gulps of air before telling Nova that yes, I'm okay.

"Good." He slides an M4 through the partition. "Mind taking care of our company?"

At once I'm back on autopilot. I sit up and grab the rifle

and turn just as the tractor-trailer's driver lowers his window and sticks out a handgun. I can't tell what kind of gun—it looks like a .38 or a .45—but that doesn't matter; what matters is that he has a gun and is now firing at us, a few random shots in the pickup's direction, Nova swerving to the farthest lane and then back to fake him out.

I lean forward and prop my weight on my knee and raise the rifle, holding it as steady as I can. I aim not for the driver but for the empty passenger seat and I let off a few rounds, the windshield cracking and then shattering, the driver leaning back so he can grab the wheel with both hands.

The BMW has swung around and is headed up our lane, directly behind us. The passenger is still hanging out his window. He's not firing because he's not at a good angle, and right now the driver is trying to do that for him, veering to the left.

I turn the rifle toward the car and let off a few more rounds, the bullets tearing up the grille and the hood, the BMW swerving back and forth, giving me enough time to swing the barrel back to the tractor-trailer and aim at the front tire. I open fire and don't stop shooting until the bullets tear away at the rubber enough that it blows.

The tractor-trailer doesn't explode or flip over like it would in the movies. Instead, the wheel goes flat. The tractor-trailer tilts with a jerk. It's already going about eighty miles an hour, and now with the flat the driver slams on the brakes, which is something he shouldn't do, not at that speed, because by jerking the wheel and slamming on the brakes it causes the momentum of the trailer to keep going, sliding toward the left, right at the BMW, the car unable to get out of the way in time that it veers straight into the median.

I've exhausted the magazine. I lean back toward the partition and ask Nova for another. He hands me one. I replace the mag and then just sit there, the wind howling around me, the destruction already a quarter mile behind us.

Despite the fact we're hooked up by transmitter, Nova shouts out through the partition: "So you got it?"

I pat my pocket, nod at him.

"Good," he says. "So now what?"

Before I can respond, I hear the approaching *chuck-chuck-chuck-chuck* of a helicopter. I look up and see it there, what looks like a modified Black Hawk heading towards us.

Nova increases the Ram's speed. He shouts back at me to watch out and cover my face. Next thing I know he smashes the window with a hammer, shards of glass flying everywhere.

"Hurry! Get in!"

I climb in just as the Black Hawk's door gunner opens fire on the bed of pillows and comforters.

SIXTY-ONE

Nova hunches over the steering wheel, pressing his foot hard on the gas pedal. As I snap in my seat belt, I glance over and see the speedometer rising, going from ninety to ninety-five to one hundred. There are cars ahead of us and Nova starts swerving around them, the door gunner in the Black Hawk pausing in his gunfire so no civilians are harmed.

"Atticus," I say, "we're not going to be able to shake this Black Hawk."

"Yes, I know. I'm thinking."

Nova says, "Well, fucking think faster."

We're on the Capital Beltway now, heading east toward Maryland. In another mile or so will be the Woodrow Wilson Memorial Bridge. In another couple miles will be Andrews Air Force Base as well as more backup.

Nova jerks the wheel hard, taking us around a tractor-trailer, and ahead of us there is a straight stretch of no traffic and after a moment more bullets rain down on us.

Despite clipping in my seat belt seconds ago, I now undo it. I lower my window and lean out, bringing the M4 with me.

Nova takes us from the far left lane to the far right, and I aim the rifle at Black Hawk, pull the trigger only three times, just a warning, a fruitless attempt because it only provides maybe a second or two of relief until the door gunner returns fire.

We speed under an overpass, an exit flashing past us, Nova cursing and saying, "I should have taken that."

"Then why didn't you?"

He gives me an angry look, says, "I'm a little fucking busy right now, in case you haven't noticed."

Another straight stretch, another opening of no traffic, and the Black Hawk dips lower.

Atticus says, "I've reviewed the upcoming highway exits and attempted to calculate a proper escape, or at least some way to ensure you more time."

"Yeah," Nova says, "and?"

"And I'm sorry to say right now it doesn't look very good. Tell me, Nova, what kind of soldier are you?"

"What the hell kind of question is that?"

"A simple one. Would you consider yourself selfish or selfless?"

We're out over the Woodrow Wilson Memorial Bridge now, right above the Potomac, passing cars and trucks, Nova leaning on his horn to try to clear the way. The Black Hawk is still on our ass but the door gunner hasn't fired at us in the past several seconds.

"Well?" Atticus says.

We swerve around another tractor-trailer and there is yet another open space ahead of us. The door gunner opens fire again, some of the bullets this time striking the top of the cab, whizzing down between us into the bench seat.

Cursing, Nova says, "Just get on with it. What's your plan?"

"The objective here is saving Walter's children, correct? And the only way to do that is ensuring Holly can get away safely with the flash drive intact."

Nova glances at me. I glance at him. We stare at each other for a moment. Then Nova nods and says, "Screw it, what's your plan?" and when Atticus tells him, he says okay and presses the gas down even more, speeding us across the bridge, the speedometer going up to one hundred five, one hundred ten, one hundred fifteen. Seconds later the Maryland side of the bridge appears and for some reason I'm expecting there to be an army of police cars. There isn't. Nova veers us off the exit, the Black Hawk having to pause in midair to follow our progress. Nova leans to his left as he veers us around the off-ramp, passing a few cars in front of us, the pickup feeling like it might tip over. Then we're around the entire way and entering the Anacostia Freeway, the Black Hawk dipping low again, and Nova punches the gas.

The highway is two lanes now, making it more restrictive than before. Trees stand tall on both sides of the freeway. We pass over another bridge and the door gunner fires at us again and some of the bullets strike the hood, Nova cursing and clenching his fingers around the steering wheel.

Driving faster, swerving from lane to lane, he says, "Holly, can I tell you something?"

He says, "If we both make it out of this alive, you're buying me a new pickup."

He says, "A real fancy one, too, all the bells and whistles."

He says, "Got it?"

"Yeah," I say, as the freeway splits with a large divider, trees everywhere, "I'll buy you the most expensive one. Satellite radio and GPS and everything."

"Good," Nova says, moving over to the right lane, "just so we're in agreement," and then he cuts the wheel hard to the left, steering us across the two lanes, taking us over the grass median and into the stand of trees, Nova's headlights picking out an open space, and as he goes between them he has to slow, the terrain rocky, and that's when I start to open my door but pause when Nova says my name, Nova pulling out his Beretta, handing it to me, and I take it and push open the door and jump out right before a tree slams the door shut, all the trees now tearing the pickup apart, the Black Hawk trying to follow his progress, until he reaches the freeway and the gunfire starts again and he punches the gas and heads back in the direction he came, the growl of the pickup's engine massive until it fades away into a whisper and then is gone.

SIXTY-TWO

For the longest time I don't move. I just stand there in the shadows of the trees, traffic speeding back and forth, the *chuck-chuck-chuck-chuck* of the Black Hawk fading away just like Nova's pickup. I still have the transmitter in my ear and can hear Nova, cursing, talking to himself, cursing some more. Then, suddenly, his voice cuts off.

"Atticus, what just happened?" Thinking that the door gunner finally got him.

"I severed the connection between your transmitters."

"Why?"

"The last thing you need right now is more distractions."

Right, so now instead of knowing what's happening to Nova, my imagination is making it up, creating different scenarios that all end with Nova taking a bullet in the head.

"I will keep you informed," Atticus says.

I still have Nova's Beretta in my hand. I drop the magazine, make sure it's fully loaded, slap it back in. I holster it and ask Atticus what time it is.

"Four eighteen."

Which means I have almost an hour and a half before

Zane's deadline. Which shouldn't be a problem, now that I have the flash drive. But which still is a problem, because I have no way of contacting Zane and can only wait for him to contact me.

"I need transportation."

"Yes, I know." Atticus pauses. "Do you know how to hot-wire a car?"

At this I can't help but smile. "After everything that's happened so far, you still underestimate me, don't you."

"I was simply asking for clarification, Holly. I would never underestimate the daughter of Jian Lin."

The mention of my father wipes the smile off my face. I start toward the highway going southbound, stepping over roots and rocks.

"Where's Nova now?"

"He will soon be headed back over the Woodrow Wilson."

I wait for a lull in the traffic before running out across the asphalt to the trees on the other side. My body is sore, my muscles tight. Maybe I'm not in as good of shape as I think I am.

I enter the trees and work through them. Atticus doesn't speak. Neither do I. I try to keep my mind clear. I try not to think about Nova and the Black Hawk. I try not to think about Casey and David and how they might already be dead. I try not to think about what my father and Zane have become, how it must have been so easy, so simple, that it could happen to anyone.

I come out of the trees into a residential area. Houses are spaced apart along the tree line, almost all of them with their lights off. A few cars sit in driveways but I don't want to chance it. What I'm looking for now is a parking lot, something with a dozen cars, something that won't quickly go noticed.

As I walk I pull out the cell phone. I hit a button to illuminate the screen: 4:30. Now exactly an hour and a half. And still no call from Zane.

"Talk to me, Atticus. What's happening with Nova?"

No answer.

I stop, place my finger to my ear, make sure the transmitter is still there. "Atticus?"

He clears his throat. When he speaks, his voice is barely a whisper.

"A few minutes ago his pickup went over the Woodrow Wilson. I'm afraid I've lost contact."

SIXTY-THREE

By the time I find a car and hot-wire it—a '99 Ford Taurus parked along the street, its doors unlocked—it's almost five o'clock and Zane has yet to call.

I drive north on 295, passing Bolling Air Force Base, the Anacostia Naval Station. I think about Nova taking on heavy gunfire. About losing control of the pickup. About driving over the bridge into the Potomac.

I want to believe that he's safe. That he somehow got out of the pickup in time. That he somehow didn't drown.

And if he didn't drown (God, please be the case), then what happened? They probably took him into custody. I know he won't say anything. Not a word. They can torture him all day and night, he won't break. It won't matter, though; they know at least one other person is involved. And if the tranquilized agents come to, or the tractor-trailer driver is still conscious after his collision, one of them will be able to give a description of me. Which means right this second, half of Washington will be looking for an Asian American woman in her late-twenties.

And silly me, I'm heading right back into the lion's den.

The owner of the Taurus seems to be a big Rolling Stones

fan. Every single album of theirs is scattered across the backseat. I punch the power button on the CD player, and, I guess appropriately enough, "Sympathy For the Devil" starts up.

I punch the power button again, cutting the music off. I lean over, pop open the glove box, and am rewarded by a pack of Parliaments that I immediately light up with the help of the car's cigarette lighter. I take a couple long drags, relishing the taste, then clear my throat.

"Atticus."

"Yes?"

"What do you think?"

"What do I think about what?"

I consider taking the South Capitol Street Bridge into the city but decide to keep driving up 295.

"About this whole thing. I mean … it's fucked up, isn't it?"

"Why do you use that word?"

"What—fucked? Because it is."

"I agree with you that this situation is not ideal. In fact, regardless how this turns out, James and I will have to relocate as it seems we're not as well hidden as we had thought. But what I mean is why do you use those vulgar words?"

The Taurus's owner also seems to have a thing for Hawaii. Three of those hula-hoop girls are stuck on the dash, shaking their things in rhythm with the road.

"I'm sorry, Atticus. I didn't know you're religious."

"I'm not religious, Holly. And based on your judgment there, it's clear what one of your biggest problems is."

The last thing I want to do right now is discuss what my biggest problem is. Still, I ask, "What's my biggest problem?"

"You assume too much. You don't take time to assess people properly. You might think you're not making snap judgments, but you do, and because of that you are disadvantaged when it comes to truly reading someone."

Irritated now, I say, "You mean someone like you?"

"And the vulgarities?" Atticus says, ignoring me. "That is simply a lack of self-control on your part."

"A lack of self-control."

"Yes. Controlling your language, what words come out of your mouth, is one of the most difficult things a person can do. They almost always speak before they think. Your father was the same way."

I drive up the ramp for the 11th Street Bridge, taking me over the Anacostia River into Washington. Once again I'm expecting there to be a squad of police cars waiting for me. Once again I'm wrong.

"How well did you know my father?"

"Quite well. As I told you, I trained him to kill."

"Have you ever killed anyone?"

Atticus doesn't answer. Again I think something has gone wrong with the transmitter and touch my ear, just to make sure it's still there. I glance at the dashboard clock: 5:15.

"Atticus?"

"He talked about you a lot. It was clear he loved your mother and sister very much. But you … you seemed to be the apple of his eye."

"Is that supposed to make me feel better?"

"Not at all. But the reason I bring it up is that one time your father mentioned how he saw something strong in you. He said it was something he didn't see in your sister. You had this strength, this … this fortitude that he said he didn't even think he had himself."

I decide to get off 295, take the exit to D Street SW.

"To be quite honest, I don't give a shit what my father once said about me. I'm sorry I have to curse like that—I know it shows lack of self-control—but fuck him. He turned out to be an enemy."

"He's a conflicted man, I won't argue that. He is a man who has made his own bed and now he has to lie in it. I feel responsible, in a way. Perhaps if I had trained him better, or if I had looked deep into his heart and soul, maybe I could have foreseen him going the other way."

"Do you know why he did it?"

"I can only speculate."

"And?"

"And nothing. Speculation is merely what it is. It won't benefit either of us to continue in that train of thought."

I continue down D Street, turn up North Carolina Avenue toward Seward Square.

"But he turned, didn't he? He became … evil. He became a monster."

Atticus clears his throat. "Do you see that as his fault?"

"What?"

"Your father did everything he could to keep this country safe. He was asked to do a great deal and he came through, every time. That's why he was held in such high regard."

I stop at the traffic light, watch cars pass back and forth on Pennsylvania Avenue.

"Are you defending him?"

"No. But to paraphrase Nietzsche, whoever fights monsters should see to it that in the process he does not become a monster."

"Yeah, and if you gaze long enough into the abyss, the abyss will gaze back into you."

"Why, Holly"—Atticus sounding pleased—"you are full of surprises, aren't you?"

I don't get a chance to answer him, because right then the cell phone rings.

SIXTY-FOUR

"Hello, Holly."

"Zane."

"How are you doing this fine evening?"

In my ear, Atticus says, "I need thirty more seconds for a trace."

"I've been waiting for you to call." I've finished the first cigarette and light up a second, taking a long drag. "I have what you want."

"Are you smoking?"

"What does it matter to you?"

"I always told you those things were bad for you."

Atticus: "Fifteen more seconds."

"Look, I have it. I have the flash drive."

"Do you?"

"Yes."

"And how do I know you really have it? How do I know you're not bluffing?"

The light turns green. I pull forward, driving slowly.

"I guess you're just going to have to trust me."

"Trust," Zane says, a chuckle in his voice. "I guess that was never our strong suit, huh?"

Atticus: "I got him. He's north of you, right near Union Station."

I press my foot down on the gas. Speaking calmly, I ask, "How are the kids?"

"Very good."

"I want to talk to them."

"I'm sure you do. First, how do I know you have the flash drive?"

I take a left onto 8th Street.

"I have it, Zane. You know I do."

A pause. Then, "Yes, I suppose I do. Like I said before, you're the wild card. You always come through in a pinch."

I take a left onto East Capitol Street.

"Besides," Zane says, "I've been keeping up with the news. I know some bad shit went down on 495 about an hour ago. I'm assuming that was you?"

Speeding past trees, buildings, parked cars. Pausing at red lights long enough to ensure I don't hit anyone and then driving through.

"Let me talk to the children."

"You know, I had a bet placed with your old man. I really didn't think you'd come through. I mean, I knew you'd try and everything, but … shit, they must have had that thing locked up tight, huh?"

In my ear, Atticus says, "He's moving west on E Street. I'm accessing satellite imaging now. Should have a visual momentarily."

Pushing the Taurus harder, swerving around slower-moving vehicles, wishing to God I don't encounter any cops, I say, "Let me talk to the children."

"Hold on, Holly. Listen, I'm trying to tell you something here. Because like I said, I didn't think you'd come through. But your old man? He said it wouldn't be a problem for you. Said it'd be no problem at all. Isn't that something?"

Turning right onto 2nd Street, heading north, I take the corner a little too hard and feel the back fishtailing.

"Zane, please. Let me. Talk to. The children."

"Okay, okay. Hold on."

A pause that lasts a couple seconds, feels like it lasts a couple hours.

"Hullo?" says a timid, tired, terrified voice.

Flying up 2nd Street, my fingers tight around the steering wheel, I say, "David, are you all right?"

"Holly?" The voice waking up, gaining strength. "Holly, is that you?"

Before I can answer him the phone is taken away and it's Zane's voice I now hear, Zane asking, "Good enough?"

"We now have visual," Atticus says. "A black utility van, still on E Street and currently passing over 6th Street."

"Casey," I nearly shout. "I want to hear Casey's voice, too."

"She's sleeping."

"Wake her up."

I have to stop for the light on Constitution Avenue; I don't have a choice. Too much traffic is passing back and forth, including a police cruiser, and I'm stuck there waiting for the light to change, the cell phone to my ear, my heart racing, my body shaking, doing everything in my power not to scream so loud it will shatter every window in a hundred-yard radius.

The sound of shuffling, then another tired voice, barely even audible, Casey sounding like she's talking in her sleep.

"Casey!" I shout. "Casey, wake up!"

"Wh-Wh-What?"

"Casey, can you hear me? Are you okay?"

"H-H-Holly?"

The light changes and I gun the engine, taking a left down Constitution Avenue, Atticus saying in my ear, "They're now heading south on 9th Street," and me saying, "Casey, it's all right, baby, everything will be okay," and then Zane taking the phone away, clearing his throat.

"Now that that's settled, let's get down to business. The Lincoln Memorial, six hundred hours. Do not be early, do not be late. That gives you a little under thirty minutes. Do you think you can be there in time?"

"Why are you doing this?"

"Because it needs to be done."

"You used to be a good guy. You used to believe in doing the right thing."

"And what is the right thing, Holly? Working as a puppet like you?"

"I'm not a puppet."

"No? Then what are you? You take orders from a government that doesn't even know why they're giving those orders in the first place. I mean, this is the same government that doesn't give a shit for the lives of two kids. Goddamn it, Holly, isn't that fucked up? Two children are being held hostage, and Walter … his hands are tied. He can't do shit. Now you tell me, what's the right thing there?"

"That's not a good enough reason for becoming what you've become."

"I haven't become anything. I've always been this way."

My foot jamming the pedal to the floor, pushing the Taurus forward, Atticus in my ear saying, "Four blocks away … three blocks away … two blocks," Zane clearing his throat again and saying, "You should know how it is. Work is work, right? Remember, six hundred hours sharp," and then disconnecting the call, the world going silent, no noise at all, everything around me a blur, tears in my eyes, and then Atticus saying, "One block away … Holly, why aren't you slowing down?" and I reach the intersection, slamming on the brakes, flinging off my seat belt, jumping out of the car, Nova's Beretta already in hand, walking toward the street Zane is coming down, the black utility van slowing at the stop sign, the driver somehow not seeing me, not as I'm twenty feet away, not as I'm ten feet away, not even when I walk right up to his window and raise the gun and pull the trigger.

SIXTY-FIVE

My first two bullets take out the driver. My second two bullets take out the man in the passenger seat, the guy reaching for his weapon as pieces of the driver's head splatter all over him, then jerking as he's shot too, one in the throat, the other in the head.

The utility van is still in gear. The now dead driver releases his foot off the brake, and the van starts to drift forward.

I hear the rear doors opening, the sound of footsteps on the pavement. Zane's voice, speaking rapidly, then a figure appears around the corner, a man with a rifle. I fire two more rounds before jumping for cover in front of the van, the van still drifting forward, now out into the middle of the intersection.

Zane's voice again, much louder now, cursing at the children, and when I peek around the corner I can see him dragging both of them by the arms up the street.

I start to turn that way but then pause when the man with the rifle takes a few shots at me, the utility van picking up speed now, heading toward the corner of the intersection. I keep pace with the van, walking sideways, using it as cover. The man on the other side does the same, waiting for me to make my move.

I hear Zane cursing again, telling the kids to stop fucking around. They're already one block up and that's where I want to be headed. But I'm stuck here, the van twenty feet from the curb, moving even faster now, ten feet from the curb, the thing going to crash right into a telephone pole. I'm thinking the guy will expect me to come around behind the van so I take a breath and sprint toward the front, duck down, dive on the ground just as the van rolls into the pole, the guy not expecting me to be there, coming up in a shooting stance, both hands on the Beretta, firing one two three rounds into his chest.

I take off running then, right up the street, Zane and the children already a block up from me. Zane is still dragging them, a hand on each arm, and in the dim light of the street lamps I can see duct tape over the children's mouths, which makes sense, because so far I haven't heard either one of them scream or cry out.

Zane keeps looking back over his shoulder, trying to track my progress. When he sees that I've taken care of the last man and am headed his way, he has no choice but to let go of Casey so he can grab his gun, fire off a few wild, random shots.

None come close to me but I take cover behind a car anyway, waiting for the lull, then jumping back up, the Beretta aimed. But I can't shoot. Not with the children so close to Zane ... only Casey is a few yards ahead of Zane, already running, Zane looking back and forth between us, deciding which is more important. He sees me again and fires off a couple more rounds but he can't get a good shot, not while holding onto David, the boy struggling now to free himself from Zane's grip. Zane looks disgusted as he pushes David away, raises his other hand, squares himself to knock off two more rounds at me, these much closer, the car I duck behind this time getting hit, the rear windshield shattering, the car alarm going off.

When Zane threw David aside, David tripped over his feet and hit the ground. He recovers quickly, back on his feet, and sprints after his sister. Casey is still running, though she's not getting very far. David has no trouble reaching her, scooping her up in a bear hug, running forward.

Okay, good. Now the kids are out of the way, at least somewhat. I can't fire directly ahead—too much chance of hitting the kids straight behind Zane—so I make a run across the street, ducking as Zane fires at me, more car windows shattering, more alarms going off.

I hop up and slide across the hood of a car, landing on the other side, staying down as Zane fires a few more rounds. When there's another lull I pop back up, the angle better now, only a building behind Zane, and I take careful aim and squeeze the trigger twice and one of my bullets grazes his arm.

The kids are now a block ahead of us, David looking like he'll never slow down. I start toward them but Zane shoots wildly again. I drop down behind the car, wait for the next lull. When it happens and I stand up, Zane has taken off up the block, sprinting after David and Casey, the children already halfway up the second block.

David looks back quickly, sees Zane coming, pushes himself even harder. Between the buildings is an alleyway and he ducks into it, taking his sister with him, the two disappearing and leaving Zane a block behind them, running even faster.

I start after them.

Zane reaches the alleyway, disappears inside.

One block away, pushing myself, a half block away, almost there, and I'm running so fast, the kids so close, I don't pause to think about what I should do next, I just do it.

Coming up to the edge of the alley, pressing myself against the building, raising the gun, listening a moment. Hearing nothing. Then turning, bringing the gun around, but Zane is already there, waiting for me, knocking it out of my hands, the

Beretta clattering to the sidewalk, Zane grabbing the front of my shirt, throwing me to the ground.

"Where's the flash drive, Holly?"

I have a split second to notice that this alleyway leads to a dead end. Maybe fifty feet from the street, it ends in a brick wall. The children are there, crouched around some trashcans.

"Where's the fucking flash drive?"

When I don't answer, Zane reaches down, picks me up by my hair, drags me forward. I kick my feet, reach up and press my nails into his skin. He yells out, lets go, turns and kicks me in my side. Falling to his knees, he wraps his hands around my throat, leans in close.

"Where's the motherfucking flash drive?"

I bring my right foot up, connect my knee with his head, send him reeling. Sitting up, I lean forward, reaching for the Kimber strapped to my ankle, but Zane is already on his feet, grabbing me by my hair again, dragging me forward.

"Don't make me kill you in front of these kids, Holly."

Dragging me, strands of hair being ripped from my scalp, Zane notices me trying to reach again for my ankle and stops. Lets go of my hair. Kicks me again in the ribs. Reaches down, lifts up my pant leg, seizes the Kimber and holds it up in front of my face.

"Always with the same tricks, huh?" He smacks me in the face with the gun. "Always with the same fucking tricks."

He tosses the gun away, behind a trio of trashcans. Cocks his head at me, shakes it and says, "You are one stupid bitch, you know that?"

Stands up, lifts back his foot and kicks me again in the ribs.

"Where."

Kick.

"Is."

Kick.

"The."

Kick.

"Flash drive!"

Despite the pain, despite at least one broken rib, I manage to turn my body on his last attempted kick. I grab his foot and twist.

He loses his balance, falls to the ground. It doesn't slow him, though; he's back on his feet even before I can sit up and he reaches down again, grabs me not by the hair this time but by my shirt, pulls me to my feet.

Leaning in close, his breath hot, he says, "I am not fucking around here."

He says, "I will kill these kids."

He says, "I will break every single bone in their bodies."

He starts to say something else and that's when I spit, the saliva going right into his mouth. Zane scrunches up his face in disgust, pushes me back toward the trio of trashcans. I stumble, can't catch my balance, fall right into them. The sound is immense, the pain even more so. The back of my head knocks against the cement and I see stars for a moment, just floating there in front of my face, and then I feel a pressure on my chest, Zane's knee there, pushing down, his hands crawling around my body, searching my pockets.

"Where is it? Where the fuck do you have it?"

He finds it seconds later, feeling it there in my breast pocket, the flash drive, his eyes lighting up, a smile creeping onto his face, pulling it out and then holding it up, the faint light just enough to illuminate the gold.

The flash drive disappears into his fist. His eyes shift down to meet mine. "You've just made me a very happy man, Holly." He smiles again. "Now to thank you, I'm going to give you the chance to choose which kid dies first."

He steps away and I try to sit back up, my body not cooperating, wanting to shut down. Zane turns back, says, "I don't think so," and kicks me again, the tip of his shoe connecting with my chin, sending me back to the ground.

The world goes in and out of focus. I think I can hear Atticus speaking in my ear, his voice tinny and faint. I think I can hear the children, screaming through the duct tape covering their mouths. I try to sit back up but can't, my body completely useless. I lie there in the trash, turning my head to the left and to the right, to the left and to the right, to the left ... and stop.

The discarded Kimber is only a few feet away.

I open my mouth, attempt to speak. Nothing comes out. I swallow, clear my throat, try again.

"Zane?"

The sound of his footsteps stop. "What?"

"Did you know it's a dog-eat-dog world out there?"

"What the fuck are you talking about?"

"Scooter told me that." I let loose a wild, insane laugh. "A dog-eat-dog world."

I try to reach for the gun but my hand doesn't want to move. I try again, and it starts moving.

Zane says, "Which kid do you want me to kill first, Holly?"

"Don't you know ... what goes around ... comes around?"

"What is that supposed to mean?"

"If you send it"—grasping onto the Kimber, holding it tight—"you better duck."

And I sit up, raising my arm, aiming the gun at Zane— who's now standing there with David in front of him, the barrel of his own gun pressed against David's head.

"You waited too long," Zane says. "You forced me to pick for you."

David is struggling to get out of Zane's grip, his eyes wide and full of tears.

I stare back at him, just stare, hoping that my lesson from yesterday is still fresh in his mind. Hoping that he'll stop struggling. Hoping that he'll go completely still and then bring his elbow back and smash it into Zane's crotch.

"Say goodbye, Holly," Zane says, cocking the hammer back, and I realize that I'm being unfair, expecting David to be a hero when he's just a scared six-year-old boy. I'm his nanny, and like any nanny, it's my job to take care of him.

So I say, "Goodbye," and place two bullets between Zane's eyes.

PART FOUR

TU TIENES SUERTE PERRA

SIXTY-SIX

By the time I make the turn down Arbor Drive, it's almost seven o'clock and the light of the morning sun is crisscrossed by all the branches towering over the street. The circus of vehicles in front of the Hadden residence is gone, all except two unmarked cars taking up the driveway. I'm forced to park along the street, in another stolen hot-wired car, a Toyota Corolla that I had no choice but to grab because the police had converged on the other car and the van two blocks away by the time we came out of the alley.

David and Casey are in the back, David with his arms wrapped tight around his sister, who has dozed off. Now, as I stop the car, turn off the engine, David nudges her awake.

She opens her eyes, blinks, looks around. I watch her from the rearview mirror, rubbing her eyes, and then she looks out the window and her face lights up and she shouts, "Mommy! Mommy! Mommy!"

Marilyn Hadden is coming out the front door, hurrying down the porch steps and sprinting across the lawn. She must have been waiting and watching all night, she looks so tired.

But she isn't alone.

Four men follow her, soldiers, their weapons drawn.

When Marilyn reaches the car, she doesn't put on the brakes; she smacks into the side, definitely hurting something, but she doesn't show it, opening the back door, saying, "Oh my babies, my babies, are you okay?" leaning in and kissing Casey on the forehead, then David, then Casey again.

I have my door halfway open by the time the soldiers arrive. Their weapons are aimed now, right at me, and one of them tells me to freeze, show my hands, slowly get out of the vehicle.

I do as he says, and once I'm out of the car, one of the soldiers pushes me down on the hood. Pain flares from my broken rib. My arms are yanked behind my back and hand-cuffs are snapped around my wrists and then one of them starts frisking me and I'm barely aware of Marilyn talking to the children and the children crying, and I'm barely aware that some people along the street have stepped out onto their porches to see what the fuss is about, and then I hear Walter's voice:

"Let her go."

The hands frisking me pause, wait a moment, then disappear.

"Take those cuffs off her, too."

"But sir—"

"Do it now."

The cuffs are taken off, my hands set free, but still I don't move. I stay on the hood of the stolen car, watching as Sylvia rushes across the yard, meeting Marilyn and the children. Marilyn holding Casey with one arm while she grips David's hand with the other, David looking over his shoulder at me every few seconds, Casey not taking her eyes off me at all.

"Go back in the house."

"Sir—"

"Don't make me tell you again."

When the four soldiers have left us, Walter tells me to stand up. I don't. Instead, I ask him a question.

"How hard did you try to get them back?"

"What?"

I push off the hood, turn to face him. "Casey and David—how hard did you try to get them back?"

He's wearing his uniform, only it looks worn, just like his face and eyes, the man having aged more than ever since the last time I saw him.

"They're my children," he says.

"That doesn't answer the question."

"You don't understand. I was powerless. My hands weren't tied on this. They were chopped off. I was up all night making calls, begging and pleading …"

"They were just going to let them die, weren't they." I don't bother making it a question.

Walter can't look at me, staring at something over my shoulder. "Our government doesn't negotiate with terrorists."

"That's a sorry excuse."

His old eyes shift to meet mine. In a voice barely a whisper, he says, "Thank you."

"Nova's dead, you know."

"What?" A whiteness spreading across his face.

"His pickup went over the Woodrow Wilson."

"That was him? If that was Nova, he's not dead."

My legs start to shake. "What … what are you saying?"

"I heard about the chase on 495 last night. I heard about the driver of the pickup that went over the bridge too, how they got him out of the water and took him into custody." He shakes his head. "It never once crossed my mind that it was Nova."

"So he's alive."

"Yes."

"And they arrested him."

Walter nods.

"What are you going to do about it?"

He doesn't say anything.

"Walter, Nova didn't have to do what he did. I never could have done it without him."

Looking at whatever's over my shoulder again, Walter says, "I know."

"And?"

"And I'll take care of it."

I shake my head and glance at the house, then glance at all the houses down the street. Those few who had ventured out onto their porches have gone back inside.

I reach into my pocket, withdraw the golden flash drive. Walter, looking relieved, reaches for it. I pull it back.

"What's on it?"

"Holly ..."

"What's so important on this thing they would let your children die?"

Walter opens his mouth. Shuts it. Goes back to staring at whatever's over my shoulder.

"You don't even know, do you?"

He says nothing.

"You're a puppet, Walter. You just follow orders, never ask any questions. You don't know why one person needs to die, or why another person needs to live. Shit, I can't blame you for that, because I'm the same way. Or, at least, I was."

His eyes shift again to meet mine.

"I'm starting to see why Zane and my dad walked away from this shit. Not that that's an excuse, but ... fuck, Walter, your own children?"

Now glaring at me, he extends his hand, the palm open. "Give it to me."

I shake my head.

"Holly, I need it back."

"Why? What's on it?"

Again Walter doesn't answer, just keeps glaring at me, and I can't help but laugh.

"Does anybody even know what's on this thing?"

Still no answer.

I say, "Fine, you want it back, here you go," and I drop the flash drive on the ground, step on it with the heel of my boot, and grind it back and forth until there's nothing left.

SIXTY-SEVEN

"You probably shouldn't have done that."

"He was pissing me off."

"That still isn't a good enough reason."

"Wait a minute. Are you actually defending him?"

"No. But remember, not too long ago, I was once in his position."

I'm headed back home in the stolen car, talking to Atticus via the transmission piece still in my ear. Now that my body is no longer active it has become sore, and I think when I get home I'll just drop in bed and not wake up for a couple days.

"So now what's the plan?"

"The plan? There is no plan, per se. All I know is that James and I need to relocate, like I told you."

"Where will you go?"

"We won't know until we get there. As for you, I suggest you go to the hospital so they can take care of your wounds."

"I'm okay."

"Holly."

"If I go to a hospital, there will be a lot of questions. I'd prefer not to deal with that right now. Besides, I think the worst of it is just a broken rib. I can take care of that on my own."

I pull into the gas station on the corner, park in one of the spaces off to the side. I look around but don't see the trio of poser nitwits anywhere.

Shutting off the car, I lean over and open the glove box. I pull out the registration card and read Atticus the name and the address. I feel bad about stealing the car—not to mention the Taurus—but sometimes you have to do what you have to do.

"Okay," he says. "I'll make sure he's contacted. Now get yourself home."

I take the transmitter out of my ear, turn it off. I lock the car and start walking the three long blocks home. My apartment complex doesn't look any different. Not even at this time of morning, where the tall buildings block out the sun and swallow my apartment in shadows.

As I walk, my hand brushes the slight bulge in my pocket. Besides Delano's flash drive, it's the one thing I pulled off Zane before we left the alleyway: a cell phone. And saved inside on the recent calls list are only three numbers: my apartment, the cell phone Zane had waiting for me in my car, and another number. This last has a 011 + 33 in front of it, meaning a foreign exchange, and it's been taking everything I have not to dial the number and see who's on the other end.

Despite what Atticus says, I do have self-control.

For some reason I'm expecting the elevator to be out of service again. It's not. I think this is a good thing, a nice reward, and even though the thing is so slow it would be faster to take the stairs, I ride it up to the third floor, my body wearing down now the closer I am to my bed, becoming heavier, weaker.

I reach for my keys but realize I don't have them on me, that in fact when I left I didn't even lock the door.

I step inside, shut the door, turn around and place my fore-head against the wood.

I close my eyes. Take a deep breath.

And feel the soft cold kiss of a gun barrel as it's placed against the back of my neck.

SIXTY-EIGHT

"Hands flat against the door."

The voice is male, heavily accented with Spanish. Should have figured.

I open my eyes, take another breath, and place my hands against the door. Footsteps sound, a different pair, and then hands run all over my body, searching for a weapon. All they find is the cell phone, which is pulled out and tossed on the table in the hallway.

"Now," says the voice, "walk," and I'm yanked back, turned around, and yes, there are two of them, both whom I recognize from yesterday, and I'm pushed forward to walk down the hall toward the living room, knowing before I even get there who will be waiting for me.

"Miss Lin, *buenos dias!*" Javier Diaz sits on my sofa. He's wearing another freshly pressed suit, one leg crossed over the other, and he smiles at me like we're old friends who haven't seen each other in decades. "Please, please"—moving aside, patting the cushion beside him—"have a seat."

The barrel of the gun has been making love to the back of my neck this entire time. Now it's lifted, and I turn my head, slowly, to the left, to the right, noting the two men standing aside with weapons in their hands.

I walk to the sofa, sit down beside Javier. This close I can smell his aftershave, something that smells cheap but which is probably very expensive.

"You," he says, wagging a finger, "are a very big pain in my ass, you know that? Lucky too, I would say. *Tu tienes suerte perra*—you are a lucky bitch."

"Are you here to kill me?"

"No."

"Then get out of my apartment. You're not welcome."

Javier leans forward, clears his throat into his fist. "You know, this isn't the best neighborhood. A young woman like you should really be more careful and lock her door when she leaves, yes?"

"Get out. Of my. Apartment."

Javier gives his men a tired, disgusted look. He leans back, crosses his leg over the other, and says, "Do you realize how easy it would be to kill you right now?"

"All due respect, I don't think it would be as easy as you think."

"Perhaps. But fortunately for you, that isn't going to happen. At least not today. If I had my way, you would be dead already. You know this. You know how much I … loathe you. But that party I mentioned before? Apparently he doesn't want you harmed. He made a deal with my father, and as you can imagine, this deal does not please me at all."

"So you came here just to tell me that? You know, an email would have been easier."

A brown envelope lies on the coffee table. Javier leans forward, opens it, reaches inside. Somehow I know what's in there, and what he pulls out doesn't surprise me at all.

"Your sister and her husband have two very lovely boys, yes?"

The first photograph he places on the coffee table, right in front of me, is a snapshot taken from a distance, Matthew and Max together in their backyard.

"Even your sister is a lovely piece of work."

The next photo shows Tina, stepping out of her car.

"And her husband"—this photo showing Ryan coming out of Markham & Davis—"is quite successful at what he does. Yes?"

For some reason I think that's it for the pictures, but it's not. Javier pulls out more, spreads them across the photos of my sister and brother-in-law, of my nephews. Shots that are barely recognizable for what they truly are.

"I told you I would show you those pictures, yes?"

Broken bones. Gouged eyes.

"You can keep these, if you'd like. As a … reminder."

Pieces of flesh. Dried blood.

"From what I'm told, she was a strong woman. Put up quite a fight."

Cracked teeth. Bits of brain.

"But she wasn't strong enough, was she?"

Javier sets the envelope aside, pats me twice on the knee, then stands. He doesn't look back as he walks toward his men, doesn't say anything else as he passes them. The men follow him; they leave my apartment, shutting the door so quietly behind them it doesn't make a sound.

SIXTY-NINE

The moment after they leave, I jump to my feet. The world has gone out of focus again. My hands curl into fists. I scream, lean down, brush the photographs off the coffee table, pictures of Tina and Ryan, Matthew and Max, Rosalina, floating everywhere. I hurry around the coffee table, through the living room to the kitchen, to the counter where the butcher block sits, five knives nestled into the wood. Without slowing I grab two of them, the longest, and I make a beeline straight for the apartment door, step out into the hallway just as the elevator doors close. I sprint for the door leading into the stairwell, the stairs that smells of mildew and piss. I start down the steps, taking two at a time, three at a time, holding one knife in each hand, running, running, my blood boiling, my heart racing, my entire being shaking so hard I don't think it'll stop. I pass the second floor and then make it to the first floor and tear open the door, not caring if anybody is around—which there isn't—and I head straight for the elevator, gripping the knives as tight as I can, so tight I think I might snap them. I reach the elevator just as the ding sounds and the doors start to open, and Javier's men are positioned right behind them, just as I knew they would be, and they see me at the last moment but they're not quick enough to grab for their weapons. I jam the blades into their throats, blood gushing everywhere, and as they fall down I pull the knives out, step over their bodies, bring the knives together and push them straight into Javier Diaz's chest. His eyes go wide. His face pales. His mouth drops open. And I keep the knives there, don't pull them out, don't move them at all, as the elevator doors slide shut, hiding us from the rest of the world.

SEVENTY

"God*damn*, you sure know how to make a mess."

Nova has just stepped out of the elevator, the elevator that now has the OUT OF SERVICE sign back on it, shaking his head at me.

"So do you think you can take care of it?"

He shrugs. "I don't see why not."

"James will be here any minute. He's bringing back my car. Atticus said he'll help you."

Three hours have passed since killing Javier Diaz and his two men. The first thing I did was made sure everyone in the building knew the elevator wasn't working again. The second thing I did was start cleaning up the mess, which was easier said than done. I called Nova but there was no answer on his cell. I then called Atticus, explained the situation, and for the last hour I'd been calling Nova again and again, thinking maybe Walter was wrong, he had drowned, until Nova showed up himself. Said he had just gotten out and wanted to see if I had bought him his new pickup yet.

"You know," Nova says, "you're starting to take advantage

of me being a nice guy. All these favors you're racking up … I don't know, it's becoming a bit excessive."

"Put it on my tab."

"So what did these guys do to you again?"

"They pissed me off."

The lobby door opens, an old Korean woman coming in with a bunch of groceries. She gives us a suspicious look, probably because we're standing in front of the elevator that is once again out of order, then she shakes her head, sighs, and starts for the stairwell.

Nova says, "You really going to go through with this?"

"I can't stay here anymore."

"But where are you going to go?"

"I don't know. California, maybe."

"Do you have money?"

"Enough to get me started."

"And"—he clears his throat—"what about the other thing?"

"Atticus said he'll give me a hand with that."

Nova's eyes get really big, and he pouts his lip. "What—you don't want my help?"

"Like you said before, I'm starting to take advantage of you being a nice guy."

"I was just saying that."

"I know. But you're not involved in any of this shit. I started it, which means I need to finish it."

"It's not going to be easy."

"I know."

"The man's going to be very well protected."

"I know."

"But that's not going to stop you at all, is it?"

I shake my head. "When he finds out what I did to his son, that truce my father set up will be finished. Nobody in my family will be safe. So I have to kill him before he kills them."

Nova looks away at a stain on the wall. "And then that's it?"

I nod. "That's it."

"You really think you can walk away from it, just like that?"

I think of that gradual decline I've been on, the slope so steep Walter said I could never find my way back. "I hope so."

"Because … I mean, this is what you do. What you are."

"Every time I take a life, a piece of me falls away. I don't want to get to the point where there's nothing left."

Nova touches the stubble on his chin. "It could be the opposite. Every time you take a life, a piece is added on. You grow stronger. Did you ever think of that?"

"I have."

"And?"

I step forward, place my hand on Nova's arm. "And I'm still not changing my mind."

The lobby door opens again; this time James walks through.

I nod to him, then think of something and glance back at Nova. "I'm glad you didn't die."

"Gee, thanks."

"For a while there I thought you were dead."

"Yeah, and let me guess—for a while there you regretted never sleeping with me."

"Not quite. But I did miss you. You've been a good friend to me." I pause, then say, "So what did they do to you in there?"

"Locked me in a room, asked me a bunch of questions."

"How did you get out?"

"Walter came in."

"Oh yeah?"

"Yeah. He came in and sat down at the table and offered me a job."

"What'd you say?"

"Me?" Nova grins. "I told him I'm retired."

CODA

Despite the fact this is my car, it has a different feel to it, a car that is mine but is not mine. When I get the chance, I'll get rid of it, buy a new one. A new used one, because it's not like I have that much money. But still, first things first …

I pull into my mother's driveway. It's almost noontime. Thankfully this is one of her days off work. She's probably sitting in the living room, watching her soaps, or some talk show, or some game show. Maybe she's knitting. Maybe she's reading. Maybe she's playing video games.

Fact is, I don't know much about my mother.

I don't know her favorite song, her favorite color, her favorite meal. I don't know what kind of prayers she says before she goes to bed. I don't know how she spends her weekends or who her friends are. All I know is that she is my mother, I am her daughter, and to save her—to save my sister and my brother-in-law, my nephews, to save everyone I care about—I have to kill Ernesto Diaz.

How I'm going to do this, I don't know. My mother will take one look at my face, see the bruises, and immediately start to worry. No matter what I tell her, she won't believe me. In fact, it would be best to leave right now, send her a postcard, an email. But I can't do that. She deserves more. Not the truth, exactly—I will not tell her about her husband, *cannot* tell her about her husband—but a half-truth, a quarter-truth, just enough so she will understand I am going away and will never be back.

I turn off the car and then just sit there, listening to the engine tick.

I glance at the phone on the passenger seat. Zane's phone.

I pick it up and scroll through the recent calls list.

I highlight the number with the 011 + 33 in front of it, the foreign exchange.

I press SEND and place the phone to my ear and wait until it's connected and then wait four rings before a familiar yet unfamiliar voice answers with one simple word:

"Yes?"

I close my eyes. Think about hanging up. Think about crying. Think about screaming.

I say, "In case you haven't figured it out yet, Zane is dead."

Silence.

"I don't know what you've become or why you became that way, but you disgust me."

More silence.

"You are no longer my father."

Even more silence.

"You should have killed me back in that alleyway in Paris, because the next time we meet …"

Still more silence, the quiet so heavy that I wonder if maybe the connection has been lost. But no, I can hear him breathing, a soft, shallow sound, and I picture him wherever he is in the world right this moment, sitting in a chair, by a window, staring out at a world he doesn't agree with, that doesn't make sense to him, a world in which everyone else are bad guys and he is the hero.

I open my mouth, start to say something else, but then decide I've already said enough.

I disconnect the call.

I turn off the power.

I toss the phone aside.

Then I get out of the car and start up the walkway to my mother's house, up the steps to the porch, where I open the screen door and knock. I stand there, waiting, thinking how easy it would be to go back to the car, run away, never have to face her.

But I can't do that. I can't run away. I need to stay here, talk to my mother, who always knows what to say and do. And who, hopefully, will explain to me why just because everything turns out good doesn't mean it's a happy ending.

ABOUT THE AUTHOR

Robert Swartwood is the *USA Today* bestselling author of *The Serial Killer's Wife*, *No Shelter*, *Man of Wax*, and several other novels. He created the term "hint fiction" and is the editor of *Hint Fiction: An Anthology of Stories in 25 Words or Fewer*. He lives with his wife in Pennsylvania. Visit him online at www.robertswartwood.com.

www.ingramcontent.com/pod-product-compliance
Lightning Source LLC
Chambersburg PA
CBHW051332250626
47155CB00007B/2571